D1712069

SNOW KISSES

Joyce Carlow
Holly Harte
Linda Madl

Zebra Books
Kensington Publishing Corp.

http://www.zebrabooks.com

ZEBRA BOOKS are published by

Kensington Publishing Corp.
850 Third Avenue
New York, NY 10022

First Printing: December, 1998
10 9 8 7 6 5 4 3 2 1

Printed in the United States of America

CONTENTS

A FAMILY FOR JEANNE

Joyce Carlow

Chapter One

Boston—August 1, 1755

The intense August sun and clear blue sky intensified the color of the swelling sea, the bright sails on the boats in the harbor and the red brick of the dockside buildings. To Jeanne, who stood by the rail, this town looked huge. Winding roads lined with buildings and houses led up steep hills from the water, and white, gold-trimmed church steeples seemed to reach for the sky. Jeanne, intent on taking it all in, jumped when a high-pitched squealing boatswain's whistle announced their arrival in Boston Town.

Elsewhere in the city Jeanne was sure that the citizenry complained of the heat, but by the docks a crisp wind blew off the ocean. Four sailing ships lay at anchor, around them seventy or so smaller fishing vessels bobbing in the noonday sun, their colored sails rippling in the breeze. The smell of freshly caught fish mingled with the scent of the salt air and the tantalizing aroma of freshly baked bread from the dozen or so dockside taverns. It seemed to Jeanne that everywhere people were running hither and thither, pulling small carts, unloading wagons, arriving or departing in carriages or simply talking in small groups.

During the voyage she had been told that *The Gloucester Pride* was the finest ship in the colonial navy and Governor William Shirley's personal favorite since it had been built in Massachusetts and thus represented his own personal commitment to making the Massachusetts Bay Colony militarily self-reliant.

The Gloucester Pride had been anchored dockside rather than in the bay, and at this moment the crew was preparing to discharge its passengers.

"Jeanne Bellefontaine!"

"Here I am," Jeanne replied shyly as she stepped forward, glancing back uneasily at her sister, eight-year-old Yvette who had been standing with her at the rail.

"Yvette Bellefontaine!"

"Here," Yvette replied in a voice so small she could hardly be heard. She, too, stepped forward to take her place next to her older sister.

Jeanne reached down, took Yvette's hand and clasped it protectively. She calmed her own apprehensions by concentrating on her responsibility for her sister. *If I hold on to her, we can't be separated; if I hold on tightly to her, we'll always be together.*

Jeanne shook her head as if to clear it. I must be strong, she told herself for the hundredth time. But at the moment she did not feel as self-confident as she wished. Indeed, she wondered if Yvette could feel her heart pounding through her hand. She didn't want to worry Yvette; she wanted to shield her from what might lie ahead.

A million questions flooded Jeanne's mind. What was this place like? What would happen to them when they disembarked? But most important, would she find gainful employment and would she be able to keep Yvette with her? These questions had plagued her since the morning they had boarded in Nova Scotia.

Uneasily, she glanced sideways. On her right side stood one Jules LeBlanc, a short puffy little man in his forties and next to him stood his wife, Lise and their twelve-year-old son, Jacques. Yvette was on her left, and next to her sister was Marcella Dubonnet, rigidly clutching a bright red satchel. Marcella was the only one of the twenty-five reluctant passengers to even have a proper satchel. The rest, like Jeanne and Yvette, had only carefully wrapped bundles which contained all their worldly possessions.

They stood on the deck of *The Gloucester Pride* in two straight lines. Twelve in the front row and thirteen in the back row. A young officer, dressed in crisp tight-fitting white pants and a blue jacket with gold buttons, had just finished reading off their names. It seemed to Jeanne that this was a strange and unnecessary ritual. They had been placed aboard *The Gloucester Pride* in Port Royal, Nova Scotia, and at that time they had given their names and watched as each name was entered in a log. They had been at sea for three days and were now participating in this roll call as if someone might be missing. Where would any of them have gone? Still, the young officer had officiously called off each one of them and had had them all line up as if they were a part of the crew awaiting orders.

The captain, Lionel J. Gardiner, paced in front of them, clearly about to address them.

Jeanne looked about the now-familiar deck, then lifted her eyes to see the white sails of *The Gloucester Pride*. By any account this vessel was well named. Her wooden rails and brass fixtures were highly polished, and her huge square sails were white as snow under the midday sun. Deep in her heart Jeanne knew she and Yvette were fortunate. Many of her fellow Acadians had been loaded onto less clean vessels and had been taken much farther afield.

"At least we're arriving in good weather," Yvette suddenly whispered.

Jeanne squeezed her sister's small hand. "That must be a good sign," she said, trying to sound optimistic.

And please, dear heaven, let it be, she said silently to herself. Let this be the beginning of a new life for both of us, let us be able to stay together, please let me be able to find work.

As if in partial answer to her thoughts the captain began walking up and down in front of them. He paced, his hands behind him as he stared, not at them but rather at the deck.

"You twenty-five," he said slowly, "have been chosen to be set ashore here, in Boston Town, because you all speak a little English." He paused, let his hands drop and then scratched his chin thoughtfully. "This is the largest town in all the colonies. It is a place of great opportunity for the hard working. If you obey the law, apply yourselves, and have ambition, you will succeed."

Jeanne wondered if he meant women too. Still, she was here, and because she had spoken so well, Yvette was here with her. That was the most important thing—they were together. Being sent away from Acadia was one thing, but she and Yvette were orphans and had been since their father had died last year. Now they had only each other. Even in Acadia they had been on their own, but here—here they had to face many new challenges, they had to make their way in a strange place with neither family nor friends to help them.

"You will all be taken by the Greater Boston Charitable Society to a place where you can rest, have a good meal and clean up. Then tomorrow you will be taken to Faneuil

Hall, there to be interviewed by prospective employers. I wish you all good luck and God's speed."

Jeanne watched as the captain briskly walked away. Another wave of misgiving flooded over her. What if she did not find employment? What if she was not allowed to keep Yvette with her? No, she told herself. I want nothing but good thoughts, nothing but hope. Yvette and I will somehow survive and our lives will be better than they have ever been before.

To succeed, you have to be willing to take chances. She told herself again she had made the right choice when she'd accepted the offer to be taken to Massachusetts, rather than to the Carolinas where most of the other Acadians were taken. It was a difficult decision, but at the time it had seemed best. She had understood that there would be few other Acadians and that Catholics were not always welcome. On the other hand, she and her sister both spoke English, and she had been told that the opportunities for employment were far better in the Bay Colony.

"Please follow Lieutenant Danvers," the captain added. Jeanne put her thoughts aside as the young lieutenant stepped forward and signaled them to follow. He led them down a rickety wooden gangplank, looking back once and advising, "Watch your step!"

At the foot of the dock, he once again lined them up, and they stood in the sun for more than ten minutes before a fine black carriage with gold trim pulled up.

"What a wonderful carriage!" Yvette whispered. "I've never seen one so fine."

Jeanne squeezed her sister's hand. "This is a big city," she said softly. "I imagine many people have fine carriages."

Yvette smiled back. "I guess in Port Royal we have no need of fine carriages since most people are either farmers or fishermen."

"I imagine you're right," Jeanne replied.

"Quiet please!" the young lieutenant snapped.

He was not speaking directly to them. Everyone else was talking too. Jeanne was amused. By the tone of his voice she guessed he had really wanted to say "Attention!" As they were civilians and not sailors under his command, he had had to use the other words. The result was the same, however, they all stopped talking and stood stiffly with their hands at their sides.

The carriage driver climbed down and opened the doors of the elegant equipage. He offered his hand to a well-dressed lady in black. She was small and neatly coiffured, though her wiry gray hair was partially hidden beneath a sheer, white linen bonnet. Over her dark dress she wore an elegant white, tatted lace collar that matched her bonnet. In spite of the darkness of the dress, it was clearly very much in vogue. The skirt was gathered, but with a fullness at the sides and in the back. The waistband was low and buttoned in the front which made the garment seem smooth and flat. The sleeves were full, with ties at the wrists and elbows. Although black on a summer's day seemed a bit severe, Jeanne admired the style of the lady's gown. Only in Halifax, on special occasions when the governor's wife entertained, would one see a dress so stylish.

"I should like to present Madame Eugenia Lowell, president of The Greater Boston Charitable Society."

As they could not address her individually, there was instead a disjointed chorus of replies in which most of those addressed mumbled, "We are pleased to meet you" in somewhat broken English.

Madame Lowell, though small of stature seemed completely self-possessed. "Please, follow me!" she directed. Without further instruction, she turned and began walking briskly down the street, and they, like well trained sheep, followed in her wake.

They walked for several blocks, up a hill and past a fish market, several taverns and a general store. They rounded a corner onto Milk Street, and there stopped before an austere narrow red building with a tall copper steeple below which a clock looked down on the street.

"This is The South Meeting House," Madame Lowell informed them. "This is where you must spend the night."

No one said a word, but they all followed Madame Lowell through a set of double doors and up a flight of stairs. "This way." The redoubtable Madame Lowell beckoned, and again they moved forward, entering a large room which had been divided in half by a heavy curtain which extended lengthwise down the center.

On either side of the curtain a row of pallets stretched out from one end of the room to the other.

"Men on the right side of the curtain and women on the left," Madame Lowell announced crisply. "I'm sorry we cannot accommodate married couples separately. Supper will be served at five P.M. sharp and breakfast at six A.M. The dining hall and kitchen are directly below this room on the ground floor.

"You will be taken to Faneuil Hall promptly at ten A.M. tomorrow. You are free to explore Boston as long as you are not late for dinner or your interviews. You will know the time because you can hear the tower clock when it strikes the hour. In fact, it can be heard from almost anywhere in the city. You must be back in this room by eight P.M. The toilet is behind the building and water in which to wash can be brought from the kitchen. Are there any questions?"

The group looked from one to another, but no one had anything to ask. Madame Lowell, who had hardly seemed to take time to breathe, had anticipated everything.

She now surveyed them with an air of apparent satisfaction, then turned rapidly and, with a wave of her hand, said, "I shall see you all in the morning."

Like school children, they thanked her in another mumbled chorus. As soon as she sailed through the doors, each staked out a bed pallet, though these were identical so only location mattered.

Jeanne and Yvette put their personal bundles on their beds. On their last night aboard ship, Jeanne had washed their clothes and dried them on deck. They each had only what they wore and one other outfit so, when possible, washing was an everyday affair. Jeanne sat down and looked at her small pile of clothing. There was almost no choice. She either wore her simple brown dress with her crisp white apron or she wore the simple dark green dress. Each laced up the front and had an accompanying low-cut corset above which the white chemise provided modesty. They were of the commonest style, being excessively practical for young matrons who wished to nurse their babies. Yvette's clothes were equally plain. Both of her dresses were brown, had three-quarter-length sleeves and were covered with a white pinafore with a large pocket meant to hold herbs or berries she might find if walking in the woods. Jeanne smiled to herself. From the looks of Boston's cobbled streets they would not be finding any berries or herbs here.

"Can we really explore the streets of Boston?" Yvette asked enthusiastically.

Jeanne bit her lip and wondered thoughtfully if it were proper for two unescorted women to walk about. This was a strange place; she was unsure of what was acceptable and what was not.

"I'm so tired of being stuck on that ship," Yvette said plaintively. "I'd really like to explore, really. Anyway, this might be our only chance. You yourself said we might have to go and live in the country. Here we are in the biggest city in all of British North America, can't we look around, just a bit?''

Jeanne smiled. Resisting her sister's desire to explore would not be easy, no matter what the dangers. "Perhaps we can follow along after them," she whispered as she indicated Francis and Martin Vachon, two strapping young men in their twenties.

"I'm sure they wouldn't let any harm come to us," Yvette said. "Should we ask them to accompany us, or should we just follow them at a distance?"

"We'll follow them at a distance," Jeanne replied. She had no intention of looking for a male friend, certainly not now that she had to make certain she gained employment. Papa had been right, you should only trust yourself and not depend on others. In any case, acquiring a male companion without a proper introduction and chaperons would be sure to invite gossip. She was only too well aware that both Vachon boys had tried to flirt with her on board ship. But she had ignored them. Still, she decided, it would not hurt to follow them. At least that way she and Yvette could see a bit of the city.

"Put on your bonnet," she told her sister. "The sun is strong, and a lady must never let the sun tan her skin. We're not on the farm anymore, we're in Boston."

Yvette quickly tied on her bonnet, and discreetly, Jeanne and Yvette followed the Vachon brothers out onto the busy street.

They seemed to be headed downhill, back in the same direction from which they had all come, albeit on another street.

"I think they're going back to the docks," Yvette said after a few moments.

"Oh, dear," Jeanne said, halting. She watched as the two young men disappeared into a tavern.

"Why did they go in there?" Yvette asked.

Jeanne shrugged. "I don't know, but we certainly can't do that. Come along, let's go back up the hill. I heard someone say there was a public common and gardens. Perhaps we can find them."

Jeanne and Yvette walked up the hill, following King's Avenue, and eventually they came to a large expanse of green lawn.

"This must be it!" Jeanne said with delight. "Look, Yvette, it's almost like being in the country while being in the city."

"It's very pretty," Yvette agreed as they walked among the flowers and toward a large pond. For a long while they sat on a bench in the sun.

"I'm so glad to be off that ship," Yvette confessed. "I'm so glad to be able to move around."

Jeanne could not but silently agree. The park, the sun, the flowers—they should all take my mind off tomorrow, she thought. But there was no escaping it. Inside she felt queasy, full of false energy, excited yet apprehensive, hopeful yet fearful.

"I think we should go back now," Yvette said. "I'm hungry, and I don't want to miss dinner."

Jeanne got up off the bench, once again forcing the future out of her thoughts. She smiled at her sister. Yvette did not need the chimes of the clock to know that in half an hour it would be supper time.

They lined up by the kitchen door, and each took away a steaming bowl of baked beans. Bread and butter were on the long table, also large pitchers of milk. Again, they thanked those who provided the food and those who served it.

It was not, Jeanne noted, much different than their voyage had been. Although they were all Acadian, they all came from different parts of Acadia. They had not known each other before sailing, and even after three days in the confined quarters of the vessel, they still did not know one another. Vaguely, Jeanne wondered if she would ever see any of them again, and, curiously, if they were as anxious as she about the future.

After dinner, the women were asked to help clean up and when that was done, Yvette and Jeanne returned to their sleeping pallets.

For many hours, Jeanne lay awake, thinking, hoping and silently praying for a new beginning, for opportunity. But finally a merciful sleep crept over her.

Chapter Two

The sun was not yet up, and darkness still enveloped the rolling hills and rocky fields that surrounded Framingham, a small village to the west of Boston.

Having finished hitching his two horses to the wagon, Matthew Schmidt stood up and stretched, breathing deeply of the cool morning air. He glanced upward at the bright morning star. This day would be a scorcher. By ten o'clock the August sun would be blazing, and the trip into Boston would be hot, dusty and no doubt uncomfortable. He considered not going, but then decided he really ought to try at least one more time.

Matthew was tall and broad shouldered. His sandy blond hair was unruly and, owing to a cowlick, had a tendency to fall over his forehead. Unlike many of his neighbors, he was clean shaven, having neither a beard nor a mustache, and his eyes were a soft brown. Though they could twinkle when he was happy, he had not known many happy days in the last few years.

His expression had grown more serious, and he was well aware that he had also grown thinner and less sociable. His life was now only about work and responsibility. He had no one with whom to share, he felt alone, tired and, sometimes, hopeless.

Daniel, Matthew's five-year-old son, was a miniature version of his father. He was tall for his age, had the same sandy blond hair and indeed the same untamed cowlick. But Daniel's eyes did not twinkle. They were serious and sad. They were also expressive, and for that Matthew was glad.

"Daniel!" Matthew called out. It was bright enough now for him to see the silhouettes of the trees against the deep purple background of dawn's first light.

"Daniel!" Again he called the boy's name, and then he saw the lad running toward him. "We're ready to go, son."

He lifted Daniel into the wagon and pulled the blanket up around him. "You won't need this for long," he said, smiling. "Soon the sun will be hot."

It was like talking to one's self. Daniel was locked in a world of silence. He hadn't uttered a sound since his mother had gone to the hospital. Before that, when he was an infant of only one year, his gurgles and baby talk had seemed perfectly normal. A dozen doctors had examined the boy, but none could cure him. All they could do was shrug and say, "Perhaps in time . . ." But time went by, and Daniel got no better. Still, his eyes and face were expressive, and Matthew understood his son on a level beyond speech. With his father, Daniel used a few hand motions to indicate yes and no. He did smile when he was pleased, he did cry if he was hurt. But both emotions were expressed nonverbally.

"There is nothing physically wrong with Daniel," doctor after doctor had proclaimed. They indicated his problem was mental. It was a diagnosis Matthew rejected, perhaps, he realized, because he did not want to admit it or even think on the possibility that maybe young Daniel had the same mysterious ailment with which his wife was afflicted.

And so, in the shadows of the early morning, Matthew continued his monologue. "We've got plenty of water and food in the wagon. We can have a picnic! Would you like that?"

Daniel silently nodded.

Matthew climbed up beside his son and made a clicking sound which caused the horses to move forward. He held the reins loosely, since both Dobbin and Myra were well trained and seemingly knew they were starting out on a long hot trip.

"Maybe today we'll find someone," Matthew said, trying to sound hopeful. "But I won't hire anyone you don't like. Do you understand that?"

Again Daniel nodded.

Matthew guided the horse to the left as they reached the end of the road that led from the barn to the main Post Road into Boston. He clicked his tongue again and the horses began to trot down the road more rapidly than before. Even they seemed to want to make time before the sun rose to its height.

Vaguely, Matthew wondered if this would prove to be a waste of time. Whenever it was announced that workers had arrived, he went to look for a suitable housekeeper. Three times he had hired one—each time a middle-aged woman with good recommendations and a sensible way. But each time it had not worked out.

Mrs. Reed had been too strict even for him. She was a woman beyond enjoyment of any kind, and Daniel grew worse under her care, while he himself grew thinner because her cooking was as devoid of spice as her life.

Mrs. Canning was too simpering. She regarded Daniel as some poor sick child, a mental defective who would always have to be looked after. But Matthew knew full well that his son, though silent, was not in any way mentally deficient. The lad was smart and caught on quickly. Indeed, it was his obvious intelligence that gave Matthew hope Daniel would one day talk as others did.

The third of their housekeepers was Mrs. Forbes, a some-what shrill woman filled with prejudices and consumed with internal anger. She lasted the shortest time of all, and Matthew had felt nothing save relief when she left. Still, he wanted to find someone. The house needed to be kept up, there was laundry to be seen to and meals had to be prepared. Earning a good living as a blacksmith took all his time. Smithing was a demanding job, for people needed help at all hours of the day and night. In fact, he seemed to be almost as busy as the town doctor. Besides, there was the farm, small though it was. The cow needed milking and the eggs had to be collected and the pigs fed. He was too divided. He could not be blacksmith, mother, father, housekeeper and farmer. He was dog tired, and every night he fell into bed and slept as if he were dead.

He stared into the sun as they traveled east toward Boston Town. "Maybe today," he said, nodding to himself. "Maybe today we'll find just the right woman to help us."

Winston Colby stood in front of the gilt-edged mirror that graced his hall and pulled his cravat through the opening in his waistcoat. He smiled at his own reflection, thinking that this green velvet suit with its silver buttons and large pocket flaps was quite in vogue and was suffi-ciently rakish to make him appear somewhat younger than his forty-five years.

"You really do admire yourself too much, darling," Milli-cent said as she descended the winding stairs. Her gown was magenta with tiny purple leaves embroidered into the fabric, and the lace that hung down beneath her sleeves was part of her elegant chemise and matched her lace cap. Her dress was of the newest style too. Most women still wore dresses with bodices that laced up the front, but this dress had a busk-shaped wooden wedge covered with cloth that had been slipped into the bodice and hid the corset laces. He raised his brow as he looked at her and wondered what this dress had cost him.

Millicent, his wife of twenty-five years, was still a handsome woman, he reflected. The problem was, her demeanor was so rigid. Yes, she was as rigid as the panniers that held out her full skirt. A trifle shrewish as well.

"Are you not a bit overdressed for the occasion?" he asked. "After all, we're simply going to Faneuil Hall to hire a new maid. If she judges our wealth by your clothes, she'll want a fortune in wages."

One of Millicent's dark brows lifted contemptuously. It crossed his mind that her brows seemed all the more expressive since the hair on her head had grown gray and her brows had remained dark.

"I'm simply dressed well. It is you who look like a peacock. In any case, we're rich enough to pay a good wage. And I hear they're all Acadian. I really want a French maid for my boudoir."

"They are, as you said, Acadians. The Acadians may speak French, but they are not French. Besides, we're virtually at war with the French."

"I don't care! They make the best maids. Everyone knows that!"

That is an absurd proclamation, he thought. Still, he believed that little French maids made the best lovers so, with luck, they might both find what they desired by hiring a single person.

"Are you ready?" he questioned impatiently.

"Quite," Millicent replied crisply.

* * *

By noon, the lower section of Faneuil Hall was filled with a milling crowd. Those available for work stood on a wooden platform and carried signs with numbers on them. All around the room were tables and straight-backed wooden chairs.

"Why did we have to come here so early?" Yvette asked.

"I have no idea," Jeanne answered as she shook her head. She only knew she was tired of standing. Then she added, "Perhaps so everyone could get here and . . . well, look us over."

Jeanne was both curious and surprised. It seemed this was a weekly event. She had assumed that only she and her compatriots from *The Gloucester Pride* would be here to meet prospective employers, but that was not so. There were over fifty men and women from *The Dover* which had just arrived from England. These people could not afford to pay their passage, and they would work off the cost of their transport as indentured servants. And there were fifteen or so others who had come from Edinburgh and Glasgow in Scotland. These, as she understood it, were freemen who were simply seeking work.

A man wearing long black robes and a tightly curled white wig approached the podium and banged a large gavel down as if he were a judge about to hold a trial.

"Now what?" Yvette whispered.

"We're getting started at last," Jeanne answered. "Do stay close to me. There's such a crowd."

"When you want to interview one of those offering services, step forward and give me their number," the man in the robes announced. "I'll call it out and you may take a seat for your interview. In the case of those who will be indentured, there are lawyers in the back to witness the contracts. The Acadians among the workers have numbers from one to twenty-five. Those with special skills such as woodcutting, carpentry or experience with animals are holding numbers twenty-six through fifty-two, and the rest are seeking contracts for indentured service.''

I feel as if I'm being sold, Jeanne thought. But at least I will not be indentured, I am free of obligations and debt. She forced the indignity of the employment process out of her mind. What mattered was finding honest labor and keeping Yvette with her. She had to remain focused on the essentials.

"She looks quite perfect," Millicent Colby cooed as she tugged on her husband's velvet jacket and pointed at Jeanne.

Winston Colby took stock of the girl his wife indicated. She was small of stature, certainly no more than five feet two, and her masses of dark brown hair, though tied back modestly, clearly fell in ringlets. Her eyes were large, dark brown and expressive; her small pale face was heart shaped. And, most important from his point of view, her figure was excellent. Even though her dress was modest and plain, he could see that her breasts were full and her waist tiny. Her skin was like milk and she looked down submissively. Submissiveness—ah, it was a quality he adored. "She does seem quite the right type," he agreed, afraid to sound as enthusiastic as he was. "Number fourteen. Shall we speak with her?"

Millicent nodded, though her eyes wandered over the others. No one else among the Acadians seemed as suitable as this girl.

"Number fourteen! Table two!" the man in black robes called out.

"That's us," Jeanne said. "Come on, and keep your fingers crossed."

"Twenty-four! Table six. Fifty-one—table thirteen!" The

man's voice droned on as people left the platform to join prospective employers.

Jeanne made her way through the crowd to the table. There she stood with Yvette for a long moment until she saw the well-dressed man and woman approaching.

"I'm Mr. Winston Colby, one of Boston's best-known traders. I have a shop on Tremont Street. This is my wife, Mrs. Colby."

Jeanne was not sure how to respond. They were both so elegantly dressed she felt as if she were addressing royalty. She curtsied politely. "I'm Jeanne Bellefontaine and this is my sister, Yvette."

Millicent frowned. "We can't afford two of you. And besides, she is far to too young."

"It is only I who seek work," Jeanne quickly said.

"Well, she couldn't come with you. There is simply no room, and we can't be feeding two when only one is working."

Winston fought to keep from staring at this young girl's full breasts. She was charming! Youthful! And desirable! "Surely we can think of something," he muttered. "Perhaps she could work in the mill and only sleep at the house."

Jeanne shook her head quickly. "No, I don't want her to work in the mill."

"Well, then, she'll just have to go to the local orphanage. We're prospective employers, not a charity."

Jeanne felt the coldness in the woman's voice, and her own hesitancy rose.

"But, my dear, surely we could make some accommodation," Winston heard himself say in a louder voice. But no sooner had the words escaped his lips than he realized he had gone too far. His wife knew exactly what was in his thoughts. She might well acquire a French maid, but it

would not be this girl. This girl was far too pretty, and
Millicent had sensed his attraction.

"I think not," Millicent said. Then, turning toward
Jeanne, "That will be all, thank you," she said in an offi-
cious and final tone.

Jeanne squeezed her sister's hand and turned back
toward the platform. It was almost empty now, and those
seeking workers had also thinned out. A feeling of panic
seized her. She had to fight the urge to turn around and
once again ask Mr. and Mrs. Colby to give her a chance.
But she could not bring herself to do it. Yvette was all she
had, and she was all Yvette had. They were a family, and
even if there were just the two of them, she vowed to keep
them together no matter what.

"It's my fault," Yvette said sadly. "You could do well
without me."

"Nonsense," Jeanne said, forcing an air of confidence
she did not feel. "There will be no 'without you.' I didn't
really want to work for them anyway."

"They did look rich," Yvette reminded her.

"Rich but not kind," Jeanne concluded as she climbed
back on the platform. She had not asked what would happen if she didn't find work that day. How would they live
until next week?

"We're late," Matthew said as he and Daniel stepped
into the hall. He couldn't believe it had taken him so long,
but he acknowledged that it was hot outside and the horses
had needed to be watered more often. He wiped his own
brow and unbuttoned the top two buttons of his shirt. He
had long ago discarded his leather vest.

He looked up at the platform. There were several older
women and a couple left as well as a comely young woman
and a child. But the two older women looked strict, and

he mentally rejected them. He turned back, looked at the young woman. She was, he thought, very attractive and very young. Too attractive and too young.

Matthew reminded himself that he had no right to look at any other woman, that he needed no temptations. Furthermore, taking care of Daniel as well as the house and all the meals was a real chore. Far too much responsibility for one so young.

"I think we've made this trip in vain," he said, turning about. But Daniel pulled on his shirt and pointed toward the young woman with the little girl who stood at her side. In fact, Daniel was pointing at the little girl who was smiling at him.

"The older one is too young," he said, leaning down to look into Daniel's eyes. But Daniel only kept pointing and shaking his head.

"Far, far too young," Matthew said. He took Daniel's hand and pulled him from the hall. "It's a long way home too," he said dejectedly as they stepped back outside.

Matthew lifted Daniel back onto the wagon before he himself climbed up. "We can get home before dark, if we hurry." With that, he picked up the reins and turned the horses toward home.

Jeanne walked toward the man who had presided over the interviews. "What happens to those who didn't find work?" she asked.

He looked appraisingly at her and then at Yvette. "You would stand a better chance without your sister."

Jeanne shook her head. "We must try to stay together."

"I gather you're destitute."

Jeanne nodded.

"Return to the Meeting Hall and wait for Mrs. Eugenia Lowell. I'll send her around to see you. I doubt the Society

can keep you for more than another week, but she'll give
you all the details—and find you some temporary work
scrubbing the floors of public buildings to pay your keep."

Jeanne nodded, though in truth she was fighting to hold
back her tears. She was tired and on edge. She had hoped
they would find something today. Now it would be another
difficult week, though the work would be the least of it.
Still, she supposed she should be grateful. At least they
would have a bed to sleep in and food to eat. But what
would happen if she did not find a position by next week?
Would they take Yvette away from her?

She let her arm drop around her sister's shoulders, and
she hugged her. "Don't worry," she whispered. But in
truth, she wasn't saying it to Yvette, she was saying it to
herself.

Matthew turned the horse back onto the Post Road. He
stared straight ahead, lost in thought.

Suddenly he became aware of Daniel next to him, and
he turned suddenly. Daniel was not sitting on the wagon
seat, but rather kneeling and looking backward toward the
city. He clutched the back of the wagon seat for balance,
and huge tears were running down his small round face.
When he turned and saw his father was looking at him,
he pointed back toward Boston and cried even harder.

Matthew reined in the horses and then pulled them to
a complete halt at the side of the road. What did Daniel
want?

"What is it, son?" he asked with concern.

Daniel continued to point back toward the city. He
seemed agitated.

"Was it that little girl?" he asked, thinking of the child
who had stood next to the attractive young Acadian
woman.

Daniel nodded.

Matthew closed his eyes. Somehow the little girl had appealed to his son. Perhaps because she had a sweet smile, perhaps . . . Well, conjecture would not answer his question. Only if Daniel could talk would he really know what the boy was thinking. He thought about the young woman. She was probably capable enough. Why had he not spoken with her? He knew it was because he had found her attractive. Was she really too young? He had hired older woman, and not one of them was satisfactory. Perhaps someone younger would be better. No, her youth was not a sufficient reason to reject her, he told himself. After all, his previous attempts to find a suitable housekeeper had failed because the older women he had hired were too set in their ways. That alone seemed a good reason for trying someone more youthful. As for her looks, well, he could keep busy enough to force that out of his mind. And just so no one would think it improper, he could move into his shop and leave her in the house with the children. Yes. He had initially not given her enough thought. He owed it to Daniel and to himself to at least speak with her.

"All right, you win," he said, turning the horses about. "We'll go back to Boston and see if we can find them."

He glanced at Daniel. The little boy wiped the tears from his cheeks and smiled. He lifted his hand and once again pointed toward Boston.

Jeanne sat cross-legged on the end of her pallet, and Yvette sat next to her. Yvette played with her knotted string, weaving it over and through her fingers, then turning it. Jeanne just stared into space, trying to sort matters out, trying to regain some of her confidence, a confidence badly shattered by the fact that she had not yet found employment. And then there was her anxiety. Time was running out.

"Miss Bellefontaine?"

Jeanne looked up and into the eyes of the man who had conducted the interviews. He was no longer wearing his official black robes, but now stood before her in a purple suit that made him look like a member of the king's own court. His leggings were light violet, his shoe buckles glistened. His waistcoat and jacket were a darker violet while his vest was the same shade as his leggings. His ruffled shirt was gleaming white, and his four-cornered hat covered his bald head. Before he had looked like a darkly clad frog, but now he looked like an elegant, if bald, fop.

"Miss Bellefontaine?" he repeated.

Jeanne struggled to her feet. "Yes, sir."

"There is a gentlemen here to see you. He says he was late this morning and only caught a glimpse of you. Will you please meet him outside? You can't receive a male guest here."

"Of course not," Jeanne answered. She scrambled to her feet. "I think you had better come, Yvette. We can go together."

"I'm not sure that's a good idea," the man told her.

"We're going to stay together," Jeanne said with determination. "We're family."

"As you wish." He turned about and headed down the stairs.

Jeanne, with Yvette at her side, followed.

In the vestibule Jeanne saw a tall man with light hair and a kind face. He appeared to be in his mid thirties. He was dressed plainly in soft leather moccasins, leather leggings, suede pants and a long-sleeved white shirt. He carried his vest. A small boy stood by his side. The little boy was almost his miniature, and it seemed to her that they were father and son.

"Miss Bellefontaine?" he asked shyly.

"Yes, I am Jeanne Bellefontaine." She curtsied ever so slightly. "And this is my sister, Yvette."

"I'm Matthew Schmidt. I'm a blacksmith from Framingham. This is my son, Daniel."

"Bonjour, Daniel," Jeanne said, smiling warmly at the little boy.

"I saw you earlier, but then I thought you too young."

"I'm eighteen," Jeanne said, thinking he had asked her age. He was a tiny bit difficult for her to understand because he spoke so quickly.

"Eighteen," he repeated thoughtfully.

"Almost nineteen," she added.

"Can you cook and clean?"

"Oh, yes. I took care of my uncle's house. And before my father died, I took care of our house."

Matthew nodded. "How about my son? Do you read?"

"I read French, and I am teaching myself English. Yes, I can read."

Matthew bit his lower lip. "My son . . . he, well, he doesn't speak."

Jeanne looked at Daniel. She had thought him quiet for a boy of his age. "Is he able to speak?" she asked.

"The doctors think so. There is no medical reason, and he's quite bright even though he doesn't speak."

Jeanne smiled. Matthew thought it was a sweet smile that revealed her concern. And her sister, little Yvette, was holding Daniel's hand. He looked up at her and Matthew sensed that somehow there was already some strange relationship between these two motherless children. Daniel had been enchanted with her from the beginning, and she had taken his hand right away.

"Will you come and work for us, then? On a trial basis, of course."

"I should be pleased, Mr. Schmidt. But there is one

thing. My sister and I are orphans and must stay together. I can go nowhere without her.''

Matthew smiled. ''Of course she can come. I think she'll be a special help with my son. He's very lonely.''

''I would like to know the wages. I want to send my sister to school.''

''Room and board of course—for both of you. And I'll pay the school fees. There will be a bonus at Christmas if you do a good job and a sovereign a month.''

''That's very generous.''

''If you work out, it will be worth that and more,'' Matthew replied. ''Can we leave now? It's a long way back to Framingham, and I fear we won't arrive before nightfall as it is.''

''We'll get our things right away,'' Jeanne said.

She hurried up the stairs with her sister at her heels. He seemed very nice and he had soft eyes. The little boy was well behaved. Besides, he liked Yvette. Vaguely Jeanne wondered what his wife was like and why she had not come to help him make such an important decision. But it didn't matter, really. No matter what her apprehensions, she and Yvette would be together. They would have a roof over their heads, food to eat, and Yvette could go to school. At least for the time being, it seemed as if the black clouds that had hung over them just a short time ago had lifted and now the sun was shining.

We do indeed have a future. We're going to make a new beginning, Jeanne thought.

Chapter Three

It seemed the wagon had been bumping along forever. Matthew honestly felt they might never get home.

"Are you thirsty?" he asked. He was now aware that he had to speak slowly so that Jeanne could understand him. "I know it seems like a long way, but it's not so much farther. I guess the wagon's uncomfortable." What would she think of him? He was babbling. Why was he bringing up the matter of thirst, of distance and discomfort? He couldn't really do anything about any of them. I could stop at a tavern if she's thirsty, he thought. Not only was he babbling, he knew his thoughts were muddled.

"No, no. We're fine. The children seem fine." Jeanne had glanced back into the wagon only once. Yvette had been teaching Daniel how to play cat's cradle with the string. Then, after a time, the motion of the cart combined with the heat of the day and they had both fallen asleep against a pile of straw.

Matthew stared ahead. The sun was setting now in a

blaze of pink and gold glory over the mountains in the west. He felt awkward and unable to converse. It's just because she's a stranger, he told himself for the tenth time. But it was more than that. It was the fact that she was young, seemed to exude a joy of life even though she was painfully shy. And, yes, was even prettier than he had first realized.

On the one hand he was aware of having lost his own enthusiasm for life. His days were too long. The blacksmith shop took too many hours, and when he finished work he had to wash the clothes, clean the house and cook. The neighbors were kind, but their gifts of prepared food were sporadic while his need was constant.

I am a creature of pure habit, he thought.

Each day began at the same hour, each day the chores had to be done once again and nothing ever changed save his own mood which grew more morose daily. But it was more than just the routine; it was the dullness of his life combined with his concern for Daniel and his constant guilt and worry over Edwina. Sadly, he simply seemed to have no choices. He had put Edwina in the hospital because he could not care for her himself. She had to be hand fed like a child, she could not stand alone and she constantly spilled things because of her palsy. In the end, he had had to choose between Edwina and Daniel. He had chosen Daniel whose life was just beginning because Edwina's life was nearing the end, or so the doctors told him.

He glanced at the young woman. Would she make a difference in their lives? Again, he wondered if he had made a mistake. Still, Daniel needed someone, and the young woman's sister appeared to like him, while he seemed quite smitten with her. Again guilt spread over him like a blanket. What would people say when he arrived home with a comely eighteen-year-old? How could he have

allowed a five-year-old to make a decision for him? Everyone would talk.

Jeanne drew her light shawl around her as the sun set
and a purple half-light covered the uneven land. "Is it
much farther?"

"Not at all. It will take another half-hour."

"That's good." She did not want to complain that her
bottom hurt from sitting on the wooden seat for so long,
or that her legs were quite stiff. But it was all temporary.
Soon they would arrive, and surely Mrs. Schmidt would
offer her tea. She stared into the distance and wondered
about Mrs. Schmidt. She must be nice, Jeanne decided.
This man would not marry a woman who was not nice.
She thought of the Colbys who had almost hired her and
smiled at her narrow escape. They would not have been
good employers, she decided.

In less than half an hour, when it had grown completely
dark, the wagon turned down a rutted path. The horses,
recognizing their home turf, speeded up and trotted
toward a white clapboard house which stood on a slight
knoll and was in total darkness. It was a reasonably large
home, and because the night was bright, Jeanne could
make out the bushes that surrounded it and could see that
there was a small garden. Next to the house was another
building and outside it a sign that read Schmidt's Blacksmith Shop.

"Has your wife gone to bed so early?" Jeanne asked as
Matthew lifted her down from the wagon.

At that moment, Matthew froze. Did she not realize he
had no wife? Of course she didn't. What had seemed obvious to him, was not at all obvious to her, and he hadn't
told her anything; he hadn't mentioned a wife at all.

"My wife . . ." he began, but did not know exactly what

to say. He felt completely tongue-tied. The girl was looking up at him expectantly, and even though it was dark, he was sure there was a look of deep concern on her face. "Ah, the children are asleep," he said. "Let me carry them into the house and unhitch the horses. We'll go inside and I'll explain everything."

Jeanne felt rooted to the spot where she was standing. Should she do as he asked? She bit her lip and tried to think. There was no choice in any case. Well, surely nothing would happen. After all the children were here and would serve as chaperons of a sort, if indeed chaperons were needed. Perhaps, she reasoned, his wife was away or upstairs ill. Certainly the explanation seemed to involve more than he wished to go into while they stood outside in the dark.

"All right," Jeanne agreed. She took her bundle of clothes and her sister's as well. Matthew Schmidt easily lifted Yvette and headed for the door. He opened it and carried her upstairs. Then he returned and carried his son upstairs. When he came down, he lit the lamps.

Jeanne walked into the house and down a center hall. To one side was a nicely furnished parlor and to the other side was the staircase that led to the second floor. She proceeded down the hall.

"The kitchen's in there. You'll find all you need for tea, and if you want something else, help yourself. I'll put the horses in the barn and come back and we'll talk."

Jeanne nodded and watched him as he went out. Then she looked around. This main room was most certainly comfortable, though, she allowed, a little cluttered. It was large, with a big fireplace, a sink and cupboards. It had a long dining table and an alcove with a window that looked outside. Off this room was a pantry, the back stairs and a door that seemed to go through a covered connector to the barn. She had noted that type of design as they drove

along. Here, in New England, the houses were all con-
nected to the barn so that one did not have to go outside
in the cold to milk the cows or fetch the eggs. Not so in
Nova Scotia where the barns were always some distance
from the houses.

This main room which served as living room, dining
room and kitchen was not unlike the main rooms found
in Acadian homes. People always had big kitchen-living
areas because they virtually spent all their time in them,
especially in winter. The fireplace was large, and the ovens
on either side were of a good size. That this house lacked
a mistress seemed painfully evident. The ovens looked
reasonably unused, and although there were dishes in the
cupboards, there were only two in evidence and they were
on the counter within easy reach. The long table was uncov-
ered, and the kitchen had a cold, unused appearance. No,
there was no woman in this house. The vases lacked flowers,
though clearly the garden was in bloom. The furniture was
a little dusty, and there were dirty pots on the counter.

Jeanne poked at the embers in the fire and added some
wood. When it was again burning hot, she filled the kettle
from the pump on the sink and hung it over the fire. In
a few minutes, just as the tea kettle began to boil, Matthew
came into the kitchen.

"I'm sorry. I had to feed and water the horses. It is I
who should be fixing the tea. You've only just arrived."

"It's all right, the horses had to be put away."

Now that they were suddenly alone, Jeanne was doubly
aware of her discomfort. She poured the hot water into
the pot with the tea and then sat at the other end of the
long table.

"My wife," Matthew said without daring to look up,
"passed away two years ago. Daniel and I are alone." It
was a lie, a partial lie anyway. Edwina was dying, or so the

doctors said, and he and Daniel were most certainly alone. But somehow it seemed better to tell her Edwina was dead.

"Oh, dear." Jeanne put a hand over her mouth. What was she to say? It was quite impossible for her to live alone in a house with a single man. But then, as she thought about it, if he had a wife why would he need a housekeeper? She chastised herself for being so stupid and, indeed, for leading him on.

"I can see you're distressed," Matthew quickly said. "Please, don't be. This is my fault. I should have said something before I brought you all the way out here."

"I should have asked," Jeanne said, staring down at the table.

"I understand your hesitation, Miss Bellefontaine. I thought about it before I hired you. But you have no cause for concern. I'll move into my shop and you and the children will have the house to yourself."

Jeanne lifted her eyes for just a moment to look into his face. He had a good face, in fact she had to admit he was quite handsome. His eyes met hers, and she felt his honesty and decency. He seemed an honorable man. The offer he made was certainly an honorable one. "You wouldn't mind living in your shop?" she asked.

"No, it's the proper thing to do, Miss Bellefontaine. Of course, I would expect to eat here—and spend some time with my son after dinner before I went to the shop to retire."

Jeanne shook her head dumbly. "That would be—I guess it would be all right," she mumbled. She still felt ill at ease, but she reminded herself that finding another position that would enable her and Yvette to stay together would not be easy. This will work, she said to herself. Yes, I will have to make it work. "What about the neighbors?" she asked.

"I suppose some of them will talk at first. But I'll speak to the minister at the church. I think in time people will realize that we—I—am behaving properly."

Tongues would wag, Jeanne decided. Certainly in Nova Scotia if a young woman moved in with a handsome older man everyone would talk and talk. But she also supposed that when the situation became obvious, and people realized that Mr. Schmidt lived in his shop, they would stop talking. And again, she admitted that her choices were limited. She would have to try it, at least for a while.

"We shall stay," Jeanne said, looking into his eyes.

"Fine. No, wonderful. I really do need help."

Jeanne looked around and laughed lightly. "Yes, you do."

"When you finish your tea, you can take the larger bedroom upstairs. Tomorrow I'll move my things out so there will be room for yours."

Jeanne again smiled in spite of herself. "I'm afraid there is little for me to unpack. What I brought is all there is."

Matthew's face reddened. " I . . . I thought there might be a trunk coming, or something."

Jeanne shook her head.

He looked at her for a long moment. She was certainly shorter than Edwina, but with little alteration there was no doubt use could be made of Edwina's clothes. He had never touched them, though more than once he had considered giving them to the poor. It was a terrible thing for clothes to go to waste, and clearly Miss Bellefontaine would require more that two dresses.

"Please don't misunderstand," he began with hesitation, "but upstairs in the closet are a number of dresses that belonged to my wife. My neighbors would all say 'Waste not, want not,' so I can't throw them out. I think with a few alterations they'd fit you."

Waste not, want not. Jeanne could all but hear her own

frugal grandmother speaking those words which had been her motto. "That's very generous of you," Jeanne said, still staring at the table.

He drained his teacup and stood up, tipping over the chair in the process. "Sorry," he muttered as he picked it up. "I'll just go and get some things, and then I'll leave."

Jeanne finished her own tea, then washed the cups. By the time she had finished, he was walking through the kitchen with a few shirts and some long red underwear over his arm.

"Good night now," he managed. And then, like a frightened deer, he was gone, darting into the blacksmith shop and leaving her standing alone in the kitchen.

Jeanne sighed. Then she extinguished the lamp and went upstairs. She felt incredibly weary, more tired than she would have admitted if asked. It was as if everything that had happened in the last six months had overtaken her and the false energy that had driven her had now fled. And though this was an odd situation—a very different situation from the one she had imagined herself being in—she felt suddenly quite relaxed, as if, for the moment at least, a great weight had been lifted from her.

"Lunch!"

Matthew put down his tools and wiped his brow. Jeanne's voice had a lilting musical quality. "I'm coming!" he called back.

He smiled as he lifted a damp cloth from the always warm water he kept near the forge. He washed his face, arms and hands. The outside temperature was high, and it was doubly steamy here in the shop where the fire had to be constantly stoked in order to remain hot enough to forge steel. He wiped himself dry with another cloth, then discarded his leather vest, under which he wore nothing. He pulled on his shirt and headed for the house while buttoning it.

As he walked across the grass that separated the house from the shop, he saw the freshly washed clothes on the line billowing in the summer breeze. He opened the door and looked around the parlor. In just the three weeks that Jeanne and Yvette had been here, it was a house transformed. The clutter was gone, the house was clean to the point where it almost sparkled, and vases of fresh flowers were on every table. More important, Daniel wore clean mended clothes and seemed more at ease than he had been since the day his mother left. He ate heartily of the tasty food Jeanne prepared, listened when Yvette read to him and even smiled now and again.

Yes, Matthew thought with gratitude, his life had been changed. A wave of guilt spread over him. He ought to tell Jeanne the truth about Edwina. He couldn't think why he'd made up the lie. It plagued him; yet he was somehow afraid to tell her the truth now, afraid she might leave.

He walked into the large kitchen and sat down at the end of the table. A clean red and white cloth covered it and the polished pewter milk jug shone so that he could see his distorted image in it. Abstractedly, he brushed the cowlick off his forehead.

Yvette and Daniel were already seated, and Jeanne turned away from the stove and came to the table, carrying a large platter. The roast chicken upon it was surrounded by vegetables from the garden. It was their custom to eat the main meal in the middle of the day. Supper was a lighter meal, often just soup and bread.

Matthew stole a look at Jeanne. She was wearing a blue and white checked dress and a snow white pinafore. Her mass of dark curls was only partially hidden beneath her lacy, dust cap. Her large expressive eyes danced with happiness even though she said nothing as she sat down. It had once been Edwina's dress. But on Jeanne it looked completely different.

"Will you say grace?" Yvette asked.

He bowed his head. "We thank the Lord for our food," he said simply. As always, Yvette and Jeanne crossed themselves. He wasn't a deeply religious man, though in fact his own parents had been Catholic before they had left Germany. But Catholics were not welcome in Massachusetts, and eventually they had simply begun attending the Church of England.

Matthew knew Jeanne and Yvette were both Catholic, and it occurred to him that when he had time, he would take them into Boston. There was no church there, but there was a priest; and a few Catholics met for religious services at the home of one of their number. But he said nothing now.

He spread the hot bread with butter and ate it. "It's good," he said gratefully. "You would laugh if you saw what I used to make before you came."

Jeanne looked at him and blushed ever so slightly.

"My bread could be used for a hammer, right, Daniel?" he said.

To his surprise, Daniel nodded back and grinned.

Jeanne wondered where in the world he'd found time to make bread before she came. He worked such long hours! It seemed to her that his shop was always full of people waiting to have their horses shod. And last Wednesday he had been gone all day. He told her that he would, in fact, be absent all day every other Wednesday. Vaguely, she wondered where he went when he disappeared early on those Wednesday mornings twice a month. It occurred to her that he might be courting someone in a nearby town. That thought bothered her slightly, and she found she hoped it was not so.

"There's a big market-fair in Natick next Saturday, would you all like to go?"

"Can we?" Yvette asked, turning toward her sister.

Jeanne smiled. "I guess so."

"It's a good chance to buy anything we might want to have for winter," he said, "and there's usually plenty to do and see. Pie-eating contests and three-legged races— swimming in the lake if it doesn't rain."

"Oh, it sounds like fun. Daniel, maybe we could row on the lake. Are there boats?" Yvette looked into Daniel's eyes.

Much to Matthew's surprise, Daniel made a motion as if he were rowing. Matthew said nothing, but he was truly amazed. He had thought only he could communicate with Daniel in this rather personal sign language. But it seemed that little Yvette had a magic way with his son.

Matthew began eating his vegetables and chicken. Neither Jeanne nor Yvette talked much, but he knew they were contented and that he was happy to have them. Jeanne was becoming less reticent, but he could not blame her for being shy because it was a trait he shared with her.

Matthew watched as Jeanne cleared the table. "You know, you make the best apple pie I've ever tasted. It's . . . well, it's not only different, it's special!"

"Thank you. My grandmother taught me," Jeanne replied. "I'm so sorry I didn't make any today."

"No, I didn't mean I wanted it today. I meant, well, why don't you enter the pie-baking contest at the fair?"

Jeanne turned toward the sink. "I don't really think mine is good enough."

"Of course it is," Yvette chimed in.

Jeanne was aware of feeling more at home than an

employee should. Still, she had met almost no one from
the community, and she was a stranger to the neighbors.
Not just a stranger, but a stranger who had a distinct French
accent and who was a Papist, as Catholics were called by
so many. Perhaps, she reasoned, entering the pie-making
contest would provide an opportunity for her to become
a part of the community, to show others that she was not
so different from them. She turned, wiping her hands on
the towel. "Do you really think it's good enough?"

Matthew looked at her and quickly reassured her. "Yes!
It's delicious—and with the spices you use, it's unique."

"All right, I'll do it."

Matthew nodded and then stood up. He hated leaving
the table to go and finish the chores. It was as if, for the
first time in three years, he had a family. Jeanne was loving
with little Daniel and so was Yvette. When Jeanne came
into a room, it somehow seemed to be filled with warmth.
And she was so pretty! Her large dark eyes were both
inquisitive and expressive, while her skin was like that of
a china doll, milky and white. And though he forced himself to turn away from the obvious and not dwell on it, he
could hardly deny the fact that she was petite and well
proportioned, with full breasts, a small waist and rounded
hips.

These were quite improper thoughts, he reminded himself. He stood up and hurried away from the table. The
horses had to be watered, the pigs fed, the cows milked.
There was much to do before he returned to his shop.
There was no time to think about what might have been
or what might be someday in the distant future. He was a
married man; he had to keep reminding himself of that
fact over and over. This woman who made his house a
home was not his wife. His wife—moisture filled his eyes
as he walked between the house and the barn—his wife
had deteriorated so. The last time he had seen her he had

been shocked by her appearance. It was as if she had aged twenty years in a matter of months. He forced his thoughts away from Edwina. Thinking about her and the future they had lost was just too painful.

Chapter Four

It was the last Saturday in August, the symbolic end of summer, though in fact summer showed no signs of leaving. The sun was bright, but not as hot as it had been a month ago. The sky was cloudless, and a light breeze ensured comfort.

"I've never been to a proper fair and market!" Yvette exclaimed as she tied on her crisp white bonnet and then turned to straighten Daniel's vest. "Have you been before?"

Daniel nodded and smiled.

"Oh, I can tell it will be fun! And when it's over, we can write down what we liked best in our secret book."

Daniel smiled again.

It was their secret, Yvette thought proudly. But one day she would let the others know. Daniel might not be able to speak, but he was learning to print. And every night, when they were alone, they wrote down their favorite things about the day. She helped him, but he was really getting

quite proficient. Ever since she had been here she had
helped him. Next week they would both start school. She
knew Daniel was afraid because he did not speak, so special
arrangements had been made before the teacher would
accept him in the class. Yvette took joy in their secret
and felt quite proud of her accomplishment. The teacher
would surely be surprised that a child who could not speak
could print and actually write some of his thoughts. Not
that he had a large vocabulary yet, but he would have. And
the teacher would likewise be surprised at how quickly she
had mastered reading English. Teaching Daniel was the
reason, one had to learn oneself before teaching another.

"I love you," she whispered in Daniel's ear. He put
his arms around her and hugged her back. "We have
something special," she confided. Daniel squeezed her
hand to show her he had understood. Yes, Yvette thought.
Little Daniel understood as no one else could. After all,
Jeanne had been ten when their mother died. Jeanne had
known their mother, but she had not. Jeanne tried of
course, but no matter how hard she tried, she was a sister,
not a mother. Daniel's mother was ill when he was an
infant, and then she died. Neither of them had known
that special love. But now they had each other, and what
they felt for one another was unique.

"It's time to go!" Jeanne sang out.

Yvette took Daniel's small hand in hers. "Let's go have
fun," she said happily as they hurried off.

"Oh! It's wonderful!" Jeanne said, in awe. It seemed as
if everyone in Framingham and those from most of the
surrounding villages were there. The rolling lawns teemed
with people, wagons and horses.

Most homemade goods were sold from the backs of farm
wagons, though some who had wares to offer had spread

cloths out on the ground and sold their merchandise from there.

Fresh garden produce, home-baked cakes, fancy breads, candies and fudge were all offered for sale. In addition to foodstuffs, women sold embroidered samplers, crocheted aprons and doilies, dresses, fancy woven blankets and handmade quilts. Men sold chairs and desks and other pieces of handmade furniture. The sales were not limited to local goods either, several itinerant traders had come from Boston in their wagons, and they sold fine pewter, silver, ribbons and even imported Irish lace.

It wasn't just the sight of goods for sale that made the market-fair fascinating. It was also the variety of mouth-watering smells which filled the morning air.

A huge iron pot of freshly harvested unhusked corn boiled merrily. It was to be eaten on the cob with freshly churned butter. A short distance away, a pig roasted on a spit, over hot coals. The cooking aromas mingled with the smell of newly scythed grass and the scents of the wildflowers.

As promised, there were activities for all. Children, under the watchful eyes of their parents, swam in the lake while couples, anxious to escape the crowd, paddled about in canoes, seeking the privacy of the tall cattails on the far side of the lake. Not far from the shore of the lake, men and boys took part in races, while girls arranged the entries in the various contests on tables. Tables of preserves, pies and cakes were all placed in competition for the blue ribbons that would proclaim the best in each category.

No sooner did they arrive than Yvette and Daniel were off toward the lake.

"She's a fine strong swimmer," Jeanne said when she saw the look of concern on Matthew's face.

"You can read my thoughts."

"We'll go down there too, just so you'll be comfortable. As soon as I've entered my pie."

Matthew walked with Jeanne toward the pie table. His neighbors greeted him and eyed Jeanne, not unkindly but with curiosity.

"It's quite all right, Charity. He's moved into the black-smith shop. It's all very proper," Matthew heard Mr. Waltham tell his wife rather too loudly.

"Shhh!" his wife admonished. "They'll hear you."

But Mr. Waltham was quite deaf and thought everyone as hard of hearing as he. "What does it matter?" he grouched. "He knows where he sleeps, and she doesn't speak English."

Jeanne glanced at Matthew. He was slightly flushed and so was she. Still, it was rather funny. "Should I surprise them?" she asked playfully.

He shook his head. "It will only result in a long, loud and public conversation." Then he looked into her large dark eyes and saw they were twinkling. He realized she was joking and he smiled back at her. "I'm too, too serious, am I not?"

"Yes," she agreed.

Jeanne put her pie on the table and the woman behind the table put a number on it and then handed Jeanne a scrap of paper with the same number. "I guess I am entered," she said.

Matthew led her down to the lake and there spread out a blanket on the grass. She folded her skirts around her and sat down. He selected the farthest corner of the blanket and sat there. He suspected they looked rather silly, but still it was only prudent. Everyone gossiped, and he wanted her reputation unsullied. In any case, he knew she, too, was sensitive and anxious that no one should misinterpret their relationship.

After a while, Jeanne left Matthew to watch Yvette and

Daniel swim and play. She went walking amid the many items on sale, and in the end bought some ribbons for Yvette's hair and a new brush for her own hair.

It was when she was walking back that she heard her name being shouted out. She had won the pie contest! Jeanne, in a burst of enthusiasm, picked up her skirts and ran.

Matthew was already there when she came up, breathless, to claim her prize of a handmade pillow cover.

"Best pie I ever tasted," one of the judges said, licking his lips.

The women who gathered around nodded their approval and murmured their congratulations. Suddenly, for the first time since her arrival, Jeanne was aware of a new acceptance. She had not missed the looks she was given on the street, nor the comments she overheard on the two occasions Matthew had taken her into the village. But now everyone seemed to know that she worked for Mr. Schmidt who lived in his shop, she was a good cook and there was no more to it than that.

"Thank you," Jeanne managed as a matronly woman in a crisp white apron handed her the pillow cover and her blue ribbon. "It must be a good pie," the woman said, smiling. "We're all pretty good cooks too."

Jeanne laughed softly. "I know you are," she replied.

At five o'clock, Matthew loaded everyone back in the wagon.

"When's the next fair?" Yvette asked. She honestly could not remember having more fun. She rustled Daniel's hair, it appeared to have grown even blonder in the strong sun.

"It's not a fair," Matthew answered. "But we have a harvest festival—we call it Thanksgiving."

"Is it soon?"

Matthew laughed. "Not till November, I'm afraid. But there's All Hallows' Eve in October. That's when we start making Christmas baskets for the poor."

"What a nice idea," Jeanne said.

"We'll have to make four this year, because there are four of us. We take them to the church for distribution."

"What goes into them?" Jeanne asked.

"Preserves, bread—of course that can't be done till the last minute—a homemade doll, candy and a chicken. And sometimes special things like bayberry candles or scented soap."

"I know how to make dolls out of corn husks," Yvette said.

"And old men puppets from dried apples," Jeanne added.

Matthew made a clicking sound with his mouth as he turned the horses toward home. "I think the poor will have some surprises this year."

As the horses plodded toward home, and the children slept in the back of the wagon, Matthew stole a long look at Jeanne's profile. Her features were delicate, indeed everything about her seemed delicate. Nonetheless, he knew she was strong of intellect, will and spirit. It was abundantly clear that her life had been hard and that she came from a community where every family's survival depended on ingenuity.

Much to his surprise, she dried the fish he caught rather than taking it to a family in town whose specialty it was to dry fish. Her garden flourished, she put up preserves and she was in the process of making something called fir beer which she assured him he would like.

In addition to her homemaking skills, she read, was wonderful with Daniel and her own younger sister, and when they conversed she could contribute interesting bits of information or ideas. She talked now and then of her own people, but he did not press her for details since the mention of family seemed to make her sad.

I admire her, he admitted to himself as he thought of the day they had just spent together. He knew one of the reasons why was her ability to win over the often tight and all too proper New Englanders. Her smile melted their disapproval of her French accent, her intelligence belied their previously held views of Acadians and her propriety had quelled any possible talk around town. Still, he worried. All day he had feared someone would ask about Edwina.

I have to tell her the truth, he told himself again. It was wrong of me to have lied. No, not yet, he thought. He couldn't tell her now, they were too close to home, and when they arrived, the children might wake up. They had to be put to bed in any case. No, this was a conversation which required not only privacy but preparation as well.

He shook his head. He dreaded it and knew he would put it off a while longer.

"It's the biggest pumpkin in the world!" Yvette said as she looked at the giant orange gourd.

Daniel explored the pumpkin with interest. Then without a moment's hesitation, he ran to the bookshelf and returned with a worn copy of English nursery rhymes.

Matthew put down the gourds Jeanne had asked him to bring in to decorate the house, and Jeanne put down her mending. Both of them looked surprised that Daniel had gone to the bookshelf.

They watched with amazement as he opened the book and began turning the pages. Then he stopped and took the open book to his father.

Matthew looked at the page, and Jeanne could see he

was completely taken aback. She glanced at her sister and saw the smile on Yvette's face.

"He's picked out a rhyme about a pumpkin!" Matthew said. "Son, you have an excellent memory!"

Yvette exchanged a knowing glance with Daniel which neither adult saw.

"I think he wants you to read it to him," Jeanne suggested.

"All right. Come here, son."

Daniel climbed up beside his father. And then, quite unexpectedly, put his small finger on the word "pumpkin."

"Good for you!" Matthew praised. "He knows the word 'pumpkin.' "

Yvette glanced at her sister. "He knows other words too," she revealed.

"You mean he can read?"

Yvette nodded. "I believe he can."

Daniel tugged on Matthew's leather vest.

"He does want you to read it," Yvette confirmed.

Matthew pointed to the black and white drawing that accompanied the rhyme. " 'Peter, Peter, pumpkin eater, had a wife and couldn't keep her. Locked her in a pumpkin shell, and there he kept her very well.' "

"I shouldn't like being locked in a pumpkin shell," Yvette said.

Matthew gazed at the words and the illustration, and then he looked at his son. He felt ill at ease and wondered if the selection of this particular rhyme had been a result of seeing the pumpkin or if it had something to do with his mother. Did Daniel think he had locked Edwina up? A wave of guilt shot through him. In a way, he had. He had shut her away. All the old questions surfaced. How could he have taken care of her and still run the blacksmith shop and the farm that supported them? Edwina required care he could not give. Daniel required care.

Now there were other considerations as well. Daniel seemed to be progressing under Jeanne's loving supervision and Yvette's constant attention. How would he react to seeing his mother—a mother who would not even recognize him?

"Is something the matter?" Jeanne asked with concern.

Matthew shook his head quickly. "No, I'm just surprised. You're a good teacher, Yvette."

Yvette glowed. "There are other rhymes he likes too."

"You have time to read a few more before dinner," Jeanne said as she put her sewing aside and got up to go into the kitchen. "I think my meat pie must be almost ready."

Matthew turned the pages and then began reading. Daniel curled up next to him, seemingly enraptured with the sound of his father's voice. Matthew thought to himself that he had never had time to do this before. And in spite of his thoughts about Edwina, he knew he was more relaxed than he had been in a long while. Jeanne had brought order out of chaos, and order had brought him a new peace of mind.

The fire glowed in the fireplace, taking the evening chill off the house. It had been a long day, a day filled with happiness and satisfaction.

"This is my favorite time of year," Matthew said. "I love the fall, the warm days and cool nights, the trees ablaze in orange, red and yellow. There's a wonderful smell in the mornings—the early morning frost and smoke as it curls out of the chimney."

Jeanne smiled. "Oh, you're a romantic. Perhaps you should write poetry."

Matthew laughed self-consciously. The truth was, All Hallows' Eve marked the beginning of the holiday season. Thanksgiving would be next and then Christmas. Once he'd adored all three, and this was the first time he had expressed his love of the season since Edwina went to the hospital. These holidays were family times, and for years he and Daniel had been alone. Now suddenly they were a family again. I do think of us as a family, he admitted to himself. And Jeanne . . . He knew he was beginning to think of her as his wife in all but one way. It was wrong, so wrong, but he wanted her to be his wife—his in all ways.

"My favorite holiday is Christmas," Yvette said wistfully. She turned toward Daniel. "That's when Père Noël comes. He's an old man with a white beard, and he wears shiny black boots, bright blue knickers and a red coat trimmed with fur. He brings candy and presents to good children. One year before my grandmother died I got a red pair of mittens and a matching hat with a long, long top and a tiny bell on the end."

"Père Noël," Matthew repeated. "My parents came from Germany. We call your Père Noël, Sintar Klaus. Every year we used to get a special calendar in December called an Advent Calendar. Each day we opened a little door on the calendar and found a new verse to memorize. Then, on Christmas Eve, we went into the woods and cut down a small fir tree. We decorated it with candles and cookies and put presents for one another under it."

"What a lovely custom," Jeanne said. "Tell me what special foods you ate?"

"Fruit bread and puddings. Usually a goose was our main course."

Jeanne smiled. "I can try to make those things." Secretly she thought, Yvette and I will cut down a small tree and decorate it. If she started now, she could make enough little candles. Certainly someone hereabouts knew how to make this fruit bread of which he spoke. And then she remembered Mrs. Brun. She was German too, and she was said to be a very good cook. She lived a few miles away.

She looked at Matthew and then quickly away since he was looking at her. He was very handsome, but he was more than just handsome. He was a good man. A hardworking intelligent man who seemed lonely. Or maybe, she thought, it is I who is lonely. Sometimes in the early morning hours she would wake before the cock crowed and would lie in bed and think about him. She wondered how he felt about her. Perhaps he thought her too young. Yet clearly he liked her—no, more than liked. She sensed he was attracted to her and she knew she felt the same about him. But time would tell. Yes, she admitted, if she thought about his strong arms around her, it sent a chill right down her spine. But she hoped she was not obvious. Perhaps, she thought, I am wrong. Perhaps there is someone else he cares for, or perhaps he still mourns his wife and cannot yet let go of her memory.

"What do you want for Christmas?" Yvette asked, turning toward Matthew.

"Ah, I want . . ." Matthew flushed slightly. He wanted Jeanne, wanted to hold her and kiss her. He wanted her for his wife. But he had no right to do so, no right at all. He had lied to her, and when she found out she might well go away forever. No, he had no right to want or even dream about this beautiful, vital young woman.

"You want what?" Yvette pressed.

"I want a good harvest and a good business over the winter."

"I want Daniel to talk," Yvette said, pressing Daniel's hand.

Matthew looked at Yvette and Daniel and inexplicably tears filled his eyes. He sniffed. "Yes, oh, I seem to have a cinder in my eye." He got up and went into the other room to blow his nose. Grown men were not supposed to cry.

"Enough of Christmas dreams for tonight," he heard Jeanne say. "Yvette, you and Daniel have to go to bed now. Tomorrow is a school day and you have to be well rested and well fed to properly learn."

Yvette scrambled to her feet and took Daniel by the hand. Both children hurried up the stairs.

Matthew came back into the parlor. "I suppose I should be going to bed too," he said.

Jeanne looked up from her sewing. "Please don't go so early. It's much nicer here by the fire. I found a checker game the other day. I put it over there. Could we play?"

Matthew grinned. It was the first time she had ever asked him to remain after the children went to bed. "Of course!" he replied. "I'd love to play."

Jeanne put down her sewing and went to the shelf. She came back with the board and wooden pieces. "I've only seen people play," she admitted. "You'll have to teach me."

She looked up at him with her large brown eyes, and he felt drawn into them. They were soft, loving eyes, beautiful eyes, each with a golden ring around the pupil. Her hair was loose tonight, and it fell over her shoulders in a profusion of thick dark curls. Her skin was like ivory. He reached out instinctively and touched her neck with his hand. Then he leaned down and touched his lips to hers. They were warm and moist, and he drew her into his arms, holding her tightly and kissing first her lips and then her neck.

At first she tried to pull away, but then she returned his kisses. He could feel her warmth in his arms, feel the rounded softness of her body. "Oh, Jeanne," he breathed.

She was silent as he held her. Perhaps she was stunned or too surprised to say anything. No, he had felt her return

his kiss. She wasn't upset or shocked. She had wanted him
to kiss her, he knew it. But this could not go on. The time
had come not just for self-restraint but for honesty.

He pulled back and with his large hands on her shoulders he looked into her face. She was slightly flushed and
looked a tiny bit confused.

"We shouldn't . . ." Jeanne managed to get out as she
looked back into his eyes and tried to fathom the conflict-
ing emotions that surged through her. First and foremost
was a feeling of elation she could not quell. She had wanted
him to kiss her! Now she realized much more. She wanted
him to love her, to make love to her. She wanted to be his
wife and perhaps even give him more children. But she
might be wrong. Perhaps his attraction to her was only
physical, maybe it was because he was so very lonely. She
warned herself against jumping to conclusions—against
giving her heart too soon—although she admitted, it might
well be too late.

"Oh, Jeanne," he said as he closed his eyes. "I have no
right. I have no right to—"

Jeanne could see the pain on his face. He was still holding her shoulders. But he was shaking his head and his
expression was one of remorse.

"You have no right to what?" she asked softly.

"I have no right to love you. I've lied to you, Jeanne.
Oh, heaven forgive me, I've lied to you."

Jeanne reached up and touched his cheek. "Tell me,"
she murmured. He loved her? She was touched deeply by
his words and apprehensive all at the same time.

"My wife is not dead," he managed.

Jeanne could not move. She felt as stiff as a bit of wood.
A chill passed through her. But in spite of his shocking
words, she could not pull away.

"Edwina is very ill, both physically and mentally. I had
to put her in a hospital in Boston. She is cared for. I

couldn't look after her and take care of Daniel too—it was impossible."

"This is not right," she murmured. "It is not right for us to be together."

Matthew dropped his hands, but continued to look into her face. "I know—I know it's not right. I have no right to my feelings for you. I've been so lonely, Jeanne. Edwina does not even know who I am."

Jeanne dropped her eyes to the floor. What was she to say to him? She felt as he did, but she knew she could not allow herself to love him, not now, perhaps not ever.

"If you want to leave I'll find another position for you," he offered. "I never should have lied to you."

Jeanne could hear the pain in his voice. It was not an offer he wanted her to accept. "I don't know what to do," she answered honestly. "I want to think about this—about what you have told me. It is not just you and I, Matthew. I must think of Yvette and we must both think of Daniel."

Matthew nodded. "He stopped speaking when his mother went away—I mean he didn't talk before that except for baby talk. But when she left he never learned to talk and he gave up all vocalization. He was so sad before you and Yvette came. I was so sad."

Jeanne could not speak. Her own emotions warred with one another. "We'll talk tomorrow," she said as she turned and ran upstairs.

Matthew watched her. She was crying.

Chapter Five

The day had passed more slowly than Matthew believed possible. He cursed himself for kissing Jeanne and then telling her about Edwina. He should have told her first . . . He should have told her long ago. And he had no right to kiss her, to want her; he had no right to feel so consumed by the love he felt for her. He looked at the clock. He had spent every second of this day wondering if she would leave. Finally, he heard her call him for dinner. He washed and hurried inside.

As they ate Yvette talked about school and how hard it was to memorize all the names of the English Kings and Queens. Then, at Yvette's request, he read to both of them while Jeanne cleaned the kitchen and cleared away the dishes. Finally, he put them to bed.

When he returned to the main room he found Jeanne standing by the fireplace, staring at the dying embers of the fire. He went and stood next to her. She turned slowly and looked into his eyes.

She reached out across the distance that was now between them, her fingers lightly touching his arm. "We won't leave," she murmured. She shook her head, and tears began to run down her cheeks. "I will suffer eternal damnation if I stay with you, but I love you too much to leave."

As he had the night before, Matthew drew her into his arms. She trembled against him as she sobbed. "You should have trusted me with the truth."

"I love you so much. I was afraid you would leave. I should have told you everything from the beginning," he said, touching her hair. "I'm so glad you're staying . . . I need you and love you. But I'm going out to the shop as I always do, Jeanne."

She nodded and then again touched his cheek. "Take me to see her," she said softly. "I want to see your Edwina."

"I don't deserve you," he replied slowly. "Are you certain?"

"I'm very certain."

Matthew gazed into her eyes for another long moment. It wasn't a kiss, but to Jeanne it felt like one. He was mentally caressing her, and she knew in her heart that he was too honorable a man not to be torn apart by his duty to Edwina and his feelings for her, feelings he had expressed quite clearly. It tore at her too, but they would have to refrain from a repetition of last night's short sweet pleasure. There could be no more kisses and, for her, no more dreams. He was married, his wife was ill. They loved each other, but it was a love that would have to wait. Perhaps, she thought sadly, it was a love that would have to wait forever.

Matthew closed the door of the blacksmith shop behind him. He carried the lantern in one hand and for a moment looked around the familiar place. The fire still burned, and the room was still warm. He walked to the back of the shop and stood by his makeshift bed. Slowly he undressed, thinking about what had happened—and what had not happened.

He sat down on the side of the bed and held his head in his hands for a few minutes. He hadn't really told her anything about his relationship with Edwina, and now he wondered if he should have. She was so trusting, so honest and so caring. "I do love you," he said aloud. How could he tell her that in spite of being married, in spite of having a son, he had never felt this emotion before? How could he tell her that he had felt only duty, but never love?

"Later, after she's met Edwina," he said to himself. Yes, he thought that would be the time to tell Jeanne about Edwina and how they came to be married.

"This is where you go when you disappear," Jeanne surmised as they approached the outskirts of Boston.

"Yes. Every other Wednesday. I drive to Boston and I sit with her. At first I hoped she would get better and would remember—would return to normal. But as time went by, well, I guess I just accepted the truth that Edwina will never be right again."

Jeanne had wondered where he went on Wednesdays. He was always gone a full ten hours. She had assumed it had something to do with his business, although she couldn't think just what. Then, for a short time, she had decided he might be courting someone, and she acknowledged that she had felt jealous. Now she knew the truth— or at least most of it. It is strange, she thought. When she had believed Matthew might be courting another woman, she had felt envy, but she felt no such emotion toward his ill wife even though she knew that Edwina might prove a permanent impediment to their mutual love.

It had been a relatively silent ride into town. At first they had discussed the unusually warm fall weather, then the maple-covered hills which Jeanne said, "Rivaled Joseph's coat of many colors." Then they had gradually lapsed into quietude as they explored their own thoughts.

Matthew drew in the reins and brought the horses to a stop in front of a two-story gray stone building. Its windows were without curtains, and from the cobbled sidewalk outside it looked uninhabited and cold.

He helped Jeanne down from the wagon and led her up the stone steps. They passed through heavy wooden doors, and Jeanne suddenly felt as if the odor of the place would overcome her. The smell of vinegar permeated everything, and she detected a strange smell that she could only describe as decay.

Matthew saw the expression on her face and took her arm gently. "After a few minutes you won't notice the odor," he assured her. "There are many sick or old people here, people without families to care for them."

He stopped in front of a desk and signed his name in a book. Then he led her down a long dull corridor and around a corner. He opened the door of a room and Jeanne followed him inside.

Before she saw another thing in the room, Jeanne saw the frail woman lying on the bed. She was tied in, her blond hair spread out around her tiny face on the pillow. Her lips were dry, and when she opened her eyes and saw them, she began struggling to get free. Her eyes were almost animal-like—frightened and furtive. And most distressing was the fact that she looked twenty years older than Matthew. Her skin was yellow and wrinkled, her nails long and uncut. She appeared unkempt and uncared for, save for the basic necessities.

"Edwina," Matthew said, leaning close.

Edwina regarded him with dull eyes, and her hands trembled.

Jeanne poured some water into the tin cup on the stand, and going round to the other side of the old iron bed, she held the cup to Edwina's cracked lips. The woman drank noisily, half sipping, half lapping as if her thirst was intense.

"She can't reach her water," Jeanne said with concern. "She's terribly thirsty."

"They're so busy here. I don't like it, but it's actually the best of such places."

Edwina was exactly the way Matthew had described her. She stared blankly into space, her body was shriveled and shaking; still it seemed clear that the care she received was less than it should be.

"They don't know what she has," Matthew said softly. "They only know she remembers nothing, her body is wasting away and she has terrible tremors and cannot eat by herself."

Jeanne moved Edwina a little and Edwina cried out in pain. "Oh, dear. She has terrible bed sores." Jeanne shook her head. "It's because she isn't turned enough. Matthew, we must take her from this place and bring her home with us."

Matthew frowned; he could hear the concern and determination in Jeanne's voice. But did she really understand what she was saying? "She requires a good deal of care. Jeanne, I can't ask you to take this on."

"You are not asking me. I am volunteering. She cannot stay here. I couldn't sleep at night just thinking about this place. I can take care of her, Matthew. I took care of my grandmother for a year before she died. Believe me when I tell you I do know what is involved."

Matthew looked into her heavily lashed, doelike eyes.

He was so touched by her concern that he wanted to hold her—not out of passion, though heaven knew he felt that, but out of gratitude. She was a veritable angel, willing to give of herself. And heaven knew she was right. He had hated having Edwina here. He was racked with guilt each time he left her. Yet he had not even noticed the bed sores.

"Are you sure you want to do this?" he asked. "Jeanne, be honest, please."

"I'm sure, Matthew. We must take her home, and the sooner the better."

"And Daniel? How will he react to seeing her this way? How will he respond when she doesn't recognize him?"

"I don't know. We'll have to try to explain to him. Daniel's been through a lot, I don't think we should underestimate him. Most important, I think he should be with his mother regardless of her condition."

"When I brought her here, Daniel knew she was ill. But he was too young to understand. I thought I was doing the right thing."

Jeanne touched his arm. "You were, but the situation has changed." She didn't say because now you have me, but it was what she meant. Whatever she and Matthew felt for one another would have to wait, perhaps for a very long time. In the meantime, the expression of her love for him would have to be manifested in the care of Edwina. Although, looking at the pitiful little woman in the iron bed, she knew she would have wanted to help in any case.

"We can't take her home today," he said. "I don't think she could make the journey in the wagon."

"We'll hire a carriage and take her home in a few days. It will take me a short time to prepare for her. I think she should have her bed in the alcove off the main room. That way, we'd always be nearby and she would feel a part of—" Jeanne stopped short because she had started to say our family.

Matthew touched her arm. "It's all right. We are a family—an adopted family."

Unspoken was their mutual desire to be a real family. Unspoken were the emotions they felt for one another, emotions they now willingly disregarded.

Jeanne looked with satisfaction on the alcove. The bed was against the wall and the window that looked out onto the front yard was at the foot of it. Edwina, sitting up in bed, would be able to see the flowers in the spring, the changing leaves of fall, and the snows of winter. She would be able to see Daniel and Yvette come home from school or at play.

For safety's sake, Matthew had put a rail around the other side of the bed so that Edwina would not fall out. Not only was the atmosphere cheerful, but everything was spanking clean. Unlike the gray sheets at the hospital, these sheets were white as snow. Instead of a scratchy old blanket, this bed was covered with a gay patchwork quilt of many colors. The crockery pitcher on the bedside table was not grim and cracked but new and clean, and inside it was crystal-clear well water.

Beside the bed was a rocker. Jeanne hoped that Edwina could spend some time out of bed, sitting up.

Anxiously, Jeanne looked out the window. Matthew had spent last night in Boston so he could get an early start back. Generously, Mr. Williams, who owned the local mill, had loaned Matthew his carriage.

Again Jeanne looked out the window. She hoped Matthew would bring Edwina before the children got home from school. It was a wish that came true. She had just turned her back to finish arranging the fresh flowers in the vase by the bed when she heard the sound of the carriage coming down the dirt road from the main Post Road.

In a few seconds the carriage came into view and in only another few minutes, Matthew was carrying Edwina's shriveled unconscious form into the house.

He gently placed her on the bed. "They gave her some sleeping powders," he explained. "They said it would make the trip easier."

Jeanne pulled the curtains she had put over the entrance to the alcove. "Leave me with her, Matthew. Let me give her a sponge bath and put her into a clean night dress."

He began to protest, but Jeanne touched a finger to her lips. "Just leave it to me. You go back to the shop and ask the children to stay outside for a while. I want to get her fixed up a bit."

Matthew glanced at Edwina. It seemed a hopeless task. His wife looked pitiful, and he was unsure if Jeanne, even though he knew she was determined, could do anything to make Edwina appear different. He felt helpless, but he was glad Jeanne was shooing him away. The longer he looked at Edwina, the more guilty and helpless he felt. It wasn't her disease, of course; he did not blame himself for that in any way. It was his inability to look after her that haunted him. No, it was more than that. He had sympathy for her as he would have had for any sick person, but he knew he did not feel what a husband should. Indeed, he never had. He turned and left, his mind on the past, on deeds long done.

He had been fourteen when he and his parents immigrated to America in 1734. They were German Catholics, but as there were no Catholics in the Bay Colony when they came, and indeed none were welcome, they had allowed their faith to lapse.

His parents had built this farm and the blacksmith business out of the wilderness. How well he remembered clear-

ing the land with his father. It seemed as if they would
never manage a clearing for the house and barn, and there
were no end of rocks in the fields when they began to till
the soil. But they finally succeeded. Now hundreds of those
rocks marked off the land that belonged to him.

When he was eighteen, in 1738, his parents decided it
was time for him to take a wife. As they would have in
Germany, they consulted with friends. Eventually a suitable
candidate was found.

Matthew remembered the first time he had met Edwina.
She was small and brittle and had straight blond hair. They
were the same age, and they were both awkward and unsure
of themselves. She was presented to him as a woman who
could cook and sew, a virtuous woman who would make
a fine wife. He had not objected because objection was
not an option. It was taken for granted that he would marry
the woman his father and mother picked, just as they had
done before him.

Even after the marriage their relationship was strained.
When they did make love, Edwina saw to it that it was
always in the dark and it was always furtive. She seemed
to feel there was something wrong with making love, even
when you were properly married.

Twelve long years passed, and there were no children.
His parents died in a typhoid epidemic, and he and Edwina
were alone. How he wanted children! They were his reason
for work, his reason for marriage—a loveless marriage to
a woman who seemed to grow more brittle by the day.

He did continue to make love to her, though he considered stopping since she showed no enjoyment whatsoever
in the activity. Then, as if by some miracle, Edwina became
pregnant.

But the prospect of a child did not please her as it did
him. Instead, it depressed her, and she spent much of her
nine months of confinement weeping.

Then Daniel, the joy of his life, was born. And almost as quickly, Edwina began to deteriorate. He had her examined by famous doctors in Boston. All of them only shook their heads and chattered on about premature senility and some disease of the brain that caused a terrible palsy.

Months went by and Edwina grew thinner and thinner. She stopped taking care of herself, and she suffered from terrible tremors. She drooled when she ate. Finally she could not eat without assistance. Gradually, day by day, she sank into a dismal world of her own. She reacted to nothing, she only stared into space.

Daniel, at first a normal bright baby, seemed frightened of his own mother, and Matthew knew he neglected his son in trying to care for his wife.

He remembered how he had wandered about, trying to think what to do, trying desperately to decide what was right. At last, he had taken Edwina to the hospital in Boston. It had seemed the only solution.

Then, almost as if in protest over the terrible situation, Daniel stopped making noises. He had never learned to talk, though all the physicians said he could. Matthew shook his head, he could not count the number of times he had heard the phrase, *There is nothing clinically wrong with him.* It was cold comfort. His wife was hospitalized and his son could not speak. His life had seemed a tangled web of responsibility and duty. And then Jeanne and Yvette had come. His world turned brighter quickly, and everything was different. Emotions he had never before felt surged through him, mingled with admiration and gratitude.

Jeanne carefully bathed Edwina's sore-ridden body. She put a salve she had made from herbs on each of the sores, then she dressed Edwina in a long white nightgown. It was easy to deal with her as they had given her far too heavy a dose of drugs. She slept soundly, groaning loudly every now and again.

Jeanne worked carefully through Edwina's tangled hair. At last she could comb it, and when she had combed it out, she arranged it in two long thin braids. In a few days, she decided, she would try to wash it. She looked at Edwina, perhaps it was not the most flattering of hair arrangements, but it would keep her hair from again becoming so tangled. Then, carefully, she trimmed Edwina's long nails and toenails. When that was done, she covered the poor woman with the quilt, piled pillows behind her head and then stood back and examined her handiwork.

Edwina was small and shrunken. Her eyes had deep lines under them, and her hair was faded and threaded with strands of gray. Still her skin was much improved by the herbal cream, and she was neat and clean. Jeanne was certain that when she awoke, Edwina would feel much better too.

At just that moment, Edwina opened her eyes and looked drowsily around.

Jeanne was afraid she might be frightened, having woken up in a strange place and with an unfamiliar person in attendance. But fear was not what she saw in Edwina's eyes. What she saw was something close to delight, and somehow the reaction set her at ease and made her feel good.

"I'm Jeanne," she said, leaning close. "I saw you a few days ago. Perhaps you remember?"

Edwina continued to look at her for a moment, then she moved her mouth. "Ja . . . Ja . . ."

"Jeanne" she repeated. Edwina could understand, and her short-term memory was not completely gone. "This is your home," Jeanne said. "We've brought you home."

Edwina's eyes darted from one thing to another. Jeanne stepped aside and opened the curtains so that the alcove immediately became part of the main room which served as both kitchen and living room.

"Daniel will be home soon," Jeanne told her. "And my sister, Yvette. I work here. I take care of your house and of Daniel."

Edwina did not respond, but Jeanne felt her eyes and knew that Edwina was not hostile, only curious. There was no doubt in her mind that they had done the right thing. Edwina needed to be with people. Even if she could not speak well, she needed people to talk to her and read to her. Like all humans she needed the loving care of others. In the hospital they had given her the barest necessities of life, but nothing else.

"I've combed your hair and cut your nails," Jeanne said. She leaned over and held Edwina's hand up. As she did so, she felt the involuntary tremor.

Edwina looked at her hand as if it belonged to someone else.

At that moment the door opened and Matthew stood at the threshold for a moment, hesitant. Behind him were Daniel and Yvette, quietly waiting for permission to enter. Yesterday he and Jeanne had talked to both of them and had explained as best they could about Edwina and her condition.

Matthew strode across the room and stood by the bed. Two hours ago Edwina had looked dreadful, but now she was clean and her hair was combed. She looked less fearful, more helpless. He bent over and took her hand. But she pulled it away and reached for Daniel.

Daniel stared at her and then went closer to the bed and let her take his hand. A frown took over his small face. The two of them just stared at each other in silence. In some strange way, Jeanne thought, she was sure they were communicating.

"She tried to say my name," Jeanne said. "I think she remembers me."

"Yes, sometimes she does remember, for a short time," Matthew confirmed.

Jeanne turned toward her sister. "Yvette, I want you to sit here with Daniel and Edwina. I want you to read to them while I get our supper."

Yvette smiled. "But of course!" She ran to get her favorite book.

Jeanne drew Matthew aside. "I must talk with you a moment," she whispered.

They walked across the room and then into the foyer. "I told you, I took care of my grandmother when she was sick. You know, she used to lie and stare at the ceiling and react to nothing. But she understood what everyone was saying, she just could not speak back. Edwina understands. We must make her a part of everything, and we must never speak of her as if she were not among us, or as if we're certain she cannot understand." Jeanne paused. "I know how that feels," she revealed. "When people think you don't understand, they sometimes say hurtful things."

He knew she was referring to comments she had heard in the village one day when he had left her alone to shop. Many thought she could not understand English, so they were mean and outspoken. She had told him about it, but had forbidden him to speak to the offenders. "They will learn," was all she'd said. He knew she lived by the golden rule as few others did.

Matthew reached out and touched her hair. As always it fell in a profusion of curls. He closed his eyes and pressed his lips together. "You're wise for one so young, you're gentle and you're kind. It is why I love you so," he whispered.

Jeanne stepped back. "If it is to be, we'll know when." She turned away and went back to the kitchen. "Tonight

I'm preparing *fricot à la poule* for dinner," she called back to him.

By this time Matthew knew that *fricots* were all thick, rich stews with chicken, meat or fish and potatoes or dumplings. A *fricot* was a meal in itself, though sometimes, on special occasions, they also had crepes for desert. These were his favorite. He always marveled at how thin they were compared to New England pancakes.

Matthew followed her back into the main room. Yvette was reading to Daniel and Edwina seemed to be listening. He sat down and looked from the children in the alcove, sitting with Edwina, to Jeanne bustling about and cooking. A kind of peace settled over him. And for the first time, he realized he was without the terrible guilt that had been his constant companion for so long.

Chapter Six

Jeanne tossed restlessly in her bed, reviewing the days that had passed since Edwina had been brought home. There was improvement of sorts; yet Edwina continued to slowly deteriorate.

On the improvement side, Edwina slept peacefully without the benefit of either sleeping powders or the ties that had tethered her in the nursing home. Her bed sores were healing, she smiled when Jeanne combed her hair, and she stroked the soft material on the two new nightgowns Jeanne had made for her. Once, a few nights ago, she had even run her long bony fingers through Daniel's hair, and Jeanne had seen the tears in the little boy's eyes. Between mother and son a silent bond existed.

But Edwina put on no weight, and her tremors were often more violent than they had been at first.

Matthew, like all of them, took turns reading to Edwina and every few nights he took his turn feeding her. In fact, Jeanne thought, apart from the extra laundry and the time it took her to change Edwina's clothes and wash her, Edwina was less work than she had anticipated. When the children were in school and Matthew was working, she talked to Edwina and while Edwina did not answer, Jeanne was certain she understood. Jeanne understood that caring for Edwina was far easier for her than it had been for Matthew. Most of her work was in the house, while his was in the blacksmith shop which was always filled with customers. He had been unable to divide himself, whereas she easily fit the extra chores into her schedule.

Jeanne again turned onto her back. It was hard to get to sleep. Matthew's face appeared to her, and abstractedly she touched her lips with her finger. His kisses still lingered, stolen kisses, kisses that should not have happened.

"We shall be eternally damned," she said to herself. But she knew he could not help himself just as she knew she had hungered for his kiss. It was like a pleasant affliction with them, this need they had for one another, this desire that welled in both of them and which, from time to time, had to be fed with a silent embrace, a kiss, a soft touch. It was as if their love were a newly planted seedling that each day grew in their hearts. Yet they both knew it was a love that could not be, a love that had to be denied.

"Is it wrong for me to see his face in my dreams so clearly?" she breathed into the darkness. "How I love that lock of hair that always falls on his forehead." She thought of his broad shoulders and chest, his muscular arms and his twinkling soft brown eyes. She recalled his gentleness with Edwina and with the children, and she concentrated on how he looked at her when they were alone. It was a look of great longing, of desire, of need. And it was mutual, she acknowledged. She wondered if her eyes betrayed her the way his betrayed him.

"Fate brought me here," she whispered as sleep began to overcome her.

She wished, as she let sleep carry her away, that she would dream of Acadia—of her parents who had died, of her grandmother, and of all the hardships they had endured. She would dream of festivals and of the village where she had been born, of the rock-strewn shore and the soft fog, of all that was good and all that was bad in her former life. And as she drifted back in her dreams she faced a new reality. She did not want to go back to Nova Scotia or to the life she had known. For better or for worse, no matter how it turned out, this was where she belonged.

The cedars had begun to turn golden, and the maples had lost their red, gold and orange leaves. Their branches, now naked, quivered in the night winds that swept down from the Berkshires where snow had already fallen at the higher elevations. In the mornings now, the grass was covered with a light white frost, and the window panes were etched in thin ice. Daniel liked to draw on the window ice with his fingernail. Still, Indian summer came to Massachusetts, and during the days the sun warmed the fields, melted the frost and made everyone forget that it was mid November.

"I love it up here," Yvette said as she looked around. "This is a wonderful tree house. Your father built it in just the right tree."

The old apple tree was on the crest of a grassy knoll, and its gnarled branches rendered it a perfect tree to climb. Matthew had constructed a small wooden tree house. It was quite a proper little house, Yvette thought. It had a door, which she and Daniel had to crawl through, four sides, a roof and a small window. Inside, she had put some books. On warm weekend afternoons she and Daniel climbed the tree to their fortress, and there she read to him and tried to cajole him into speaking.

"Our secret," she said. "Make the noise again, Daniel."

Daniel made a noise from deep inside and pressed his lips together.

"That's very good. It almost sounded like Merry. Now remember, even if you learn to say it, you have to wait till Christmas when we exchange gifts. Now watch my tongue and lips, I'll say it very, very slowly. Merry Christmas, Papa.

"P . . . pa . . . pap," Daniel said. He flinched slightly as if afraid of the sound of his own voice.

"Oh, that was wonderful! Papa . . . Merry Christmas, Papa."

"Mmm . . . mmmmaree kristmmmmas, Papaaa."

Yvette threw her arms around him. He had truly spoken! She hugged and kissed him till he shook his head and pulled away.

"You did it! Oh, Daniel, this will be the best Christmas your papa ever had, I just know it!"

Daniel grinned. "Mmmaree kristmmas, Papaaa," he said again.

Tears welled up in Yvette's eyes. She had worked with him for weeks now, and then suddenly just a few days ago he had really spoken. "I know I can teach you to talk," she said confidently. "And I'll bet once you get started you won't stop for anyone."

Daniel laughed. "Taaak," he said.

"Talk," Yvette repeated slowly.

"Taalk."

"That's almost it! Oh, Daniel, I'm so excited." She smiled gently. "But remember, it's our secret till Christmas."

Jeanne pulled the box out from under her bed and took the lid off. Inside were all the little candles she had made for the tree. Matthew, she thought with happiness, would be utterly and completely surprised. In the attic, when she had been preparing for Edwina, she had found a hand-carved wooden box. Inside were forty little candle holders that were meant to be attached to the Christmas tree. She knew they were candle holders because there was wax inside most of them. She had taken them and laboriously cleaned them, and now she had made new tiny little candles for them. Matthew, she thought happily, would no longer have to miss his German Christmas. She had picked out just the right tree in the woods and intended to cut it down on Christmas Eve. Yes, she had the candles. She intended to make gingerbread men to hang on the tree as well. Matthew had talked about them; he had told her and Yvette all about German Christmas celebrations.

They, in turn, had told him about Christmas in Acadia. "On Christmas Eve, the whole town goes to decorate the church. When the church is all ready, we have a party with fir beer and piles and piles of food. The fiddlers come and step dance till it's time for mass!" To illustrate, she had demonstrated the dance for Matthew. He had laughed and even tried it. But Yvette's and Daniel's clapping of hands was not enough. They needed the fiddlers, and their dance dissolved into laughter before they collapsed on chairs to catch their breath.

"Jeanne!"

The sound of her name brought her out of her thoughts. Jeanne quickly slipped the box beneath her bed and hurried downstairs in response to Matthew's call.

He was standing next to Edwina's bed, a perplexed look on his face.

"What is it?" Jeanne asked, leaning over to examine Edwina.

"She remembered," Matthew said. "She knows me."

Edwina blinked. "I do. I do . . . remember . . . some things."

Jeanne smiled. "Oh, it's a blessing! Do you know me as well?"

Edwina nodded. "You are the nice girl who looks after me. You're Jeanne."

"Are you feeling better?" Jeanne asked. She touched Edwina's brow with her cool hand.

"No . . . I'm the same, but my mind seems suddenly clearer. As if a fog has been lifted, or a veil." She shook her head. "I can't see well."

Jeanne could plainly see that her hand still quivered. In fact, the tremors which shook her body seemed to have gotten worse by the day. What a strange quirk of fate! Her mind improved while her body grew weaker.

"I'm going to fetch the doctor," Matthew said.

"Yes, he should be told," Jeanne agreed.

Jeanne sat down by Edwina's bed. "Is there anything I can get you?"

Edwina shook her head even as her eyes focused on the window. Outside, Daniel and Yvette were returning to the house. "That's my little boy," Edwina managed. And then tears began to roll down her hollow cheeks.

Jeanne saw Matthew through the window. He had ridden off to bring the doctor back with him.

"Yes, that's Daniel."

"He looks like his father. He sits with me . . . He can't speak. My fault . . . my fault," Edwina murmured.

Jeanne frowned, wondering what she meant. Did she mean it was her fault because she had become ill?

"No, it's not your fault," Jeanne said, putting her hand on Edwina's arm. Edwina seemed suddenly agitated, and then she was racked by a terrible tremor. It was like a long terrible shiver from the top of her head to the end of her toes.

"My fault," she managed again. "My fault."

Jeanne took her frail hand and held it tightly. But all while she wondered what Edwina meant.

Dr. McGilvery was a short rotund man with a heavy Scot's accent. He came from Edinburgh, and his lilting brogue reminded Jeanne of Nova Scotia. So many of those who lived there were also Scots.

He examined Edwina behind the closed curtain of the alcove, and when he came out, he motioned to Jeanne and Matthew.

"Does this mean she's getting better?" Matthew asked. "She seems weaker. It's so puzzling this sudden return of memory."

"It's not unusual. No, I'm afraid it does not mean she is getting better. Indeed she is truly weaker, and her palsy is even worse. Sometimes, in fact quite often, a patient suddenly appears to be getting better just before growing worse and passing on. It's a short remission—a sort of gift from God that gives the person time to say goodbye."

Matthew said nothing. He could only think of Daniel who would soon lose his mother for a second time.

"You've done a wonderful job of caring for her, Miss Bellefontaine. Her bed sores are gone, and she's much more comfortable than before."

"Thank you," Jeanne replied. "I want to do my best for her."

The doctor looked from Matthew to her and back again; then he patted Matthew on the arm. "God gives and God takes away," he said reverently. "You're a lucky man, Matthew Schmidt."

Jeanne felt the color rise in her cheeks. It seemed clear that the good doctor had guessed how she and Matthew felt about one another. She thought she ought to deny the doctor's words, though in no sense were they accusative. But she said nothing.

Matthew also remained silent, although it was clear he felt self-conscious. Awkwardly, he cleared his throat. "When your horse needs shoeing bring him around."

"I wouldn't go anywhere else," the doctor replied.

These New Englanders seldom spoke of money or exchanged it, Jeanne noted. Barter was the most common way of doing business. It was understood that the doctor did not charge Matthew for the visit and that Matthew did not charge the doctor to shoe his horse. In her homeland, it was a little different. Services were indeed traded, but there was more haggling involved, and a blacksmith would want to know just how many times he would shoe the doctor's horse in exchange for one visit.

The doctor picked up his bag and they followed him down the hall. He had driven his own carriage so Matthew would not have to take him home. He tipped his hat and bid them farewell.

Jeanne pulled her woolen shawl around her and she and Matthew stood on the porch in the cool air, looking at the stars which filled the clear night sky.

"Walk with me," Matthew asked.

Jeanne nodded and followed him down the steps.

They stood for a moment and watched as the doctor disappeared in the distance. Then Matthew began walking down the road with Jeanne at his side.

"Next week is Thanksgiving," he reminded her. "We'll be having a turkey."

"We have much to be thankful for," she said softly.

"I have much to be thankful for," he corrected. He stopped, and drawing her into his arms, he kissed her. It was a long slow kiss, a kiss that spoke of the things they were not free to say to each other.

As his hands moved over her, a slight chill ran through

Jeanne. They both knew this was just another fleeting
encounter, a stolen moment, an expression of promise. "I
love you," he said into her ear.

Oh, how I want him! But her momentary desire was
quickly pushed aside. She stepped away from him. This
time neither of them apologized for their need. They both
knew the yearning they felt would be buried for now.

Matthew looked at her, and then he took her small hand
in his. "I have to tell you how it was with us," he said
slowly. "It's important to me that you understand."

"You don't have to tell me unless you're sure you want
to."

"I want to tell you. I don't want us ever to have secrets.
It was an arranged marriage. I never loved her, Jeanne.
Till I met you, love was just a word for an emotion I never
felt. At least where a woman was concerned. I love Daniel,
but that's a different kind of love."

"Many marriages are arranged and people grow to
love."

"I know. I never would have left her. I have a duty toward
her. I would never do anything so dishonorable."

"I know that, Matthew. It is one of the things I love
about you. You are honorable, and you have done as much
as anyone could have done for Edwina."

"You've done more."

"I want her to have peace," Jeanne replied.

Matthew smiled at her. "And to think that when I first
met you I thought you were too young. You're wise, Jeanne
Bellefontaine."

"I have known sadness, and sadness is a good teacher."

Again, he wanted to hold her. But he restrained himself,
fighting off his need for her, his love for her.

He knew her mother had died after her sister had been
born, that she had reared her sister; he had learned her
three older brothers had been killed in an Indian raid

and, finally, her people had been dispersed from their homeland. She had lost everything, yet she had lost nothing because of her strength. She was spirited and no one could ever take that away from her.

"Matthew, Edwina said something odd to me. Something I don't understand."

Matthew, too, stopped and looked into her eyes. "What did she say?"

"She said it was her fault Daniel couldn't talk. Do you know why she would say such a thing? She said it over and over."

Matthew shook his head.

Jeanne shrugged. "Maybe she'll tell me more."

He took her arm and they headed back to the house.

The respite of Indian summer ended suddenly and banks of dark clouds filled the sky as the days of December grew ever shorter.

"Jeanne ..." Edwina's tiny voice seemed somehow pleading.

Jeanne, who was sitting beside Edwina's bed, put down her knitting expectantly. "May I get you something?"

Edwina lifted her skeletal palsied hand. "Hold my hand," she croaked, as if she were choking. Edwina's voice was always weak, but now it had become raspy too.

Jeanne got up and moved her chair even closer. "Edwina," she said, clasping her hand.

"I was a bad mother," she said slowly, painfully. "My hands always shook . . . I dropped him. That's why he can't talk."

"Daniel?" Jeanne was so surprised she didn't know what to say.

"I dropped him," she repeated.

Jeanne grasped both of Edwina's hands and held them

tightly. "No, listen to me. You had palsy, you couldn't help it. You were a very good mother, a very good mother. Daniel loves you."

Edwina's eyes searched hers. It was as if she were trying to say something she couldn't quite phrase. Then, very slowly she said, "It's all right that you love Matthew. It's good. We never really loved each other. Tell him I said that, please tell him it's all right."

Tears filled Jeanne's eyes, and she squeezed Edwina's hands which seemed to be growing cold even as she held them. "I'll call Matthew . . ."

"No. No. You . . . listen, please. Take care of Daniel," she gasped. "Take care of my little boy. Oh, how I wish I could see him grown . . . take care . . ."

Edwina's voice faded off and Jeanne let her hands drop. She heard Edwina draw a long deep breath, and then her head fell sideways.

How sudden it had been! How quickly it had come! Yet Jeanne could not deny that as her mind seemed to gain in strength, Edwina's body had seemed to get weaker and weaker. But so suddenly! She had spoken her name and said a few words, then as if she knew in advance, she had died with a single request on her lips.

"Yes, I'll take care of him," she heard herself say even though she knew Edwina could not hear. "I promise, I'll love him as if he were my own." Jeanne sobbed and made no attempt to stop her tears. How terrible this was! How much Edwina had wanted to see her small son become a man . . .

She sat for several minutes, then she folded Edwina's hands and reached down and closed Edwina's eyes. She crossed herself and, still crying, got up. As she turned, her mouth opened in surprise. Matthew was standing by the doorway, tears running down his face.

"Did you . . . ?" Jeanne questioned.
He nodded. "I heard everything."

The burial ground was atop a hill behind the white clapboard church. Winter had truly come, yet the dark skies and chilling wind seemed entirely appropriate to the occasion.

Jeanne wore a dark brown dress and cap. Over that, she wore a heavy wool cape. Yvette too wore a dark dress, and both Matthew and Daniel were dressed in dark suits. Dr. McGilvery was there, and so were most of the neighbors. Such good people, Jeanne thought. They had brought breads and soups, roast meat and cakes, cookies, and pies to the house. "It's the custom," Mrs. Anderson explained. "You won't feel like cooking," Mrs. Henderson had said. And so each of them had brought something.

Jeanne's hands were folded in front of her, and Daniel stood by her side, clinging to her skirt. Yvette stood on the other side but she stared at the ground.

Slowly, the plain wooden casket was lowered into the ground. The Reverend Henley picked up a handful of soft dirt. " 'Ashes to ashes, dust to dust. Dust thou were, and to dust thou returnest . . .' " He threw the dirt on the casket.

Matthew bent over and did the same. Moving round the circle, each of them followed suit. Then the reverend said a final prayer, and after that, they all sang a hymn.

At the end of the hymn, they walked slowly back down the hill. They would go home and others would come to pay their respects. Jeanne took Daniel's hand. He didn't cry continuously, but now and again she saw tears running down his cheeks.

"It's all right to cry," she had told him last night. But

no matter. Daniel retained his silence, and he fought not to cry.

"This is terrible," Matthew said, once they were sitting alone in the wagon. Yvette and Daniel had gone in the carriage with the McGilverys. "It's so soon before Christmas."

Jeanne nodded. "The time was not ours to pick, Matthew. You must be strong for Daniel. We must still celebrate Christmas for him."

Matthew didn't answer, he just made his familiar clicking sound, and the horses began to move.

Matthew turned the horses onto the short road that led to the house. "You're right," he said finally. "We will celebrate Christmas. Daniel and Yvette deserve Christmas and so do you."

Jeanne touched his hand. "You deserve it too," she said, thinking again of the little tree and the candles. She hoped it would take his mind off Edwina. She hoped it would make him happy.

"Edwina knew about us," he said after a few moments. "She knew we love each other."

Jeanne nodded. "It was so sad, she so wanted to see Daniel grow up."

Matthew looked into her eyes. "We both chose you," he said, touching her hand. "It must be right."

Chapter Seven

The sky was gray from horizon to horizon and a cold wind rattled the trees and made the barn creak. The promise of the first snow filled the air. There was no doubt it was December.

Jeanne finished putting the final touches on the four baskets that sat on the table. Each one was filled to the brim, and on the top was a big red ribbon.

"Christmas got here too soon this year," Jeanne said. "I hardly had time to finish everything."

"We'll take them to the church this afternoon. Then we'll come home and have our own Christmas Eve together," Yvette said, repeating the day's schedule. She had just come inside, and her nose was red and her cheeks rosy.

Yvette was aglow with the holiday season. Daniel, having absented himself from the filling of the baskets, was outside with his father in the blacksmith's shop.

"We'd better check them one more time. It wouldn't

do to have more in one than in the other," Yvette said as she leaned over the brimming baskets.

Jeanne smiled. "I suspect you just like to look at what's inside," she said to Yvette.

"I do. It makes me happy."

Each basket had a long loaf of Christmas fruit bread, a jar of strawberry preserves, a corn husk doll, a rag doll, a little bag of candy, a pair of bayberry candles and a bar of bayberry scented soap. On the very top was a fat roast chicken wrapped up in a clean cloth.

For the fourth time, Yvette inventoried the contents of each basket. "All right. I've checked them all, we're ready to go."

Jeanne laughed lightly and put on her heavy cloak. Yvette followed her and they each took two baskets and put them in the wagon.

"When we get home," Jeanne whispered, "we'll have to hurry to get the tree ready before Matthew comes in, otherwise it won't be a surprise at all!"

Yvette smiled slyly. "I have the biggest surprise of all," she said, hardly able to bear keeping her secret a minute longer.

Jeanne just smiled and wondered what Yvette had made Matthew. Whatever it was, it was quite a secret. She never saw her working on anything; yet there was constant reference to Matthew's surprise.

They drove the wagon to the church and hurried into the church hall to deposit the baskets.

"These look lovely!" Mrs. Henley, the minister's wife, exclaimed in delight. Then she smiled enigmatically at Jeanne. "I'll be seeing you later."

Jeanne just smiled, assuming she meant the next morning at church. Catholic or no, she had decided she and Yvette would attend. "Better to be in one of God's houses than none," she had rationalized.

They went back to the wagon and hurried home.

"We really must move quickly," Jeanne said as she and Yvette went into the woods to cut the tree.

"Brrr, it's really cold. You know what? I think we're going to have snow for Christmas, that's what."

"I think you may be right," Jeanne agreed.

Jeanne stopped in front of the little tree. She bent down on the damp ground and began to saw it. It wasn't a large tree so it took her very little time to finish. Then she shook herself off and they hurried to the shed. She had already made the little stand, the tree just had to be nailed to it.

As soon as they were done, they brought the tree in the back door of the house and set it down in the alcove where Edwina's bed had been. They quickly put on the Christmas candles and hung the decorated ginger cookies.

"It's getting dark," Yvette said. "Matthew will come at any minute."

"I know, I know," Jeanne breathed. "You light them now and draw the curtain. I'll run and get my gifts and put on my other dress."

"The pretty one!" Yvette called after her. "You absolutely must wear the pretty red one!"

Jeanne ran up the stairs. She took off her housedress and slipped into the pretty red gown she had just altered. She brushed her hair and quickly tied a ribbon in it. When she was finished, she gathered up her presents and hurried back downstairs.

She piled her presents under the tree and saw that Yvette had added some packages of her own. They both stood back and silently admired their handiwork.

"He'll be so surprised!" Jeanne said. And she was aware that for the first time since the death, the sadness of Edwina's passing had left her.

"I smell something really good!" Matthew said as he came into the house, announcing himself from the hall.

Jeanne and Yvette exchanged furtive glances. The roast pork with apples was almost done, and there were two pies cooling. Tomorrow, Christmas Day, she planned to have a goose.

Matthew came into the main room and looked around. "My two girls look as if they're keeping a secret. What do you think Daniel?"

Daniel, who stood by his father's side, nodded, then he ran to Yvette.

"Close your eyes," Jeanne said.

Matthew closed his eyes, and Jeanne pulled aside the curtain. "Now you can open them!"

Matthew opened his eyes to see the little tree with its candles aglow and the cookies and candies hanging from its limbs. Tears filled his eyes. "It's the Christmas tree of my boyhood," he said in awe. "I don't know where you found the time."

Jeanne just smiled.

He walked over to her and kissed her on the cheek. Their eyes locked and for a moment it was as if they were alone.

"I want to give Matthew my gift now," Yvette said.

"It's customary to wait till just before we go to bed to open gifts," Matthew answered, "but considering everything, I think we might make an exception tonight."

Everything? What is everything? Jeanne wondered.

"This is not a customary gift," Yvette replied.

Jeanne looked at her sister and felt puzzled. It was unlike Yvette to insist. And what could it be? She did not see any package under the tree addressed to Matthew from Yvette.

"All right," Matthew allowed. "Let's make a compromise, we'll each open one gift now."

Yvette took Daniel's hand and led him to his father. She stood behind the little boy with her hands resting gently

on his shoulders. "My gift is really our gift," she said slowly.
"Daniel?"

Daniel opened his mouth and Yvette held her breath.
He could speak when they were alone, in fact he could
now say quite a few words. At first nothing came out but
a weird guttural sound.

Yvette froze like a statue. *Oh, what if he can't?*

Jeanne frowned slightly.

"Mmmmerry Christmassss . . . Paapaa," Daniel stuttered
nervously.

Matthew's mouth opened wide with delight, and his eyes
filled with tears. "Oh, son!" He bent down and embraced
Daniel tightly.

"Papa . . . Mmmerry Christmas!"

"Merry, merry Christmas Daniel!" Matthew's voice
cracked with emotion. Then he looked up at Yvette. She
was crying too and so was Jeanne.

"That's my surprise gift," Yvette whispered. "I taught
him, he's worked very hard."

Matthew bit his lower lip. "You couldn't have given me
a more wonderful present." He pulled her into his arms
too and gave her a big kiss on the cheek.

"Oh, this is a wonderful Christmas!" Jeanne cried.

Matthew went to the closet and came back with three
packages. One small, and two of medium size. He gave
the medium one to Yvette. "You open this one," he urged.

Yvette carefully opened the beautifully wrapped package. "Oh!" she exclaimed as she took out an elegantly
dressed doll. It had a delicate china face and a smooth
satin dress. "This is the most wonderful doll I've ever seen!
All my life I dreamed of a doll like this!"

Matthew grinned with satisfaction. "It came all the way
from London. I bought it in Boston."

Yvette hugged him again, even as she cradled her pre-
cious doll.

Matthew then handed Daniel his box.

Daniel was not as careful as Yvette. He enthusiastically ripped open the box and withdrew a pair of ice skates. "For this winter," Matthew said, smiling. "It's time I taught you to skate."

Daniel's eyes glowed. "Th . . . th . . . thank you, Paa . . . pa."

Again Matthew embraced and then kissed both Yvette and Daniel.

Then he stood up and turned to Jeanne. He dipped into his pocket and handed her a tiny box. "Something special," he said, looking into her eyes.

Jeanne opened it carefully and then stood staring at it, her mouth slightly open. "Matthew," she whispered. It was a gold wedding ring.

Children or no children, he slipped his hand around her waist and bent down and kissed her on the lips. "No more hidden kisses," he breathed in her ear. And then quite loudly so the children would hear, "Will you marry me?"

Jeanne again wiped tears from her eyes as she leaned against him, aware that her face was flushed. She could hardly speak. "Yes," she whispered. "You know I will."

"Ah, but I wanted to hear it from your lips."

Both Daniel and Yvette clapped.

"We have witnesses," Matthew said, smiling.

"I only got you the tree," Jeanne confessed. "I should have made you another gift."

Again he embraced her and unashamedly kissed her and then looked deep into her expressive eyes. "You are my gift, Jeanne Bellefontaine.

Then he smiled and winked. "My surprises are not over. We must eat before the others arrive."

"Others?" Jeanne said, taken aback.

Matthew grinned. "You'll see. I promise."

"But I have nothing to serve . . ."

"Don't worry . . . Here, here, let me have my little surprise. You'll understand soon enough. Won't she, Yvette?"

Jeanne looked from one to the other. "The two of you have been keeping a secret from me?"

"And it's not easy. Now hurry up woman, we must finish before anyone arrives."

Jeanne nodded and turned toward the stove. The table was already set, and she quickly put on the food. The children sat down to eat.

Matthew checked the clock. "No need to hurry too much, we have enough time," he assured her with another wink.

No sooner had the dirty dishes been washed and put away than the door knocker sounded. Matthew hurried to respond and admitted a wagonload of people.

Dr. McGilvery and his wife, Martha, the Reverend Henley and his wife, Agnes, the Rutledges and all their other their neighbors came in. They carried plates of food, homemade wine and a large cake.

"What is all this?" Jeanne asked, her eyes large.

"Our wedding," Matthew said. "We're going to be married right now, right here, in front of that tree."

Jeanne's eyes glistened and everyone laughed merrily. "Oh, this is a surprise!" She turned toward Matthew. "A wonderful surprise."

"I knew about this. That's why I told you to wear your pretty dress," Yvette said proudly.

"You're a little devil," Jeanne said cheerfully.

"And why I said I would see you later," Mrs. Henley added.

Matthew took her hand and led her to the tree. The

Reverend Henley followed and the witnesses all took their places.

The reverend opened his book and began to read the marriage ceremony in a low voice.

Jeanne was hardly aware of anything save Matthew's hand holding hers.

When the moment came, she whispered "I do," and heard him promise the same. Then he wrapped her in his arms and kissed her. It was a long slow kiss and everyone clapped and laughed and she heard the wine bottle being opened.

At midnight, Daniel and Yvette went up to bed. At twelve-thirty the last of their guests left.

Jeanne extinguished the candles on the little tree and Matthew cleared the tables. Then they stood together in front of the fire.

He gathered her into his arms and kissed her again. This time it was not a kiss to be broken off, this time there was no backing away or pulling apart.

Jeanne felt his strength against her, felt his arms around her, his warm breath on her neck. Above all, she felt the promise of what was to come.

"I love you," he said, lifting her up. He carried her to the bedroom and set her down gently on the bed. "I'm sorry there was no priest for the wedding."

Jeanne smiled up at him. "It's all right. I feel quite married just the same."

"One day, maybe next summer, we'll go south by boat to Maryland and be married again in a Catholic Church."

"Could we?" She lifted her large eyes to his.

"Yes. I want to do that," he admitted.

He sat down beside her and kissed her again as he loosened the ribbon that held her profusion of dark curls back, away from her face. Then he slowly undressed her, kissing her as he did so, marveling in the alabaster delicacy of her skin, the silky feel of her leaning against his bare chest.

"You are my true beloved," he whispered as he kissed her.

Jeanne shuddered in his arms; he was warm and strong and good. He was everything a woman could want in a man.

"I was once so frightened, so alone," she confessed. "I was so afraid Yvette and I would always be alone."

He toyed with her hair and caressed her. "None of us will be alone again, my darling. We're a family."

Jeanne yielded to him willingly, happily and with a passion he easily inflamed. She could not control her desire to return his caresses.

"It's wicked to love as much as I love you," he told her.

"Then we are both wicked," she whispered back.

They touched and kissed, and then they were locked together in a strong embrace, each aching for the other and yearning for fulfillment. When it came, they trembled together and kissed again, deeply.

After a long while, Jeanne turned about and cuddled into the curve of his body. The last things she saw before she drifted off into a deep satisfied sleep were the huge snowflakes falling outside the window. It was the first snow of winter.

RACHEL'S GIFT

Holly Harte

Chapter One

Rachel Willowby tightened her grip on the reins of the horse, her thoughts centered on her destination: the Double A ranch, owned by Spencer Adams and located a few miles west of town. Thinking of the reaction of the other members of the Ladies Aid Society when they'd drawn lots to see which of them would take the buggy ride, she smiled. The relieved looks on the ladies' faces had been almost comical. When she had asked them to explain their reactions, the answer she'd received had cramped her heart with sympathy. Learning Spencer Adams hadn't been seen in town more than once or twice in all the years since the accident that took the life of his closest friend made Rachel's determination to succeed in her mission increase. Surely Spencer Adams couldn't be as rude and foul tempered as the members of the Aid Society had led her to believe, could he? She intended to find out.

She took a deep breath, the crisp December air fortifying her determination to accomplish the goals she'd set for herself. In addition to carrying out the Aid Society's objective, to deliver the Christmas basket sitting beside her on the buggy seat and extend an invitation to the Christmas Ball sponsored by the women's group, she'd also added a goal of her own. She planned to get Spencer Adams to agree to attend the ball, hopefully without getting the door slammed in her face—something several members claimed to have experienced in past years.

As she crested another hill and the small ranch house came into view, she straightened her already stiff spine even more, her heart pounding in anticipation. Nothing like the prospect of a challenge to get a person's blood humming in her veins.

In her twenty-eight years, Rachel had never run from a challenge—even one reportedly as ill-mannered as the reclusive Spencer Adams—and she didn't intend to start now.

She pulled the buggy to a halt in front of the porch which spanned the full width of the small adobe house. After wrapping the reins around the brake handle, Rachel stepped out of the buggy. She adjusted her woolen shawl more securely around her shoulders before reaching into the buggy to retrieve the cloth-covered basket from the seat.

Drawing in a deep breath, she moved toward the house and stepped up onto the porch.

A sharp rap on the front door caused Spence's right arm to jerk in reaction, the razor in his hand slicing the skin under his jaw. "Dammit!" Laying his razor aside, he dipped a cloth into the basin of water then swiped at the thin rivulet of blood running down his neck.

The knock came again, this time with more force. "What the hell's the rush?" he said to himself. Stepping into the hall, he shouted in the direction of the front of the house. "Give me a minute, Jeb."

Bare-chested, the wet cloth pressed to the underside of his jaw and remnants of shaving soap dotting his face and neck, Spence made his way to the door.

Just as a third knock sounded, he snatched the door open.

"For God's sake, Jeb, what's the matter with—" Spence's mouth snapped shut, his eyebrows lowering in a scowl. The person pounding on his door wasn't his hired hand, Jeb Lawrence, but a woman with red-gold hair, a dappling of freckles across her narrow nose and eyes the exact color of the Texas sky on a sunny, cloudless day.

She was tall, though beside his six-foot-two-inch frame, she barely reached his shoulder. Her shawl and the basket she held clutched in front of her hid her upper body from his scrutiny. But from what he could tell, her breasts appeared to be full and her waist didn't look much bigger than the span of his two hands.

There was no need to ask why this woman stood on his front porch on the tenth of December, the basket told him all he needed to know.

"Look, ma'am, I think you'd better—"

"Mr. Adams," Rachel said, trying to keep her gaze on his face. "My name is Rachel Willowby, and I'm here on behalf of the San Antonio Ladies Aid Society. This"—she lifted the basket and held it out to him—"is for you."

He didn't accept the offered basket, but spread his legs in a wider stance, crossed his arms over his muscular chest and directed an intense glare at her.

Rachel ignored his rudeness, but gave in to temptation and took a moment to observe the man she knew so little about. Since arriving in San Antonio the past summer to begin her new position as a teacher at The German-English School, she had not only never seen Spencer Adams in town, but she couldn't remember anyone having mentioned his name.

He was tall, nearly a full head taller than her own above average height. His angular face and square jaw were deeply tanned, with frown lines creasing his forehead and the corners of his full mouth. Dark brown, slightly wavy hair brushed his broad shoulders, and thick eyebrows were knitted over hazel, deep-set eyes. She stared into his eyes for a long moment. Something in those brownish-green depths, some hidden inner pain, tugged at her middle. In spite of his intimidating pose and fierce scowl, she thought him an extremely attractive man. A curl of heat formed low in her belly and spread outward. Dropping her gaze from his face, she encountered his naked chest with its inverted triangle of dark hair. She fought against the urge to run her fingers through that enticing patch, then swallowed hard before shifting her gaze back to his face.

"There's a loaf of fresh bread in the basket," she said, her voice slightly raspy. "And some of Mrs. Gunther's wonderful anise-seed cakes, several jars of preserves and—"

"I don't want your charity," Spence replied, his voice dropping to a low rumble. "I can provide for myself."

"Of course you can, Mr. Adams. I assure you, this isn't charity. The basket is a gift. Each Christmas season, the Ladies Aid Society fills baskets with foodstuffs made by our members and gives them to the less fortunate, as well as to those folks like yourself who don't get in to town much." She flashed him a bright smile. "But this year, we have another reason for making these calls."

The warmth of her smile touched him as if she'd actually reached out and physically caressed his skin. Hoping to clear his wayward thoughts, he gave his head a quick shake.

"I'm here, Mr. Adams, to also extend a personal invitation to our first Christmas Ball. The Society has made arrangements to rent the Casino Club for what should be a gala event, and we'd be honored to have you join—"

"That's enough," he said in a clipped voice. "I'll take the damn basket, if that'll get rid of you"—he snatched it from her with his left hand—"but I won't be attending your ball. I have other plans."

"But I haven't told you when the ball will be held."

"Doesn't matter. I'm busy." When she opened her mouth to reply, he silenced her with a glare. "You've completed your philanthropic obligation, Mrs. Willowby, so now you can just turn yourself around and head on back to town."

Rachel pressed her lips into a firm line. She drew a deep breath, then exhaled slowly. "Actually, it's Miss Willowby, Mr. Adams, and why do you have to be so rude? I came out here on a social call, to extend a simple invitation, and you're acting as if I brought some dreaded disease. Didn't your mother teach you—?" Spotting the thin trail of blood running down his neck, her eyes went wide. "You're hurt!"

"Yes, thanks to you." He lifted the cloth still clutched in his right hand and pressed it to his momentarily forgotten cut. "Your knocking damn near caused me to slit my own throat while I was shaving."

"If you'll permit me, Mr. Adams, I'll see to your injury."

"No need. I can take care of myself."

"Since you hold me responsible, I think it only right that I tend your cut." One reddish gold eyebrow rose. "Wouldn't you agree?" Not waiting for him to respond, she brushed past him and stepped over the threshold. "Come inside, Mr. Adams, before you catch a chill," she said from the dim interior of his house. "I certainly don't want to be blamed for that as well."

"Hold up there. You don't have to . . ." As his voice trailed off, he blinked, momentarily stunned by the cheeky woman he'd just had the misfortune of meeting. The image of the way her full breasts rose with her sharply drawn breath niggled into his brain, making his body harden painfully.

His brow lined with a frown, Spence entered his house and closed the door behind him, wondering why he'd allowed Rachel Willowby to stay longer than anyone else who'd been brave enough to show up at his door. Even more puzzling, why did he find the notion of her touching him so appealing?

Chapter Two

Once Rachel's eyes adjusted to the dimness of the house, she moved to the center of the parlor, then removed her shawl and draped it over the back of a chair. She turned to wait for Spencer Adams to speak. When he remained silent, she said, "If you'll direct me to the kitchen, I'll put some water on to heat so I can see to your injury."

"I told you, that isn't necessary. It's only a nick." He removed the cloth from the underside of his jaw. "See there, the bleeding has already stopped."

"Then why did you tell me you nearly slit your throat when I knocked on your door?"

Spence cleared his throat, shocked by the heat creeping up his neck and face. Hoping the poor light in the room hid his flush, he said, "I . . . uh . . . I reckon I just over-reacted and spoke out of turn."

"You should learn to control the way you react, Mr. Adams," she said, moving closer. "If you don't, one day you may do something you'll truly be sorry for."

His back went rigid for a moment. Relaxing, he exhaled a weary sigh. "Believe me, Miss Willowby, I'm fully aware of that."

Rachel stared at his stiff posture, the shuttered expression on his face, the haunted look in his eyes and knew her first impression of the man hadn't been wrong. He was suffering from some inner pain, some invisible hurt which she longed to ease. The urge to reach out and smooth the deep grooves on his forehead nearly overwhelmed her, forcing her to clench her hands in the fabric of her skirt to keep herself from touching him.

She took an unsteady breath, hoping her next words would dissipate the tension in the air. "Are you sure you don't want me to kiss where you cut yourself?"

Spence's eyebrows shot up. "Beg pardon?"

Rachel smiled. "That's what my mother used to do. Whenever I fell down and skinned my knee, she'd wipe my tears and clean up the scrape, then she'd kiss my knee and proclaim it all better."

The corners of Spence's mouth twitched. "You're an adult now, Miss Willowby. Surely you no longer believe such childish nonsense."

"I don't know," she said in a low voice, taking another step closer, so close she could feel the heat from his body. "I've never had occasion to test the idea." She drew a deep breath, instantly dizzy from the heady combined scents of spicy shaving soap and the musk of warm male skin. Before he could object, she rose on her toes and pressed her lips to the tiny cut on the underside of his jaw.

Spence inhaled sharply. The brush of Rachel's breasts against his chest, the touch of her lips on his skin sent his pulse into a wild rhythm. He swayed on his feet, then grasped her upper arms to steady himself.

When he regained his balance, he held her away from

him. "I think it's time for you to leave," he said in a raspy whisper.

"But—"

"No arguing, Miss Willowby." He turned and practically dragged her to the door.

"Wait. My shawl." When she started to go back into the parlor, his hand held her firmly in place.

"I'll get it," he said. A moment later, he returned and handed her the shawl.

Rachel took the woolen garment and settled it around her shoulders. Giving him a smile, she said, "It was a pleasure meeting you, Mr. Adams, and I look forward to seeing you—"

"Save your social graces for someone who appreciates them, Miss Willowby. We won't be seeing each other again."

Though his sharply spoken words stung, she managed to keep her smile in place when she replied, "Don't be so sure." She started toward her buggy, then abruptly turned back. "By the way, you're welcome, Mr. Adams."

He stared at her for a moment, scowling. When he didn't speak, she said, "For the Christmas basket."

His face burning with another flush, he managed to murmur a belated thank you. Then much to his relief, the irritating woman climbed into her buggy and directed the horse away from his house. Yet as he watched the buggy head down the drive toward the main road, for the first time in seven years, the emptiness of the days ahead struck him with full force. Scowling, he gave a grunt of disgust then took a step back and slammed the door against both his view of the cloud of dust churned up by Rachel Willowby's departure and his morose musings about his life.

* * *

On the ride back to San Antonio, Rachel made a decision. Spencer Adams may have fooled everyone else, but she wasn't so easily hoodwinked. She'd been a teacher for nearly seven years, and during that time she'd become an expert at detecting when someone was putting on an act. So now that she knew Spencer wasn't as mean and ugly natured as he tried to seem, she had to figure out how to get him to shed the facade he'd cultivated for so long. Mulling over the situation, she realized the key had to be easing the pain she'd clearly seen in his eyes.

By the time she returned the horse and buggy to the stable and headed for her boarding house, she hadn't come up with a definite plan with the exception of one detail. No matter what course of action she took to get Spencer to change his rude and reclusive ways, she'd have to make another trip to his ranch to accomplish her goal.

Since the following day was Sunday, Rachel headed for the Double A right after church. Though the day had started out sunny, as soon as she left the edge of town, the temperature began to drop. She'd been told snow was rare in San Antonio, but the sharp bite of the wind and the strange cloud formations to the north made her wonder if the person who'd imparted that bit of weather information had been pulling her leg.

She shivered, wishing she'd worn her heavier coat and urging the horse to a faster pace. By the time she arrived at the Double A, her cheeks stung and her hands and feet were stiff from the cold. After finally managing to wrap the reins around the brake handle, she climbed out of the buggy and hobbled to the front door.

Her first knock was answered almost immediately by Spencer, his usual scowl in place.

"For God's sake, woman, don't you have any sense at

all in that pretty head of yours? This is Texas, where the weather is unpredictable at best. Sure as hell, there's a storm brewing, and you're out lollygagging around the countryside.''

Rachel knew somewhere in the less frigid reaches of her brain that Spencer's calling her pretty would normally have sent her pulse into an erratic rhythm. But right then, she couldn't think of anything except getting warm. "Can I . . . can I come in, please?" she managed to get out, hugging her shawl more tightly around herself in an effort to stop her shivering.

Spencer's scowl deepened, but he stepped aside and let her pass through the door. "Take a seat by the fireplace. I'll fetch something to help you thaw out."

A minute later, he returned to the parlor holding two partially filled glasses. Handing one to her, he said, "Drink this. It'll warm your blood in no time."

She nodded, then lifted the glass to her mouth with a shaking hand and drained half the contents. Liquid fire scorched a path down her throat, making her gasp for air. Struggling to breathe normally, she fought the urge to cough, tears welling in her eyes.

"You're supposed to sip it," Spencer said, giving her a gentle whack on the back before he dropped onto the settee beside her. "Whiskey as fine as this is meant to be savored."

The burning in her throat slowly eased, moving lower and creating a delicious warmth in her stomach. "You've had plenty of experience with whiskey, I expect," she said in a raspy whisper, dabbing at her eyes with a corner of her shawl.

He chuckled. "Enough to know you don't toss it down like that. Not unless you want one hell of a headache in the morning."

"Wouldn't matter," she replied. "I can't feel my head."

This time he laughed, a deep rich sound that did more to chase the chills from Rachel's body than the shot of whiskey. The heat in her belly intensified, spreading wider and wider, until her entire body tingled with anticipation. Another shiver racked her, this one having nothing to do with being cold.

She stared into his hazel eyes for a moment, noticing the pain she'd seen lurking there had slipped away. "You should laugh more often," she said. "My mother used to say laughter is the best—"

"Save the old adages for someone who appreciates them," he replied, his expression having gone back to the former harsh scowl, the pain from some unknown source again clouding his eyes.

Rachel bit the inside of her mouth to hold in the retort she longed to make. Instead she took a tiny sip of whiskey and stared into the fireplace. After several moments of silence broken only by the crackling of the fire, Spencer shifted on the settee.

"Damn."

"What is it?"

"Rain," he replied, getting to his feet.

Rachel also rose. "I'd better head back to town. Could I trouble you to let me borrow a blanket? I'm afraid I didn't think to bring one."

Spencer stood staring out the parlor window. "You're not going anywhere, Miss Willowby."

"It's only rain, Mr. Adams. Surely—"

"It's more than rain. With the temperature dropping, the rain will freeze before it hits the ground. Before long, everything will be covered with a coat of ice." His shoulders lifted with a deeply drawn breath. "I'm afraid you won't be able to get back to town until the weather breaks."

She stared at his back with narrowed eyes. "How long will that be?"

He turned toward her and shrugged. "Can't tell. Sometimes the ice melts within twenty-four hours, sometimes not for several days. Just depends on how long this cold spell lasts."

"Days! I can't stay here for days. I have to be in school tomorrow. My students—"

"Your students," Spencer said, crossing the room, "will have to get along without you." Lifting his coat from a peg beside the door, he added, "For the time being, you're stuck here with me."

Rachel's heart leaped to her throat, his words echoing in her head. *Stuck here with me.* She wasn't sure if the wild pounding of her pulse was from fear or excitement at the prospect of spending an indeterminate amount of time in the company of Spencer Adams. Watching him button his coat, settle his hat on his head and then reach for the doorknob, she shook herself out of her musings. "Where are you going?"

"To put your horse in the barn, before the poor beast freezes to death."

Her cheeks burning with a blush, she moved around the settee and started toward the door. "There's no need for you to go out there, Mr. Adams. I can see to my horse."

Though Spence had half a mind to agree, he couldn't make himself say the words. Instead, he said, "You've already suffered one chill, Miss Willowby, and I don't want to be responsible for the consequences of more of your foolhardy actions."

"But, I—"

"Don't argue, Miss Willowby, just stay by the fire and finish your whiskey." He opened the door, then glanced over his shoulder. "Slowly."

The door clicked shut and he was gone. Rachel moved back to the settee and sat down. After a moment, a slow smile spread across her face. Just that morning while sitting in church, she'd prayed for the Lord's guidance to help Spencer Adams, and now her prayers had been answered. Not in a way she might have expected, but by an ice storm. Her smiled broadened. The Lord truly did work in mysterious ways.

Chapter Three

When Spence returned to the house after taking Rachel's horse and buggy to the barn, he found his guest back in front of the fire. Her shawl lay beside her on the settee; her arms lifted while she fussed with her hair. She'd apparently let down the thick mass of reddish-gold curls during his absence and was in the process of putting it back to rights. Spence's mouth went dry, his heart thundering in his ears. With her arms raised and the fire behind her, the fullness of her bosom was clearly outlined for his hungry gaze.

He closed his eyes against the glorious sight, willing his body not to react and his brain not to imagine what those breasts would feel like filling his hands, what the hardened tips would . . . He shivered, instantly aroused to the point of pain. What was the matter with him? He'd never had trouble controlling his sexual urges. Not until one reddish blond, impudent do-gooder knocked on his door.

Spence drew a deep breath, then opened his eyes.

Against his will, his gaze immediately sought Rachel. He released a soft sigh, relieved to see she'd finished with her hair, her hands now lowered and clasped in her lap.

He cleared his throat before crossing to the fireplace. "I gave your horse a rubdown and made sure he had water and feed," he said, bending to put more wood on the fire.

"Thank you, Mr. Adams," Rachel replied, staring at his back and admiring the way his muscles bunched and flexed, the way the fabric of his shirt strained with his movements.

Still crouched in front of the fireplace, he turned toward her. "No need to thank me, it's what anyone would've done to help a person who doesn't have enough sense to stay inside on a day like this."

"You don't have to rub it in. I know now that I shouldn't have ventured out. But I've only been in Texas a few months, so I had no idea how the weather could change so quickly."

Spence caught a glimpse of her freckles in the flickering light cast by the fire, and another jolt of desire surged to his groin. Angry over his inability to control his body's reaction to Rachel Willowby, he lashed out in the only way he could. "Well, you'd better learn fast or else get the hell out of Texas."

Rachel gasped at the venom in his voice. Certain his words weren't meant to really hurt her, she finally said, "Then perhaps you should teach me about Texas weather, because I have no intention of leaving."

Spence stared at her for a long moment, at the proud tilt of her chin, the spark of defiance in her sky blue eyes. Turning back to the fire to hide his sudden grin, he said, "That might be arranged. This storm could last for days, so we'll have plenty of time on our hands."

Rachel relaxed. Days alone with Spencer Adams. Her shoulders rippled with a shiver of delight at the prospect. "I'm ready whenever you are, Mr. Adams."

Spence's heart skipped a beat at her statement. Glancing over his shoulder and seeing her innocent expression, he knew she had no idea how her words could have been taken. Exhaling a shaky breath, he gave the fire one last jab with the poker, then set the tool aside as he straightened.

As he brushed the dust from his hands, he turned to face her. "We could be stuck together for a while, so I think we can dispense with the formality. Call me Spencer, or Spence if you prefer."

"Yes, you're right, Mr.—I mean, Spencer. And I insist you call me Rachel."

He nodded, gooseflesh popping out on his arms at hearing his name from her lips. "Rachel. Pretty name," he said in a low voice, adding an unspoken "just like you" in his mind.

She smiled. "Why don't you sit down and tell me about yourself?" When he didn't move, she said, "Or am I keeping you from your chores?"

He finally sank into a chair opposite the settee. "No, Sundays are pretty quiet around the Double A except when we're rounding up cattle to take on a trail drive."

"A trail drive! How exciting. Tell me what it's like?"

Spence smiled at her enthusiasm for a necessary but exhausting part of owning a cattle ranch in the Texas hill country. There'd been a time when he shared her unbridled excitement over driving a herd of cattle to the railhead up in Kansas—back when he and Daniel had started the Double A. His expression abruptly changed, his smile fading, the familiar ache clutching at his heart. After Daniel's death, going on a cattle drive had lost its appeal. Guilt and longing for a friend who'd been like a brother, a friend he would never see again, swamped Spence. Several minutes passed before Rachel's voice broke through his painful musings.

"Spencer, you're frightening me. Are you all right?"

He blinked, then forced his gaze to focus on the woman sitting on the opposite side of the fireplace. Her reddish gold eyebrows were knitted in a frown, her eyes wide with concern. He cleared his throat, then said, "I'm fine."

"But the look on your face. You looked as if you were in pain. Are you sure you're—?"

"I said I'm fine, dammit," he replied in a near shout. "So, just drop it."

Rachel straightened her spine. "Well, you don't have to get so testy. I should think you'd be grateful that someone was concerned about your well-being."

Spence closed his eyes and dropped his head onto the back of the chair. "Sorry, I was just . . ." He sighed. "Well, that doesn't matter. I still shouldn't have spoken to you that way."

Rachel was silent for a moment, then said, "Perhaps if you talk about it, you'll feel better. My mother always said it was better for a person to talk about whatever's bothering them, rather than keeping it inside and letting it fester."

"Your mother is just full of quaint little pearls of wisdom, isn't she?"

Though his words were laced with sarcasm, Rachel took no offense. "Yes, she is. She has a saying for just about everything that happens in life."

Spencer stared at her for a moment. Finally he said, "If you've only been in Texas for a few months, where was home before you came here?"

Rachel recognized his tactic: take the focus off himself by making her the center of attention. Willing to go along with the ploy, she smiled, then said, "Ohio. My family still lives there."

"You came to San Antonio to teach?"

"Yes. The students at The German-English School are taught in both languages, and I was hired as one of the teachers for the English branch of the school's curriculum."

"You like teaching?"

"Of course. Why wouldn't I?"

Spence shrugged. "Just figured you'd be like most women, wanting to get married and raise a passel of kids."

Rachel's cheeks burned with the blush. "Well, maybe I'm not like most women," she said, tilting her chin upward.

"True, you're not," Spence replied with a grin.

She dropped her gaze to her clasped hands, her voice lowering to a whisper. "The truth is, I wanted those things, once, but . . ." She couldn't bring herself to admit that she'd never come close to marriage. The men she'd met weren't attracted to a woman of her height, nor did they want a wife with her intelligence. She inhaled deeply, released the breath with a sigh. "Anyway, Mother always said, 'what's meant to be, will be.' So, I turned to teaching to find fulfillment in life."

Spence heard the pain in her words, though she'd undoubtedly deny his suspicions if he confronted her with them. "You're not too old to have a family, so maybe you'll still get married and have children."

She lifted her head and gave him a wistful smile. "Thank you. I appreciate your saying that. But there aren't many men who'd want an educated, twenty-eight-year-old spinster for a bride."

"Maybe that was true in Ohio. But in this part of Texas, men are always looking for wives, regardless of their age or education. Any one of them would be proud to marry you."

His words caused Rachel's face to burn with another

blush. "That's kind of you to say," she said. "But you can stop trying to make me feel better. In the months since I arrived in town, not one man has expressed interest in courting me, so I know the—"

"Then they're all fools," Spence said before he could stop the words.

She stared at him, her jaw hanging open. Before she could form a reply, he recovered from his outburst to add, "Have you made friends in town? Someone who could introduce you to the single men in the area?"

"I have a few friends, mostly other teachers at the school."

"Any of them Anglo, or are they German?"

"There are only two Anglos at the school, myself and the other English teacher, Miss Simon. The rest of the teachers are second or third generation Germans."

"Well, there's your problem. As you've undoubtedly found out by now, the German community of San Antonio is a tight-knit group, staying pretty much to themselves. From what I understand, some of the younger Germans are starting to intermarry with the Anglos, the Irish and some of the others in town. But I still think your best bet to land a husband would be to—"

"I'm not on a fishing expedition for a husband," Rachel said, giving Spencer a fierce glare. "And I didn't ask what you think."

"Fine," he said, his jaw tight. "Stay an old maid for all I care."

Rachel flinched at his cruel words, but didn't reply. Instead, she turned to stare into the fire. She'd thought the wound had healed, that the idea of spending the rest of her life alone would no longer resurrect the deep ache in her heart. But she was wrong; the old pain was still there.

The look on Rachel's face made Spence feel like a first-class heel. Pushing out of his chair, he crossed to the settee and sat down beside her. He lifted a hand to brush a strand of hair off her face. The softness of her cheek sent his pulse soaring. "I'm sorry, Rachel. That was totally uncalled for." He watched her throat work, struck with a sudden longing to place his lips where his gaze touched her. When she didn't speak, he whispered, "Please, say you'll forgive me."

She drew a deep breath, then turned her head toward him. Seeing the truth of his words reflected in his eyes, she wet her lips with the tip of her tongue. "You're forgiven."

"Thank you," he replied, unable to take his gaze off her mouth. Her moist lips glistened in the firelight, sending a staggering jolt of need ripping through him. "Rachel, I . . ." She wet her lips again, chasing whatever he'd been about to say from his mind. He could concentrate on only one thing; her mouth and his need to kiss her.

He moved his hand to cup the back of her head, then held her still while he slowly brought his face closer to hers. He touched her lips tentatively at first, then with more confidence. Reveling in her softness and her tiny sigh of pleasure, a groan rumbled deep in his chest.

"Heaven," he murmured against her mouth. "You taste like heaven."

"Must be the whiskey," she replied, her heart pounding so loudly in her ears she could barely hear her own words.

He chuckled. "No, darlin'. Whiskey never tasted this good." He used the tip of his tongue to outline the contours of her mouth; then he pulled her bottom lip into his mouth and gently suckled the plump flesh.

Rachel gasped, feeling the tugging sensation of his mouth in a place much lower. She clamped her knees together, hoping to thwart her body's reaction to Spencer's ministrations, but with little success. And when he slipped his tongue inside her parted lips, she thought she'd expire on the spot. Such an incredibly exciting, deeply intimate kiss went not only beyond her experience but also beyond description.

Chapter Four

Rachel lay tucked in bed, wide awake. Try as she might, she couldn't fall asleep. The fact that she was lying in Spencer's guest bedroom clad in a man's shirt—Spencer's shirt—in place of a nightdress, could well have been reason enough to keep her awake. But the true reason was that she couldn't stop thinking about the kiss she and Spencer had shared earlier, the kiss he'd tried valiantly to downplay for the remainder of the day. In fact, he'd tried to act like nothing had happened between them. But she knew the truth, at least the thought she did. If she'd read his expression correctly, he wasn't as unaffected by the kiss as he wanted her to believe.

She smiled at the darkened window where a thin band of silver moonlight speared into the room through a gap in the curtains. Spencer's kiss had been both tender and fierce. Just thinking of his lips pressed to hers made her pulse quicken and the place between her thighs throb. She lifted one hand and touched her fingers to her lips.

How could one kiss cause such a heated response? Nothing in her limited experience came even close to what—

The mattress suddenly bounced gently, the weight of something or someone landing on the foot of the bed.

Rachel shrieked in terror, sitting bolt upright, then scrambling closer to the headboard where she huddled with her knees drawn up to her chest.

Before she could let out another yell, the door burst open and banged against the wall.

"Rachel, what is it? Are you all right?"

She released her held breath with a sigh. "Spencer, thank God," she managed to say through a tight throat. "There's something in here. I think it's on the bed."

She heard the soft padding of his bare feet on the wood floor, then the scratch of a match. As she blinked to adjust her eyes to the glow of lamplight, Spencer chuckled.

"I should've known," he said.

Rachel followed his gaze to a big striped cat curled up on the foot of the bed.

He bent to pick it up. "Tabby, shame on you for scaring the wits out of our house guest."

"Tabby." Rachel frowned at the cat. "My stars, coming up with that name must have taken—what?—all of two seconds?"

Spencer scowled at her mocking tone. "So the cat doesn't have a creative name. What difference does that make?"

"It doesn't," she replied, closing her eyes and exhaling a deep breath. When Spencer didn't say any more, she opened her eyes and looked up at the man still holding the cat in his arms. "So how come I didn't know you had a cat? Where's she been all this time?"

"Tabby's timid around strangers. She's probably been hiding under the bed in here all day." He rubbed the cat under the chin. "Old Tabby lives here with me, but she really isn't mine. She puts up with me because I feed her, but she'll always be Daniel's cat.''

"Daniel?"

Spencer pressed his lips together, a muscle's ticking evident in the muscle in his jaw. "Daniel Atkins. He was my friend and my partner, the other A in the Double A ranch."

"What happened to him?" Rachel said in a gentle voice, hoping his answer would give her some insight in to the reason for the pain she'd glimpsed in his eyes, the same pain now reflected in the harsh set to his face.

Spencer didn't immediately reply, his thoughts centered on Daniel. He wondered if he'd ever forget that day seven years earlier, or if he'd ever forgive himself. His shoulders rippled with a shudder. No, he would never forget, just as he'd never forgive himself for what he'd done.

He drew a deep breath, then said, "He died. Seven years ago. While we were on a trail drive." He glanced around the sparsely furnished bedroom. "This was his room. From the time Tabby was a kitten, she stayed in here with him. When I showed you to this room, I completely forgot about Tabby. After you fell asleep, she must've finally gotten brave enough to come out of hiding."

Rachel didn't correct his assumption that she'd fallen asleep. Rather, she said, "Well, other than scaring a year off my life, there's no harm done. You can put her down now."

"Are you sure?" Spence blinked, for the first time really seeing Rachel. The neckline of the shirt he'd given her gaped open, revealing a hint of full bosom, and her hair cascaded around her shoulders in a wild tangle of reddish blond waves. His body was suddenly at full attention, his blood surging to his groin.

"Of course," Rachel replied. "I'm the intruder in her

room, so she should be allowed to stay, provided she doesn't object to letting me share it with her.''

"She shouldn't," Spence replied, lowering the cat to the bed. "She likes people well enough; she's just shy at first."

"Come here, Tabby," Rachel said, extending a hand to the cat. Tabby eyed her for a moment, then moved toward the head of the bed, tail straight up, the tip flicking with each step. After sniffing Rachel's hand, she meowed, rubbed her back against Rachel's updrawn legs, then returned to the foot of the bed and lay down.

Rachel looked up at Spencer and smiled. "We'll be fine. You can go back to bed now."

Spencer cast a quick glance at the cat before returning his gaze to Rachel's face. He wished his own bed was the one Rachel occupied. The thought sent images flashing through his mind—of sliding into bed beside her, pulling her into his embrace and fitting her flush against him, exploring the curves of her body with his hands and then his mouth.

He bit his lip to hold in a groan, the throbbing in his groin pure agony. Praying she couldn't see the evidence of his arousal through his hastily donned trousers, he pulled his mouth into a frown. Damn, he needed a woman. He couldn't remember the last time he'd gone to town to seek sexual relief, so that had to be the reason for his erotic thoughts about Rachel.

After he murmured a good night and turned to leave the room, he couldn't shake the notion that he didn't want any of the prostitutes he'd sought out in the past. The only woman he wanted was Rachel Willowby.

The following morning, Rachel rose just past dawn. She moved across the cold floor and pushed the curtains aside.

Everything in sight was covered by a thick layer of glittering ice. Trees bent with the added weight, their branches nearly touching the ground, and long icicles hung from the eaves of the barn.

She sighed, then turned away from the window. "Looks like I won't be leaving this morning," she said to Tabby who blinked up at her and yawned.

As Rachel returned from the kitchen with warm water for a sponge bath, she wondered how she would fill her time until the weather allowed her to return to town. By the time she had finished dressing, she'd come up with an idea for part of the day. Smiling, she headed back to the kitchen.

When Spencer stepped into the room sometime later, he pulled up short. The smells of freshly brewed coffee and frying bacon assailed him, making his stomach rumble. He couldn't remember the last time someone had fixed him breakfast. He frowned. Probably not since he and Daniel had left the orphanage in New Orleans. After that, cooking became his responsibility because Daniel burned everything to a crisp or served it half raw.

He forced himself to step farther into the room. "You're up early."

Rachel smiled at him, cracking another egg into the skillet. "I've always been an early riser. Besides, morning is the best part of the day, don't you think?"

Spence swallowed hard and bobbed his head in agreement, caught in the snare of Rachel's beaming smile. Watching her move around his kitchen as though she belonged there, he couldn't concentrate. He finally found his voice and said, "Can I help with something?"

"No, everything's just about ready, so have a seat." Seeing him hesitate, she added, "Since the ice storm has forced you to put up with me, I thought it only right that I do what I can to repay your hospitality. I don't get much chance to practice anymore, living in a boarding house, but I used to be a pretty fair cook.''

He watched her pull a pan of biscuits from the oven, then crossed the room to the table, pulled out a chair and sat down. This was his house, his kitchen, where he'd cooked and eaten his meals for the past seven years— alone. Though he could've eaten with his hired hands, he preferred his own company. So how the hell could the presence of this woman feel so natural, so perfect?

Not liking the direction of his thoughts, Spence picked up his fork and dug into the heaping plate of food Rachel set in front of him. While he ate, he kept his gaze focused on his plate. If he looked at her, he might be tempted to kiss her again. And if he kissed her again . . . Well, he just couldn't let that happen.

To test his resolve, he allowed himself a brief glance at Rachel. She was staring at him, the look in her beautiful, sky blue eyes easy to interpret. He pulled his mouth into a frown, determined to carry out his plan. But a voice inside his head whispered, ''Even the best-laid schemes often go wrong.''

He jerked his gaze back to his plate. *Dammit, now she's got me spouting ridiculous old sayings.*

Chapter Five

For the remainder of the morning, Spencer busied himself with chores in the barn. While most of the work didn't require his immediate attention, at least it kept him away from the house, away from Rachel. He refused to analyze his need to distance himself from the woman, mostly because he already knew at least part of the answer. If he stayed close to Rachel, he wasn't sure he could keep himself from kissing her again. In fact, he wanted another chance to sample her sweet lips so badly he feared he might go so far as to make sure the opportunity presented itself.

He grunted, disgusted that he couldn't stop thinking about her. How she'd managed to wrangle her way into his every thought in such a short amount of time completely mystified him. He'd done just fine without a woman in his life all these years, and he didn't need one now. So why did Rachel constantly fill his mind and make him ache with a desire the like of which he'd never known?

After filling the feed box in the last of the horse stalls,

he turned to look around the barn. He'd already checked and repaired his tack, fed and watered the horses, mucked out the stalls and spread fresh straw, so what else could he do?

His stomach growled, reminding him of the hours that had passed since breakfast. Knowing his solitary respite was at an end, he retrieved his hat, jammed it on his head, shrugged into his shearling coat and headed for the door. As he crossed the yard, ice crunching under his boots, he bent his head against the bite of the northerly wind, one hand holding his hat in place.

Once inside the house, he removed his hat and coat, then stamped the ice from his feet. Rubbing his hands together to get the blood flowing again, he started toward the kitchen, but stopped. Rachel stood in the doorway.

"You must be frozen stiff," she said with a smile. "Come in here where it's warm." She stepped aside to let him pass. "While I finish dinner, you can thaw out with a cup of coffee."

"I told you, you don't have to cook for me."

"Don't be silly. You've been working all morning, so you shouldn't have to cook your own dinner, too." She ushered him to a chair at the table, then turned to fetch the coffeepot.

After filling his cup, she said, "I've been thinking maybe this afternoon we could do something together."

He nearly spit a mouthful of coffee across the table. The *something* that leaped to his mind undoubtedly wasn't what she meant. Wiping his mouth, he hoped his voice sounded normal when he said, "Like what?"

She took a seat opposite him. "Something for Christmas. Maybe some tradition you have."

He scowled. "Tradition? I don't have any Christmas traditions. It's just another day around here."

"Oh, but it should be more than that."

"Have you forgotten this is a cattle ranch? There's always work to be done. There aren't any days off."

"You don't have to take the entire day off to celebrate Christmas. Don't you at least have a special dinner?"

He shifted on his chair, uncomfortable with her line of questioning. "I . . . uh, usually have dinner with my men."

She smiled. "See there, you do have a tradition."

He took another swallow of coffee before replying. "My having dinner with my men doesn't mean there's something we can do about it now. Christmas is almost two weeks away."

Rachel twisted her mouth into a thoughtful moue. At last she said, "I know. We'll bake cookies. One of the other teachers gave me a recipe her grandmother brought here from Germany. She said the cookies get better with time, so her family always makes them well before Christmas." When he didn't respond, just stared at her, she said, "I hope you don't mind, but I looked through your cupboards and I know you have the necessary ingredients.

Spencer's eyebrows lifted. "What do cookies have to do with Christmas?"

She studied him silently for a moment, then said, "Didn't your mother bake Christmas cookies?"

"What does that have to do with anything?" he said more sharply than he'd intended.

"I just wondered where you got your attitude about Christmas. Cookies are made to be eaten at Christmas, of course, but they're also given as gifts and used as decorations on Christmas trees. I thought everyone knew that baking cookies was a holiday tradition."

"Well, not everyone, Miss Willowby. The orphanage never baked cookies for those of us living there, at Christmas or any other time."

The pain Rachel heard in his statement stunned her. She couldn't respond; her throat was too clogged with emotion. Finally, she found the voice to say, "You agreed to call me Rachel, remember? And I'm sorry, I didn't mean to pry."

After a long moment, Spence said, "No harm done." He drained the last of his coffee, set his cup on the table, then got to his feet. "I'll wash up for dinner."

Rachel kept the dinner conversation centered on the workings of a cattle ranch, a topic which didn't seem to upset Spencer. She longed to ask about his childhood and being raised in an orphanage, but knew he would consider this prying into his life. Maybe he'd open up to her once he got to know her better—and she did intend for them to get to know each other better. Somehow since she'd first met Spencer Adams the day before, her goal of getting him to agree to go the Aid Society's Christmas Ball had undergone a change. She wasn't certain how or why, but now she was determined to get him not only to attend the dance but also to escort her.

As she cleared their dinner dishes, then arranged what she would need for making cookies on the table, she day-dreamed about stepping into the hall at the Casino Club, her arm looped through Spencer's. Everyone would turn at their entrance. The single women would stare at the man at her side and wish they could trade places with her. Shaking her head to chase the fanciful musings from her mind, she released her breath in a long sigh, recalling the familiar words her mother had often spoken. *Slow down, Rachel Marie. You're putting the cart before the horse again.*

She smiled, remembering her mother's exasperation over her youngest daughter's impatient nature. Rachel had been told more times than she could count that there was a proper order for everything. But such reminders had never stopped her from attempting an illogical method.

"What're you smiling at?"

Rachel started, Spencer's voice jerking her back to the

present. "I was just thinking about something my mother used to tell me."

Spencer stared at her from beneath his furrowed brow. "Another of her sayings, no doubt."

"Actually, yes, it was."

When she didn't offer to explain, Spence dropped the subject. He turned his attention to the large mixing bowl she'd placed in the middle of the table. "You really want me to help? I don't know the first thing about making cookies."

"Then you can learn. Unless you've got something else you have to do." Rachel held her breath, hoping he wouldn't use the escape route she'd given him.

He twisted his mouth into a wry smile. "Well, actually, I . . . uh . . . I have the afternoon free."

"Great," Rachel replied with a grin. She turned to pick up a length of toweling like the one she'd wrapped around her waist as a makeshift apron. "Here, let me tie this—"

Spence took a step back. Holding one hand out in front of him, he said, "Whoa, hold it right there. I agreed to help you, but I'm sure as hell not gonna wear an apron."

The indignant look on his face made Rachel bite the inside of her lip. Clearing her throat to cover a chuckle, she laid the piece of toweling aside. "Okay, but just be warned, making cookies can be messy."

Spence frowned. Something about her statement, something about the sparkle he'd seen in her eyes before she'd dropped her gaze warned him to be wary, though he couldn't say exactly why. He'd just have to keep his—

Rachel's voice pulled him from his musings.

"Will you pass me the flour, please?"

He looked down on the table, located the sack of flour and did as she asked. When his hand brushed hers, he sucked in a sharp breath. The touch of her skin, even such a brief one, affected him like a lover's caress and sent a wild thrumming through his veins.

Even without any physical contact, just having her close enough to inhale her scent, to watch the way she caught her lower lip between her teeth while concentrating on her task, left him feeling slightly breathless and partially aroused.

After everything was in the bowl, Spence took a seat at the table. He was content to watch Rachel mix up the cookie dough until he realized his new vantage point put him in a dangerous position—his gaze was on a direct level with the enticing gentle bounce of her bosom. He shifted on the chair, digging his fingers into his thighs in a futile attempt to curb his body's reaction.

"So, tell me more about your ranch," Rachel said, all too aware of the man sitting only a few feet away. She leaned one hip against the table to steady her suddenly wobbly knees.

"What would you like to know?" Spence winced at the sound of his own voice, hoping Rachel didn't realize the reason for the raspiness.

"Anything you'd like to tell me. Coming from Ohio, I'm afraid I don't know much about raising cows."

Spence cleared his throat, then began speaking. "Well, the first thing you need to learn is, this is a cattle ranch. We raise beef here, not dairy cows."

"Yes, I guess you wouldn't raise cattle for milk." When Spencer didn't say any more, she said, "Have you always wanted to own a ranch?"

He nodded. "For as long as I can remember, all Daniel and I talked about was coming to Texas and starting our own ranch."

"Finally your dream came true, and then Daniel died," she said in a soft voice. "That had to be especially hard for you."

"Yeah, it was. All those years of working at whatever jobs we could find, trying to scrape together enough money to make the trip here and buy land." He paused to draw a deep breath. "Our dreams were finally taking shape. We'd started the Double A, bought our first herd of cattle, built this house. And then a year later we left on our first trail drive, which"—he rubbed a hand over his face—"which also turned out to be Daniel's last."

Rachel realized the topic of his late friend and partner was one Spencer seldom broached, so she remained silent in case he said more. When he didn't offer to continue, she turned from the table to fetch the coffeepot. Pouring him a cup, she said, "Yet, after Daniel's death you stayed here. That must have been difficult."

He took a sip of coffee and nodded. "Probably one of the hardest things I've ever done. But owning a cattle ranch had been my dream as much as it was Daniel's, so I stayed." He stared into his cup. "Some years have been rough, but on the whole, the Double A has done well since his death."

"He'd be proud of you," Rachel said in a soft voice.

Spencer's head snapped up. She saw emotions flash into his eyes, the pain giving way to pride, then the muscles of his throat working.

"Thanks."

"You're welcome," she replied with a smile. "So, tell me more about cattle ranching."

He managed to give her a weak smile in return, and after a moment, he began speaking. He told her about cattle ranching in general and the Double A in particular.

As Rachel dropped spoonfuls of cookie dough onto a baking tin, she listened to Spencer, completely entranced. She wondered if he realized the extent of his expertise, or how well he explained even complicated subjects. He would have made an excellent teacher, had his life taken a different path. But the unmistakable pride in his voice when he spoke of the ranch told her he'd made the right choice.

She opened the oven door and slipped the baking tin inside, praying she could get Spencer to make another right choice and agree to attend the Christmas Ball.

Chapter Six

After Rachel baked two batches of cookies, she decided the time had come for Spencer to get involved in the task. "It's your turn," she said, reaching for the extra length of toweling.

"We've already discussed this," he replied, getting to his feet. "I'm not wearing no damn apron."

"Okay, you don't have to," she said with a smile. "But remember my warning. Making cookies can get messy. So don't blame me if you have to change your clothes when you're finished."

Spence looked at Rachel's apron and frowned. "Your clothes aren't a mess, so why——?" A cloud of white dust suddenly appeared in front of his face. His mouth hanging open, he looked down to see flour clinging to the front of his shirt. His eyes widened at Rachel's boldness. Snapping his mouth shut, he brushed at the flour then turned to look at the woman beside him. She held one hand over her mouth, her eyes glowing with mischief.

"So," he said in a low voice. "You think that was funny, do you?"

Rachel couldn't speak. She could barely breathe. She had no idea what had possessed her to pick up a handful of flour and sling it at Spencer, but something had and she'd done it without a qualm.

Spencer's hand dipped into the sack of flour. "You want to play games? Is that it?"

Rachel dropped her hand, but refused to retreat. "I just . . ." She swallowed the threatening giggle. "I just couldn't help myself."

"Really?" His clenched hand rose over her head and his fingers opened. "Well then, I guess I can't help myself either."

Rachel sucked in a sharp breath, the cloud of flour filling her nostrils, settling on her eyelashes and cheeks. She gave a sputtering cough, then calmly reached toward the table.

Before she could reach her intended target—a bowl of eggs—Spence's hand clamped around her wrist. "Oh, no, you don't," he said in a silky whisper. "Flour is one thing, but I draw the line at your pouring eggs on my clothes." He pulled her closer, her breath warm on his face. "That's enough of your games. Now it's time for one of mine."

She blinked up at him. "What do you—?"

"Shhh. Don't talk, darlin'. Just close your eyes."

Her heart hammering a wild rhythm against her eardrums, she let her eyelids drift shut. Her last sight was of Spencer staring at her through narrowed eyes. His gaze was hot and potent, though not from anger. She resisted the urge to shiver. Then before she had time to draw a deep breath, his lips touched hers.

As Spencer deepened the kiss, she groaned into his mouth, her body melting against his, her knees nearly giving out. His arms slipped around her waist, preventing her from falling and holding her firmly pressed to his chest.

Rachel made a sound in her throat, a soft moan of unmistakable pleasure, sending Spence's desire skyward. Never had he responded to kissing a woman as he did to Rachel Willowby. She made his pulse race, his blood heat and his body hard as rock, all with just one kiss. If he didn't pull away soon, he realized, he'd lift her off her feet and haul her off to his bed.

That thought brought reality back in a rush. He jerked his mouth away from hers. How had this happened? How had he nearly lost control so quickly? He glanced down at the woman in his arms, her breasts rising and falling with her labored breathing, and he found his answer.

But Rachel wasn't that kind of woman—the kind that gave herself to a man she barely knew. She deserved more than a randy cattle rancher hustling her off to his bedroom, more than a wild romp of tangled arms and legs and cries of pleasure. Though based on her reaction to his kiss and the desire reflected in her eyes, she might not need a lot of convincing. In fact, she might be more than willing.

He squeezed his eyes closed for a second. He had to stop thinking about what it would be like to take Rachel to his bed, to nuzzle his face between her full breasts, to bury himself in her welcoming warmth until he—He bit back a curse. Drawing an unsteady breath and then another, he tried to cool the firestorm of lust still pounding in his veins.

"Spencer?" Her voice sounded strained.

He sighed. "What?"

"Are you . . . ? Are you all right?"

He dropped his arms and took a step back before saying, "Why wouldn't I be?"

"The expression on your face. You look as if you're in pain."

"I am in pain, dammit," he said before he could stop the words. Seeing the confusion in her eyes, he decided he might have hit on the answer to his dilemma. Maybe if he shocked her, he could finally put out the blaze still smoldering in his veins. Forcing himself to speak in a harsh tone, he said, "I'm so hard I'm ready to bust." Hearing her soft gasp, he knew he'd accomplished the first part of his goal. He'd managed to shock her, but the flames of desire continued to burn. He still wanted her, more than ever.

He rubbed a hand over his face, then exhaled a weary breath. "Look, I shouldn't have said that. I had no business talking to you that way. I . . . uh . . . I'm—"

Rachel pressed her fingers to his lips. "No, don't." She stared up at him, noting the strain still evident in the hard set of his jaw, the remorse clouding his hazel eyes. "Don't be sorry. I'm not."

His heart thumped against his ribs. Was she offering herself to him? He didn't think so, but the look in her eyes said—He gave his head a fierce shake. No, he had to be wrong. Besides, even if had read an invitation in her gaze, Rachel needed—she deserved—a better man than he.

Spence turned abruptly and started across the room. "I just remembered something I need to do."

Before Rachel could open her mouth to reply, he brushed past her. A few seconds later, she heard the front door bang shut. "Well, I'll be switched," she said to the empty kitchen, using another of her mother's favorite sayings. "What was that all about?" Realizing that figuring out the puzzle of Spencer Adams would take more time than she'd anticipated, she looked down at the flour-coated table and floor and sighed. Her enthusiasm for baking cookies sinking fast, she gave up the idea of making another batch. Instead, she started cleaning up the mess she'd made.

Spence sat on a stool in the barn, wondering what he'd done to deserve an albatross like Rachel Willowby hanging around. As soon as the question formed, he knew the answer. Rachel was at the Double A, being a thorn in his side, for the same reason he seldom made the trip into town, the same reason he no longer found any enjoyment in life, the same reason he worked so hard to make the ranch a success. Daniel's death.

He didn't like to think about his best friend's death, but Rachel's intrusion into his daily routine had brought back the painful memories. If he hadn't pushed and prodded Daniel into going on that cattle drive seven years earlier, even when Daniel kept saying they should wait until the herd was bigger, his friend and partner would still be alive.

Spence clenched his hands into fists, wishing for the thousandth time that he could relive that day. That he hadn't insisted they take their cattle north, that he'd listened to Daniel and waited another year.

He dropped his chin onto his chest. *I'm sorry. Daniel. God, I'm so sorry.*

Chapter Seven

When Spencer finally returned to the ranch house several hours later, he'd managed to push thoughts of Daniel, and the guilt still eating at him over his friend's death, from his mind. Determined to be civil to his guest, he found Rachel curled up in a chair in the parlor.

"Are you warm enough?" he said, moving farther into the room. "If not, I can bring in more wood."

She didn't look at him, but continued staring into the fire. "I'm fine."

Spence sat down in the chair on the opposite side of the fireplace. "Do I smell something cooking?"

"After I cleaned up the kitchen and got most of the flour out of my hair, I made stew. It needs to cook for a couple more hours. Then I'll make biscuits."

"Sounds good." When she still didn't look at him, he cleared his throat, then said, "Listen, Rachel. I'm sorry about how I behaved earlier. I—"

"Will you stop apologizing?" she said, finally meeting

his gaze. "I told you, there's no need for you to be sorry. Not for kissing me, and not for . . ."—her cheeks burned with a blush—"what you said afterward." When he opened his mouth to speak, she added, "And if you're trying to apologize for leaving me to clean up the mess we made, don't bother. You obviously had your reasons for high-tailing it out of the kitchen—reasons you don't want to discuss. So, stop fretting, okay?"

Spence stared at the woman sitting with her feet curled beneath her, at the soft smile curving the mouth he longed to taste again. "You're a unique woman, Miss Willowby," he said in a husky whisper. "Stubborn. Intelligent. Forgiving." Silently, he added perceptive and desirable to her list of attributes.

Another blush warming her cheeks, she smiled broadly. "Why, thank you, Mr. Adams. I think you're pretty unique as well."

He nearly told her the only unique quality he could claim was being responsible for his best friend's death, but he managed to halt the words.

Rachel saw the expression on Spencer's face, the flash of pain in his eyes. Deciding they needed to change the direction of their conversation before he made another hasty exit, she said, "Did you know the Germans celebrate a second Christmas?"

His eyebrows beetled in a frown. For the first time since he'd come into the house, he noticed Rachel's position in the chair pushed her bosom more fully against the bodice of her dress. He swore he could see the outline of her nipples through the layers of fabric. Jerking his gaze up to her face, he said, "Can't say as I do."

"One of the teachers at school told me it's an old German tradition. Christmas Day is reserved for church activities, a traditional service in the morning and an evening program for the children. Then on the twenty-sixth, they celebrate their second Christmas, a holiday set aside for visiting friends and relatives." She flashed another smile. "I think that's a wonderful tradition, don't you?"

Spence swallowed hard before he could respond. "Reckon so," he finally said, trying to clear his mind of the tantalizing picture of her naked breasts, their hardened tips begging for his touch, his lips. He shifted in his chair, biting back a groan and wondering how his body could react so strongly to just a thought, how he could want a woman he barely knew so damn much.

"Spencer, is something wrong?"

He snapped back to the present with a start. "No, uh . . . nothing's wrong." He shifted again, hoping to ease the throbbing in his groin. "So, what does your family do to celebrate Christmas?"

Rachel wondered at the strain she heard in his voice, but didn't comment. Instead, she said, "Well, on the day before Christmas, my father and my brothers go out into the woods and cut down a pine tree. Then, that evening, all of us help decorate the tree."

She chatted on about Christmas dinner and exchanging gifts, all of which Spence listened to halfheartedly. His mind constantly strayed to topics far removed from Christmas, fanciful notions he had no business entertaining and should avoid like the plague. Yet, he was helpless to heed his own warning.

Before he realized the passage of time, Rachel rose and announced the stew would be done soon so she'd better see about making biscuits.

After she left the room, he blew out a long breath, then rubbed a hand over his face. When he headed for the kitchen a few minutes later to wash up for supper, he prayed the weather would break soon.

* * *

Tuesday morning dawned clear and bright, much to Spencer's relief. The sun quickly warmed the frozen ground, turning the layer of ice coating everything to slush and making the icicles on the eaves drip in a steady plopping rhythm.

By mid-morning he announced the road safe to travel, then offered to hitch Rachel's horse to the buggy.

While Spencer went to the barn, Rachel waited on the front porch and pondered how she could get him to go to the Christmas Ball. There had to be something she could do. She just had to figure out what that something was.

Once he brought the horse and buggy up to the house, he jumped to the ground. "I hope the stable owner doesn't give you a hard time about not returning the horse and buggy when you were supposed to."

She came down the steps of the porch, stopping next to Spencer. "With the excellent care you gave his horse while I was here, I should think the man would be grateful I'm returning such a fit animal. Besides, considering the weather these past few days, I doubt he'll raise a fuss."

Spence nodded, longing to run his fingers down the curve of Rachel's cheek. Instead he tucked his hands into his jacket pockets.

When he remained silent, she said, "Well, I guess I should be going. If I hurry, I'll can still get to school in time for my last morning class." She turned toward the buggy. "Thank you again for allowing me to stay here. If I can do something to repay the favor while you're in San Antonio, I'd be—"

"Not much chance of that. Jeb takes care of buying supplies and most of the other ranch business. I only go into town to see my banker." His irritation compelled him to add, "Or when I need a woman."

Rachel swallowed, then stepped into the buggy and sat down, her cheeks burning, her spirits slipping.

As she adjusted her skirt around her, Spencer wanted to recall his indelicate words, to tell her how much he'd enjoyed their time together, how much he'd miss her. But he couldn't make himself say any of that. Instead he said, "Take care to stay on the sunny side of the road on the way back to town. There're bound to be some icy spots left over from the storm."

"I will," she said through a forced smile. Picking up the reins, she added, "Take care of yourself Spencer."

On the ride back to San Antonio, Rachel spent the time thinking about the stubborn man she'd just left. As the miles passed, her need to help Spencer continued to increase, but with that need came a deep sense of despair, that settled around her like the dead weight of a rain-soaked wool cloak.

She was maneuvering the horse and buggy through the streets of town before she'd finally managed to shake off the helpless feeling. She'd never let a challenge get her down, and she didn't intend to let Spencer Adams be the first. As she left the stable and headed for the boarding house and her small suite of rooms where she'd change clothes before heading for the school, she made what she considered a significant realization. Since Spencer had cut himself off from any type of social life, perhaps suggesting he attend a ball would be too intimidating for his first outing. Maybe, she should initiate his return to society with something less daunting, something he would find less objectionable.

As a plan formulated in her mind, she smiled. Yes, the idea was a good one, she decided, racing up the stairs of the boarding house and then hurrying down the hall to the door to her rooms. A bubble of doubt surfaced regarding her decision, making her momentarily fumble with her key. She still had a monumental task ahead of her. She had to get Spencer to agree.

Chapter Eight

As soon as classes were dismissed at noon on Wednesday, Rachel ate a hurried dinner, then headed for the stable to put her plan into action.

When she arrived at the Double A, her knock wasn't answered. Looking around the yard, she finally spotted Spencer working on a section of fence beside the barn. As she approached the corral, she called out to him.

Spencer stiffened when he heard the voice that had filled his head since its owner's departure the day before. Certain his imagination must be playing tricks on him, he continued with the chore of replacing a fence rail.

Rachel stopped a few feet from him, on the opposite side of the fence. "Hello, Spencer."

He started, then glanced up at her from beneath the brim of his hat, though he didn't stop working. "You're like a bad penny, Miss Willowby. Always coming back."

She chuckled. "Now who's spouting sayings?" When he didn't respond, she said, "My mother used to say that to a stray cat. Even though she fussed about it, she always put out a saucer of cream whenever the mangy cat showed up on our back porch.''

"Is that what you want? To be fed again?"

She chuckled again. "No, I didn't come here to eat."

He straightened, his eyes still shaded by his hat brim. Rachel could see only his mouth, which was turned down in a frown.

He folded his arms across his chest. "As I recall, this is a school day, so why the hell aren't you teaching?"

Rachel ignored the harshness of his words and forced herself to offer him a bright smile. "The German-English School doesn't hold classes on Wednesday and Saturday afternoons."

He grunted, but didn't reply.

Now that the time had come, Rachel fought down a case of nerves. "Spencer, I came to ask you something."

A muscle in his jaw tightened. "What?"

She took a deep breath. "I'd like you to join me in San Antonio on Saturday night."

His heart slammed painfully against his ribs. "Why should I do that?"

"Because several of the teachers at school are going to be singing Christmas carols with some of the other Germans in town, and I'm going to go listen to them. So I thought you might like to go with me."

Before Spence could reply, she added, "You could come in early, then I'll take you to supper before the caroling starts."

"I've already told you, I don't—"

"I'd really like to do this. I mean, it's the least I can do to repay you for your hospitality."

When he started to shake his head, she said, "Please, Spencer, say yes. It would mean a lot to me, and besides, it'll be fun."

"Rachel." He inhaled deeply and let the breath out slowly. "I already told you, I rarely go to town. You should've known better than to waste your time by coming all the way out here."

"I didn't waste my time, and I think you don't get into town enough. You should be mixing with society more, making friends, enjoying the Christmas season. You should—"

"No. You should stop trying so hard to be a do-gooder. When are you going to realize that you can't fix everything you think needs fixing?"

"I don't understand. What do you mean?"

"I'm not one of your charity cases, Rachel. You can't decide to correct what you think is wrong with me, and just like that"—he snapped his fingers—"make it better. Life doesn't work that way. I'm the way I am for a reason, and nothing you can say or do will change that."

Her chin came up a notch. "I'm not trying to change you, Spencer. I just wanted to show you what you're missing by isolating yourself out here on your ranch, by not going into town and socializing more. Is that so wrong?"

He stared down at her for a long, silent moment. Finally, he sighed heavily, then said, "Why do I get the feeling you aren't going to stop badgering me until I say yes?"

She flashed him a saucy grin. "Probably because I won't. I planned to throw you down and hog-tie you if I had to."

Spencer couldn't help it, the hard set to his jaw gave way to a smile, then a deep chuckle. "I'd like to know how you planned to accomplish that." When she opened her mouth to reply, he held up one gloved hand. "Never mind. I don't think I want to know."

After a few moments, he pulled off one of his gloves and ran a hand over his face. "All right, dammit," he said, though there was no sting to his words. "I'll go."

The smile lighting her face made his breath catch in his

throat and his heart rate pick up speed. He should be shot for agreeing, yet he couldn't make himself withdraw his acceptance.

She turned toward the house. "Meet me at five o'clock Saturday in front of Ernst's Restaurant on Commerce Street."

He nodded, still unable to speak, rooted to the spot while she walked away, the swaying of her backside sending a bolt of desire licking through his veins.

As he watched from the corral, he saw her buggy make its way across his yard and then turn and head down the road. He heaved a sigh. *Well, now you've gone and done it! Agreeing to have supper with her in San Antonio, for God's sake. Of all the stupid, dull-witted, idiotic*—Cutting his name-calling short, he pulled his glove as he turned back to the corral fence. *You're plumb crazy, Adams, that's all there is to it.*

He spent the rest of the day contemplating his dilemma. He couldn't decide what he would do come Saturday— not show up in San Antonio or meet Rachel as they'd agreed. He knew what he should do, he should simply send word that he'd changed his mind. Yet the anticipation of seeing her again, of possibly getting another chance to taste her sweet mouth, was just too strong to ignore.

As the week wore on, he still hadn't come to a solid conclusion, his decision vacillated with his mood. On Saturday, he awoke in a foul temper, certain he wouldn't be going anywhere come evening. But by mid-afternoon, he was heating bathwater and searching his bedroom for a clean shirt.

When he mounted his horse and started for town, the shock on the face of his foreman still played in his mind's eye. Hell, he couldn't blame Jeb for being surprised at his announcement that he was going into town to have supper. He hadn't been away from the Double A more than a dozen times in the past seven years, and never alone. If he needed to see his banker, he made arrangements to go on the day Jeb went after supplies. And if he needed female companionship, he always went to one of the town's bawdy houses with Jeb or some of his other hired hands.

At least he hadn't revealed that he wouldn't be having supper alone. If he'd let that bit of information slip out, Jeb would have bent his ear but good, asking all kinds of nosy questions—questions he'd already asked himself a dozen times.

Spencer settled his hat more firmly on his head, then urged his mare to a faster pace, more anxious to see Rachel than he would have thought possible.

Rachel resisted the urge to pace back and forth on the boardwalk in front of Ernst's Restaurant. Somehow she managed to stand quietly, hands folded in front of her, forcing herself to maintain an appearance of calm. Inside she was a bundle of nerves, her heart thundering in her ears, her stomach queasy. Would Spencer really come to town? Or would he stay hidden on the Double A, tucked away with whatever had driven him to live the life of a recluse?

She heard a clock strike five somewhere in town. Then another five minutes crept by. Drawing an unsteady breath, she decided to give him another ten minutes before—

"Rachel"—the voice snapped her out of her musings—"I hope you haven't been waiting long. I ran into someone I knew down the street, and I couldn't get away."

She longed to ask if that someone was one of the prostitutes he'd visited since his infrequent trips to town usually involved one of their number, but she swallowed such petty words. "That's perfectly all right. I haven't been here long." She looked up into his freshly shaven face and felt her heart cramp. How could it be that she was falling in love with this man? Pushing that thought aside, she looped one arm through his and steered them toward the door of the restaurant. "Come on, I'm starved."

Spence stared down into her sparkling blue eyes, the familiar burst of desire ricocheting through his body. "Me, too," he said in a low voice, though his hunger had little to do with food and everything to do with the woman on his arm.

Chapter Nine

Spence barely tasted the steak he ordered, or the rest of the fine meal the waiter set before him. His every sense was centered on his supper companion. He didn't like the notion that Rachel meant more and more to him with each passing hour. Yet, he feared that no matter how hard he fought, he could well be embroiled in a losing battle. He couldn't let that happen, he had to—Rachel's voice pulled him from his painful musings.

"Ummm, Spencer, have you given any thought to attending the Christmas Ball?" Rachel said, trying to keep the hope out of her voice.

Spence swallowed the last bite of his food, then laid down his fork. "Some," he replied, though in fact he'd never given any consideration to attending. "You're going, aren't you?"

Rachel drew a deep breath. Fiddling with her spoon, she said, "Well, yes. As a member of the Ladies Aid Society, I'm expected to be there."

"Expected? Does that mean, you might not?"

She sighed. "No, I'm certain I'll go. It's just that I was hoping to find someone . . ." She cleared her throat. "Anyway, I'll be at the ball."

A dull ache started in the region of Spence's heart, fed by the longing he detected on Rachel's face, the yearning he heard in her voice. He stared down at his empty plate with a frown. He wasn't considering actually asking if he could take her to the ball, was he? No, that couldn't be the reason for the odd pain in his chest. There had to be another explanation. Yet when he lifted his gaze to meet hers, the words that came out of his mouth took him by surprise.

"Rachel, what I've been thinking about the ball is whether you might allow me to accompany you."

Her eyes widened. Though she knew she should turn him down as a matter of principle, since she'd all but coerced him into extending an invitation, she wanted to go with him too much to do so. "Thank you, Spencer, I'd love to."

They fell silent while the waiter cleared the dishes from the table. After the man disappeared into the kitchen, Rachel dabbed her mouth with her napkin, then said, "Heinrich Kruger, a teacher at the school, invited some of us for coffee and dessert after the caroling tonight."

Spence stiffened, then shook his head. "I don't think—"

"Trude Kruger makes the best *lebkuchen*—German honey cakes. They'll melt in your mouth."

"I still don't think it's a good idea."

She reached across the table and placed a hand atop his. "Heinrich and Trude are good friends of mine. They'll be more than happy to have you in their home. Please, Spencer, say you'll come with me."

Spence squeezed his eyes closed, summoning the strength to refuse. When he opened his eyes and looked into Rachel's face, he swallowed hard. "Okay, I'll go," he finally replied, wondering why the word no was suddenly so hard to say—and how he'd lost control of his own life. First, she'd maneuvered him into inviting her to the ball, and now she'd managed to pry another agreement out of him. *Dammit, this has got to stop. First thing ya know, she'll be—*

The smile Rachel flashed him chased all self-deprecating thoughts from his mind. His collar suddenly tightened around his neck, the room grew too warm, the walls started closing in. Pushing his chair away from the table, he got to his feet. "I need some air," he said in a croaky whisper.

Rachel rose, quickly pulled some money from her handbag and dropped it on the table, then followed Spencer from the restaurant.

She found him on the boardwalk, leaning against a post and staring down the street. Pulling her woolen cloak more tightly around her, she said, "Spencer, is something wrong?"

A few seconds passed before he answered. "I . . . uh . . . got real hot all of a sudden."

"You're not taking ill, are you?"

"No. I just couldn't breathe in there, that's all."

"It does feel better out here," she replied, drawing a deep breath of the crisp evening air.

When he didn't respond, she said, "If you're feeling up to it, the carolers will be starting soon."

"Yeah, I'm fine." He straightened and turned toward her. "Where did you say they're going to be?"

"The Main Plaza."

"That's quite a walk." He held out his arm to her. "So, we'd better get going."

Rachel smiled, then slipped her arm through his. As they made their way west along Commerce Street toward the town's Main Plaza, she couldn't stop thoughts she had no business thinking from niggling at her brain. Thoughts like how much she wished Spencer returned her newly discovered love, or that they were a happily married couple out for an evening stroll.

By the time they arrived at the Main Plaza, the carolers had already assembled and begun singing. Bonfires, burning in tar barrels, crackled, their flames lighting the plaza and casting a bright yellow glow on the singers as well as the crowd gathered to hear some of their fellow citizens sing German Christmas songs.

Rachel kept her arm looped through Spencer's, reluctant to relinquish the physical contact.

"Do you know what they're singing?" Spence said, when one song ended.

Her heart pounding in reaction to the warmth of his breath on her ear, she said, "The one they just sang was 'Silent Night' and the one before that was 'O, Christmas Tree.' "

"You speak German?"

"No, though I've picked up a few words since I've been here." She looked up at him. "You didn't recognize the melodies?"

When he shook his head, her heart tightened again for the boyhood Spencer must have led. She offered him a smile, then said, "Those are traditional German Christmas carols, but they've also become popular in English. 'Silent Night' is one of my family's favorites. My mother would start singing while we decorated our tree; then the rest of us would join in."

He shifted his stance, uncomfortable with the topic of conversation. His movement made her lean toward him to maintain her balance, bringing one full breast into firm contact with his arm. Red-hot desire ripped through him, stealing his breath and replacing his mental picture of

Rachel and her family singing carols with a much more erotic scene.

By the time the singers finished their last song, Spence had finally wrestled his wayward thoughts into submission. Though the effort left him with a pounding head and a sour mood.

The walk to the Kruger house on Madison Street was accomplished in relative silence, for which Spence was grateful. If Rachel had insisted on carrying on a conversation, his sullen disposition would have become obvious. And while he would have skipped going to her friends' home in a heartbeat, he couldn't bring himself to drag her spirits down to the same level as his. So Rachel's willingness to remain quiet was a relief.

As Spence stood on the porch of the Kruger house, waiting for his knock to be answered, he wished he'd found a way to beg off. But when the door swung open he knew there was no way to do that.

Rachel had said Heinrich and Trude Kruger would make him feel welcome in their home, and she was right. The middle-aged couple—Heinrich, tall and lean with a thick mustache, and Trude, petite and slightly plump with huge brown eyes—greeted him with warm smiles, then ushered Rachel and him into the parlor to meet the rest of their guests.

At first, Spence found his first social outing in seven years awkward and uncomfortable, but Rachel seemed to sense his uneasiness and stayed close by. Her frequent smiles, her fingers touching his arm, her heady scent wafting around him all helped to lessen his unease. He'd finally started to relax when the conversation shifted from the holidays to their town.

"Someone said the old Bishop ranch has been sold,"

one of the other guests said, a stout man with gray hair and heavy jowls named Ludwig Burger.

"*Ja,* I heard that," Heinrich replied. "The new owners are planning to fix up the place, then bring in a large herd of cattle." He turned to Spencer. "Since you have a cattle ranch, perhaps you have heard something about that?"

Before Spence could reply, Ludwig spoke again. "That's why your name was familiar when Heinrich introduced us. You're one of the owners of the Double A?"

All eyes turned to look in Spence's direction. Resisting the urge to squirm on his chair, he said, "I'm the sole owner now, and as for the Bishop ranch, I haven't heard anything about—"

"I'd nearly forgotten," Ludwig said, setting his coffee cup on a nearby table. "You're the one who hid himself away after that unfortunate business about your partner. Died on a cattle drive, didn't he?"

Spence managed a jerky nod, a buzzing noise starting in his head.

"As I recall, there was talk at the time about you blaming yourself for the accident." Before Spence could find his voice, the man continued. "Well, I'm glad to see you've finally come to your senses and gotten over that ridiculous notion."

Heinrich nodded, then said, "We're all glad, Spencer. It's time for you to put the past behind you and start getting on with your—"

"You don't know anything about what happened," Spence said, the buzz intensifying in his brain. "Who are you to tell me what's ridiculous—or what I should do with my life?" Not waiting for a response, he surged to his feet. "None of you knows what the hell you're talking about." Clamping his mouth shut, he strode across the parlor, shoved his coffee cup into Trude Kruger's hands, then nearly ran from the room.

Chapter Ten

The Krugers' front door banging shut startled Rachel out of her momentary shock over Spencer's rude departure.

She slowly got to her feet. Ignoring the stunned looks on the faces of the other guests, she crossed the parlor and stopped in front of her hostess. "Trude, I'm so sorry. I didn't mean to spoil the evening."

"Don't be silly, dear. You didn't spoil anything," Trude replied, patting Rachel's hand. "And please don't be angry with Spencer. He's obviously still in a great deal of pain."

Rachel nodded, then stepped into the hallway and removed her shawl from the coatrack by the front door. "If you'll excuse me, I'm going to try to catch up with him."

By the time Rachel reached the street, Spencer was already a block away. Picking up the hem of her skirt, she ran after him.

She didn't call out to him until she'd made up some of the distance separating them. "Spencer. Spencer, wait."

He glanced over his shoulder. At first Rachel thought he wasn't going to stop, but then his long strides slowed. Just as she drew even with him, he came to a halt but kept his back to her.

Before she could say anything, he spoke. "You should have stayed with your friends. I'm sure one of them would have seen you home."

"I didn't want to stay. I want to be with you."

He snorted. "I don't know why the hell you would. Anyone with a lick of sense wouldn't want to be around a man who killed his best friend."

Her heart pounding, she said, "What do you mean, killed? I thought Daniel died in an accident."

He drew in a deep breath, exhaled heavily and then turned to face her. "A mere technicality. As far as I'm concerned, I killed him."

Rachel put a hand on Spencer's forearm. Though his muscles stiffened beneath her touch, he didn't pull away. "Tell me what happened."

"I don't think that's a good idea."

"Please, Spencer," she said, wishing she could see the expression on his face. "Help me to understand."

After a few moments, he began speaking in a low voice. "The first spring after Daniel and I started the Double A, I wanted to drive our cattle north to the railhead in Abilene, Kansas. Daniel disagreed. He thought we should wait at least another year, until we had more cattle to sell. But I said if we sold the beeves we had, we could buy a prize steer and start building up a better herd sooner than we'd planned. He still didn't agree, and we argued about it for days. I just wouldn't leave well enough alone and kept badgering him until he finally gave in."

He rubbed a hand across his face. "We'd only been on the trail drive for a few days when something spooked the cattle. Daniel got caught in the middle of the stampede.

He was riding a horse he hadn't had very long. A high-strung gelding that wasn't used to bawling, frightened cattle. I saw what was happening from the other side of the herd, that Daniel was having a hard time controlling the horse, so I tried to get to him. But I couldn't get there in time. I watched Daniel lose his seat then fall.

"When . . . when I finally got to him, he was still alive. But we both knew he wouldn't make it," he said, his voice breaking. He paused to pull himself together. "With his last breath, he told me to make the Double A the best cattle ranch in this part of the state."

He took a step back, forcing her to remove her hand from his arm. "So, you see, I'm not worth all your fussing and fretting. In fact, I'm not worth a damn thing."

Rachel remained silent for a moment, then spoke. "That's not true. You're worth a lot, especially to me."

When he didn't respond, she added, "Spencer, what happened to Daniel wasn't your fault. His death was an—"

"The hell it was!" he said in a near shout. "If I hadn't insisted on going on that damn trail drive. If I'd listened to Daniel, he would still be alive. I killed him as surely as if I'd pushed him under the hooves of those cattle."

"That's not true either." When she tried to touch him, he took another step back. Dropping her hand to her side, she said, "I can understand how you'd feel guilty about Daniel's death, especially after the two of you argued about making the trail drive. And you're certainly entitled to grieve for him. But people die when it's their time to leave this earth, and there's nothing you or any of the rest of us can do to alter God's timetable. Though Daniel's life ended much too soon, you weren't responsible, Spencer, and you couldn't have stopped his passing." She paused for a moment, before saying, "What if you'd been the one to die in the stampede? Would you want Daniel to wallow in unwarranted grief and guilt as you've been doing?"

"Who are you to say what I feel is unwarranted? He was my partner, and I loved him like a brother. I should've been able to save him, dammit. But I didn't, and I have to live with that." He pointed a finger at her. "So don't you tell me what I should or shouldn't be feeling."

The pain and bitterness in Spencer's words cut Rachel to the quick. Blinking back the sudden sting of tears, she swallowed the lump in her throat. "I didn't know Daniel, but I suspect he wouldn't want you blaming yourself for his death." She drew in a shaky breath. "Spencer, don't you see what you're doing to yourself? If you don't let go of your guilt, it's going to destroy you."

He crossed his arms over his chest. "What do you care if it does?"

"I care, Spencer, because . . . because I'm falling in love with you."

He stared at her long and hard, unable to see more than the outline of her face in the darkness. A full minute passed before he spoke. "Don't waste your time or your love on me, Rachel. Like I said, I'm not worth it."

She forced back another spurt of tears. "I'll come out to the ranch tomorrow and we'll talk—"

"No! You've already meddled enough in my life. I don't want to hear more of your preaching. Stay away from the Double A, or so help me, I swear I'll have you physically removed from my property."

When she didn't respond but stood next to him, still as a statue, he said, "Go on, Rachel. Go back to your friends and forget you ever had the misfortune of meeting me."

Before she could force words through her tight throat, he turned and stalked off.

Rachel wasn't sure how she managed to get back to the Kruger house, not with the ache in her chest hurting so much. When she stepped into the hallway and met Trude's concerned stare, she tried to put on a valiant front, but with little success. She knew Trude saw through her efforts, but was thankful that her friend, as well as the other guests, didn't ask questions. For the next hour, Rachel managed to pretend everything was fine; then she rose and quietly asked Heinrich if he would take her home.

She lay in bed that night, staring at the ceiling, tears running silently down her face. Her last conversation with Spencer played over and over in her head. If only she'd known the right thing to say to him, the right words to ease his burden of guilt, the right way to comfort him. But she'd failed at all those things, and as a result, she would have to endure the consequences.

She used to think nothing could be more painful than accepting the idea of remaining a spinster for the rest of her life. But she'd been wrong. A heart breaking for a love that could never be was worse. Much worse.

Many hours passed before the tears stopped and she slipped into a fitful sleep.

Spencer made the ride back to his ranch feeling as if he were the lowliest creature on the face of the earth. Recalling what he'd said to Rachel, he was appalled. She didn't deserve to be on the receiving end of his self-directed scorn. But dammit, all her talk of his not being responsible for Daniel's death had touched a nerve and set off his temper.

He scowled into the night. Could she be right? Was he wrong to blame himself for Daniel's death? Had he needlessly heaped guilt on himself these past seven years? He gave his head a fierce shake. No, such talk had to be just plain foolishness. Still, she'd been right about one thing. If Daniel could speak to him from the grave, his friend wouldn't mince any words in telling Spencer what an idiot he was to allow his guilt and grief to completely take over his life.

As painful as the thought was, Spencer couldn't help smiling at the notion of Daniel giving him a tongue-lashing. His smile faded, a lump forming in his throat. In a strangled voice, he whispered, "God, why did you have to take Daniel so soon?"

Chapter Eleven

The day of the Christmas Ball dawned clear and bright, in direct contrast to Rachel's drab and overcast mood. She forced herself to eat breakfast, then headed for the Casino Club to help the other members of the Ladies Aid Society decorate the hall. Normally, she loved being with the other women, chatting and laughing as they worked. But that day her heart just wasn't into lighthearted conversation.

When she left the hall later that afternoon, she longed to go back to her boarding house and take a long bath before curling up in bed for the rest of the night. But she knew no matter how much she longed to stay home, she'd have to make an appearance at the dance. She'd never backed down from an uncomfortable situation before. But that was before she'd fallen in love and had her heart trampled into the ground.

After lying down for an hour and then soaking in a hot tub, she sat down at her dressing table. "I can do this," she said to her reflection while arranging her hair. "I can go to the ball, a smile plastered on my face. And after a decent amount of time, I'll leave." She tucked another hairpin into a thick curl of hair. Yes, that was what she'd do. No one would miss her once the ball was in full swing, so she could just slip out the back door.

She rose from the dressing table and moved to where she'd hung the dress she planned to wear. As she fingered the lace trim on the neckline, she wished once again that she didn't have to attend the ball alone.

She'd heard nothing from Spencer since the week before when he'd left her standing down the street from the Krugers'—not that she'd expected to hear from him. He'd made his position perfectly clear. Still, she'd clung to a tiny flicker of hope that he'd contact her. Now that the day of the ball had arrived, she realized she'd been foolish to keep even the tiniest hope alive.

"Well, Rachel, it's no use crying over spilt milk," she said, mimicking her mother's matter-of-fact tone of voice.

She was starting to remove her dressing gown when a sharp rap sounded on her door. Holding the dressing gown closed at her throat with one hand, she moved to the door. "You came sooner than I expected, Tim. Could you give me in a few minutes?"

"Who the hell's Tim?"

Rachel started, then reached for the doorknob and jerked open the door. "Spencer!" Her gaze swept over his formal attire, her heart taking up a wild rhythm. "What are you doing here?"

"I thought we were going to the Christmas Ball? And you didn't answer my question. Who's Tim?"

"My landlady's son. He's supposed to fetch the bathtub from my room." She frowned. "And what do you mean, we're going to the Christmas Ball. After what you said last week, I thought . . . I mean, I figured . . ."

Spencer smiled. "I know. So, if you'll let me in, I'll explain."

"Oh, of course," she said. Still clutching her dressing gown, she moved aside so he could enter.

Spence stepped over the threshold and closed the door behind him. He gave the suite of rooms a cursory glance, then swung his gaze back to Rachel. She looked wonderful with her cheeks flushed, her sky blue eyes shining up at him. He longed to take her into his arms, to rub his growing arousal against her belly, to kiss her senseless, but he resisted doing all of those things. Instead, he cleared his throat and began speaking. "First, I want to apologize for my behavior at the Krugers'. I was rude to leave the way I did, but I also had no right to take out my anger and frustration on you."

When she opened her mouth to respond, he said, "Wait, let me finish. On the way home that night, I started thinking about what you said. And this past week, that's all I've thought about. It took a while, but I finally came to realize you were right."

She eyed him warily. "You did?"

He gave her a crooked smile. "I don't blame you for being skeptical. But please believe me, I now know I wasn't responsible for Daniel's death. Though I'll never stop missing him, I've vowed to stop letting guilt eat away at me. Once I made that decision, it was like an enormous weight had been lifted off my chest." His smile broadened. "I haven't felt this good in years."

"Oh, Spencer," she said with a smile. "That's wonderful."

"Yes, it is." He stepped closer, then lifted one hand and ran his knuckles down the side of her face. "And I have you to thank for the change."

"I didn't do anything. Not really."

"Yes, you did. You forced me to look at my life, to see

myself for what I'd become. And frankly, I didn't like what I saw.''

"Don't be so hard on yourself. You lost someone you loved dearly, so your reaction was—''

"Shhh, I don't want to talk about me. I want to talk about us.''

"Us?'' The word came out with a squeak.

"Yes, us,'' he said with a chuckle. "I want there to be an us, provided you meant what you told me last week.''

Rachel pulled her brow into a frown. "What I told you?''

Spencer's heart skipped a beat. "You don't remember telling me you thought you were falling in love with me?''

"Oh, that,'' she replied, her face growing warm with a blush.

"Yes, that.'' When she didn't say any more, he went on. "Well, is it true?''

"Actually''—she swallowed hard—"it's more than think. I'm sure I've fallen in love with you.''

He closed the distance between them, lowered his face to rest his forehead against hers. "You have no idea how happy you've made me, darlin'. Or how lucky I am.''

Rachel looped her arms around his neck. "Then why don't you show me?''

"What about the Christmas Ball?''

"What about it?''

"I thought you wanted to go?''

"I do, but we've got plenty of time. If we're a little late''— she lifted one shoulder in a shrug—"so what? When I walk in on your arm, everyone will understand.''

Spence laughed, then shifted his face so he could nuzzle the side of her neck. "You're a meddling do-gooder, Rachel Willowby, who doesn't know enough to keep her nose out of other people's business. But I love you just the same.'' His last words were murmured against her mouth, just before he captured her lips in a kiss.

Rachel's pique over the first part of his statement died as the last of his words sank in. With a soft whimper of joy, she pressed herself against him, reveling in the warmth of his body, the heat of his mouth, the rasp of his tongue.

When Spence finally lifted his head, he sucked in a deep breath to ease his labored breathing. Rachel tried to pull him back down for another kiss, but he resisted. "Easy, darlin'. We have to get you dressed, and if you keep kissing me like that, we'll never make it to the ball."

Rachel stared up at him for a long moment. Lifting a hand, she ran her fingertips over his lips. "I don't care if we don't go."

Spence chuckled, then kissed her fingers. "Hmmm, I'm tempted to take you up on that. But I think we should go to the ball. All your friends will be there, so that would be a good time to announce our engagement."

Her eyes went wide. "Engagement?" she said in a croaking whisper. "Are you serious?" At his nod, tears welled up in her eyes and spilled down her cheeks. "Oh, Spencer, yes, that would be the perfect time."

Later, as they walked to the Casino Club on Market Street, Rachel said, "What would you like for Christmas?"

"Nothing. You've already given me everything I'll ever want."

She gave him a soft swat on the arm. "Stop talking like that, or I'll start crying again."

He came to a halt, then grasped her shoulders and turned her to face him. "But it's true. If it weren't for you, I'd still be the same rude, foul-tempered pain in the ass I was when we first met. You forced me to see the truth about my past. You gave me the best gift a man could ask for. The chance for a lifetime of love and happiness." He pressed a lingering kiss on her lips, then lifted his head and whispered, "Rachel, I'll treasure your gift until my dying breath."

Epilogue

Five years later

Spence entered the front door of the ranch house, then removed his hat and coat. The scent of vanilla hung in the air, and voices drifted into the parlor from the kitchen. Smiling, he headed in that direction. At the doorway he paused, content to quietly take in the scene.

The table was covered with sacks of flour and sugar, jars of spices and assorted mixing bowls. Rachel stood beside a chair, holding a kneeling four- year-old Annie, the wild tangle of the girl's reddish brown hair temporarily subdued in thick braids.

In the high chair on the side of the table closest to the door, sat two-and-a-half-year-old Daniel, his green eyes trained on the star-shaped cookie clutched in one pudgy hand.

The sight of his family filled Spence with so much emotion he thought his heart might leap from his chest. Every time he walked in on a scene like this, his wife and children busy at some chore, he offered another prayer to thank God for bringing Rachel into his life. Without her, he'd still be the bitter, guilt-ridden, hollow shell of a man she'd first met nearly six years earlier.

As he watched Rachel help Annie measure flour into a mixing bowl, memories of the first time he'd watched his wife make cookies came flooding back. Recalling how she'd gotten him to agree to help, then boldly doused him with a handful of flour, he smiled. His wife was truly something. She was still a do-gooder, trying to help those in need or right the world's wrongs, but she was also wonderful at running the house, a patient and loving mother . . . and passionate—his smile broadened—extremely passionate. He rolled his shoulders, wincing slightly as his shirt rubbed across the scratch marks she'd inflicted at the moment of her climax the night before.

He bit the inside of his cheek to hold in a laugh. Like everything else in her life, Rachel had approached the marriage bed with great tenacity and eagerness. And once she'd become confident of her abilities as a lover, she'd turned into a real hellcat—always inventive and demanding but never disappointing.

He sucked in a deep breath. God, he loved her. How had he survived all those years before she'd come into his—

"Papa. Papa," Daniel shouted, snapping Spence back to the present. "Cookie." Spence blinked, then smiled at his son. All that remained of the cookie was one point of the star and the few crumbs stuck to Daniel's fingers, cheeks and chin.

"Yes, son, cookies. I just hope you aren't eating too many," he said, moving into the room and ruffling the boy's blond hair. He smiled at his son, then stepped behind the chair holding Annie and bent to kiss the top of her head. "How's my little mouse?"

His daughter glanced up at him, her greenish-blue eyes sparkling. "Fine, Papa. Mama's letting me help."

"So I see," he replied, smoothing a strand of silky hair that had escaped her braids.

"I hope you don't mind, Spencer," Rachel said. "But we're going to be eating a little later than usual. I want to get this last batch of cookies in the oven before I start dinner."

"No problem," he replied. "I'll just have a cookie to tide me over." While eating the warm cookie, he watched Rachel help their daughter add the last of the ingredients to the bowl and then stir them with the wooden spoon. When his wife moved past him to fetch a baking tin from the top of the stove, he said, "After last night, I thought you'd be too tired for baking."

She looked up at him, a gleam in her sky blue eyes. "Actually, I was full of energy this morning." She flashed him a saucy grin. "Must be the good night's sleep."

He leaned closer, his lips brushing her ear. "Or maybe it's the exercise you got before you drifted off."

She chuckled, rising onto her toes and pressing her mouth to his. "Hmmm," she murmured, nibbling on his lips. "You may be right." She lowered her heels to the floor, then cast a quick glance at the children. Satisfied they were safely occupied, she whispered, "You were pretty spectacular last night."

"No, darlin', *we* were. I'm nothing without you."

Tears sprang to Rachel's eyes. A lump in her throat, she whispered, "Oh, Spencer, what did I ever do to deserve you?"

He reached out and pulled her close. Rocking her in his arms, he whispered, "You rode out here to the Double

A, stuck your nose in my life and wouldn't stop prodding and pushing until I finally saw the light.''

"That's not very flattering," she said, her cheek pressed against his chest. "You make me sound like some kind of deranged reformer bent on saving your soul from eternal damnation."

"I don't mean it quite that way. Although you did save my hide by pulling me out of the hell I'd made of my life. Like I told you that night on the way to the Aid Society's Christmas Ball, you gave me the greatest gift I could ever ask for." Using his knuckles, he lifted her chin until she met his gaze. "Thank you, Rachel," he whispered, staring deeply into her eyes. "For the gift of your love."

Her heart nearly bursting, she swallowed hard, then managed to say, "You're welcome." With a soft moan, she accepted his kiss.

TESSA'S HEART

Linda Madl

Chapter One

The hair on the back of Tessa Jennings' neck tingled and she straightened, suddenly aware that her backside was presented wantonly—and defenselessly—toward the wagon road.

Disquieted by the sense of being watched, she forgot the cedar tree she'd bent over to examine for fullness and turned to search the prairie above the road. Nothing stirred there.

The winter wind tugged suggestively at her long skirt and caressed her cheek. The sensation of being watched remained.

Involuntarily, Tessa brushed a hand across her derriere. She was being silly, she told herself. The ridge above was bare, the swaying of brown prairie grass the only movement to be seen. She and Danny were alone. Yet, the tingling persisted. There was no mistaking the sense of being watched. Someone was spying on her and Danny; someone who refused to show themselves.

December was a cold time for travel on the prairie, and Tessa had had no expectations of meeting anyone when they'd set out from Prairie City. But she'd brought her gun just the same. Even with 1871 just around the corner, and statehood already established for ten years, Kansas could occasionally be a lawless place.

She surveyed the ridge again and debated whether she should return to the wagon for the rifle and the saw she'd concealed under a buffalo robe. She might not kill a troublemaker, but she could make him darned sorry that he'd bothered her and her brother.

Only menacing clouds stretched along the horizon, the same cloud bank she'd seen earlier—and had decided to ignore. It was Christmastime. She wasn't about to allow threatening weather to put a damper on their Yuletide spirit. With relief, she noted that the gray clouds seemed to have retreated. But the uneasy sense of being watched clung to her.

"What about this tree, Sis?" Danny called from the small forest of dark cedars and winter-bare cottonwoods that clogged the rocky ravine better known as Little Kitten Creek. The stunted stand of trees qualified as the closest thing to a forest near Prairie City. "Is this one tall enough?"

Tessa turned to see Danny dancing around a promising evergreen: his sturdy shoes crunched the dried grass. "That certainly is a big one," she said, admiring the fullness of the tree. Her Christmas mood returned, despite the tingling at the back of her neck.

Prairie City boasted several respectable oaks and a stand of cottonwoods sheltering the spring that supplied the town's water. But this rocky fold between the rolling hills nurtured the only evergreens to be found for miles and miles. In years past Papa had always cut the community Christmas tree and proudly placed it in the center of the Prairie City schoolhouse, the meeting place for the Meth-

odists, the Presbyterians and the Prairie City Church of All
Hope. Everyone shared in the delight of decorating the
solitary tree and celebrating around it. But this year
because Papa's arthritis had worsened during the fall, she
and Danny had volunteered to carry on the tradition. If
Tessa Jennings had anything to do with it, Prairie City
wasn't going to celebrate Christmas with mere oak boughs
for holiday greenery. "Just remember I'm not quite as
strong as Papa. We've got to be able to manage this tree
ourselves."

"We can handle this one," Danny insisted, peering up
at the evergreen's top. "This year's tree has to be at least
as big as last year's, don't you think? We don't want to
disappoint anybody."

"No, we don't," Tessa agreed, admiring the cedar's
great height and thinking of how pleased Papa would be
with the lofty tree. How beautiful it would look bejeweled
with candles and draped with garlands of popcorn and
buttons. No, they wouldn't disappoint anyone. Especially
not Nathan and Nellie. Tessa wanted everyone in Prairie
City to be impressed with the size and the beauty of the
tree she and Danny brought home. The Jenningses would
hold their heads high at the Christmas tree–trimming
party. Everyone would know that they were a family who
worked together and accepted pity from no one.

"No one will be disappointed by the tree the Jenningses
bring home," she vowed and grinned at her brother. The
wind slackened and the heavy, rich smell of cedar filled
her head and stirred her zest for Christmas once more.
The spicy scent inspired her with the cheer of Christmas
songs and tasty holiday foods.

"Oh, dang, here's a flat side," Danny said, frowning at
the flaw he'd discovered. A hank of hair fell across his
smooth, broad brow. He was tall and lanky for his twelve
years, strong and good-natured. Over the past year as

Papa's illness had worsened, Danny had been a great help to Tessa. He'd grown up a lot, just as she had. Between them they'd managed to keep the *Praire City Spirit* newspaper running. But at moments like this, when all his boyish enthusiasm surfaced, Tessa was reminded that Danny was only twelve—hardly a child but not yet a man.

"We can't have a dang flat-sided tree," Danny said, turning away from the imperfect cedar.

"No, we can't," Tessa agreed, smiling, amused by her brother's sudden perfectionism—and ignoring his bad language.

"There must be another here, one that's fuller and more uniform."

Before Tessa could agree, Danny loped deeper into the forest of cedars, jumping the shallow icy creek and scrambling over the rocks to the other side of the ravine. She hesitated, wondering if she should go back for the rifle and the saw before following him. They would need the saw to cut down the tree and she was still convinced that hidden eyes watched them. She would go get them.

"Danny, hold up a minute," Tessa called after her brother. She did not like the idea of his trailing off out of her sight, but he'd already disappeared into the scrub.

She turned, intending to dash to the wagon for the saw and the rifle, then catch up with Danny. Instead of thin air, she walked into a solid warm, dusty shirt front.

"I've got it," a deep voice rumbled from inside the shirt.

"Oh," she yelped, stumbling backward, hastily putting a safe distance between herself and the unexpected stranger.

He held up the saw. Its well-oiled teeth gleamed menacingly in the pale winter light. Tessa sucked in a breath and dragged her gaze from the blade to the man.

"Who are you?" she demanded, quickly assessing him. "Are you the one who has been watching us?"

He was tall and dressed like a cowboy: boots, spurs, jeans,

a plaid wool coat over a flannel shirt, a dirty red kerchief around his neck. A dark mustache hid his mouth. Indian beads decorated the hatband of the wide-brim dust-covered Stetson that shadowed his eyes. Several days' worth of dark stubble covered his lean jaw. But the gun he wore concerned Tessa most. His six-shooter, a long-barreled, sleek, dangerous-looking weapon hung low, strapped tight against his thigh in a very uncowboylike fashion. A cowpuncher, if he wore a gun, usually strapped it high at his waist and out of the way of his movements in the saddle.

When she saw what he had in his other hand, the blood drained from her face. Tessa stared at her rifle in his big gloved hand.

The cowboy swung her gun up to give her a closer look at it. "Yep, I've been watching."

Alarmed, she glanced toward the wagon, where she saw an unfamiliar, well-groomed bay gelding tied to the wheel. Silently she fought the panic threatening her composure. "What are you doing with my rifle?"

"Keeping it safe," he said, lifting his chin so he caught her gaze with the bluest, iciest, most unreadable eyes Tessa had ever seen. A deadly chill seeped into her bones as he continued to talk. "Yeah, I have been watching you, and I don't mind telling you, Sis, you've got a nice backside."

A leer spread across the cowboy's face. His use of Danny's pet name for her annoyed Tessa more than frightened her. How long had the cowboy been watching and listening to them? Inwardly she cursed the stupidity of leaving the gun in the wagon, but she clung to her bluff. "Thanks for bringing the saw and my rifle. I'll take them now."

He pulled the gun beyond her reach and tucked the saw under his arm. "You don't need it. We're just going to help Danny with that tree." With his free hand, the cowboy reached for Tessa's arm.

She stepped beyond his reach. "Who are you? What do
you want?"

The hint of indecent humor disappeared from his
mouth. "The name is Harper, and I'm just being neigh-
borly in the spirit of the Christmas season and all." His
words, uttered grudgingly, turned crisp and short. He nodded in the direction Danny had taken. "Time is a-wasting.
Let's go get that tree."

"Do we have a choice, Mr. Harper?" Tessa asked, still
mystified as to what he wanted and hoping there was some
way to get rid of him.

"No," Harper snapped, gazing in Danny's direction.
"Your brother is younger than he looks and way too inexpe-
rienced for the two of you to be out here alone in the
dead of winter looking for a damned Christmas tree."

Before Tessa could react, he latched onto her elbow
with a painful grip and dragged her deeper into the forest—farther from the road but toward Danny.

His grasp was so powerful Tessa found herself lurching
along beside him, surprised and afraid. He was right about
Danny. Her young brother could not stand up to an armed
man. She had to defuse the situation. "We don't have any
money with us," she stammered as she stumbled along at
the cowboy's side. "Take the team and wagon if you want,
but Duke and Duchess are over twenty years old."

"All I want is to see you on your merry way, Sis." His
words were low, spoken in a mocking growl.

Tessa couldn't imagine what on earth he meant, but she
was certain now that he was up to no good.

"I found another tree, Sis. This one is even better,"
Danny was calling from ahead of them, but still out of
their sight. "Over here. This is the perfect Christmas tree."

"Answer him," Harper ordered, his fingers biting
deeper into Tessa's arm.

"We're coming," she called, stumbling over a fallen

branch. Harper's grip lifted her over the dead wood, saving her from going down on her knees.

Danny suddenly appeared from behind a rich, full cedar tree almost three feet taller than he. It was a flawless Christmas tree—just what they'd been looking for—with abundant, perfectly shaped limbs and an elegant, straight trunk. But at the moment Tessa had more pressing issues to deal with. The questioning look on Danny's face told her that he'd heard her use of the plural pronoun we and the uncertainty in her voice.

"Well, howdy," her brother said when he saw Harper. A friendly smile spread across his fresh face. "I didn't hear anybody coming along the road."

"Neither did I," Tessa confessed, her mind refusing to grasp how suddenly this ordinary afternoon had turned into a nightmare. She forced herself to speak evenly so she wouldn't alarm Danny. If he panicked, she was afraid she would lose control too.

"Name's Harper. I'm here to help you and your sis get a tree." With the saw blade he pointed toward the cedar next to Danny. "Is this the one you want?"

Danny cast Tessa a doubtful frown. "Well, if Tessa thinks it's all right."

"Sis likes it fine," Harper said, without a glance in Tessa's direction. He released her so abruptly that she staggered away from him. Swiftly, he propped her rifle up against a bare cottonwood, and with the saw in hand, he knelt next to the cedar Danny had selected. "Hold the trunk up above and pull on it from your side," the cowboy ordered as he reached beneath the spiny branches and began to saw the trunk.

"Sure." Danny immediately grabbed the tree trunk in his gloved hands. "I've got it."

Over Harper's head, Tessa gaped at the rifle leaning against the cottonwood. The man kneeling with his back to her was the only obstacle between her and the gun. As soon as she heard the saw teeth bite into the cedar bark, she lurched around the cowboy and seized her rifle. With a practiced movement, she swung it up under her arm, levered a cartridge into the chamber, and whirled on him.

Just as she was about to level the barrel at Harper's back, she heard someone shouting from the road.

"Ho, there in the trees."

Tessa glanced over her shoulder, a cry of relief ready to fall from her lips. Help. Someone was coming to their rescue. She waved at the three hats she could barely see above the trees in the ravine. She jumped up and down in her excitement and relief. "Hello! We're over here on the far side of the creek."

"What in hell do you think you're doing?" Harper cursed. With quick, urgent movements he fought his way out from under the tree, uttering profanities that stung Tessa's ears and reddened Danny's face.

Rifle in hand, Tessa stepped back farther from the cowboy. Safely out of his reach, she pointed the barrel at him. "If you know what's good for you Mr. Harper, don't move."

Chapter Two

"Don't be a fool," Sam warned under his breath as he struggled to free himself of the last, prickly cedar branch. The girl didn't have the sense God gave a goose. Coming out on the winter prairie to get a Christmas tree with nobody to help but her young brother and then shouting welcome to any strange riders who came along the road. When he turned and straightened, he was unsurprised to be greeted by the barrel of Sis's gun. He almost laughed. Her rifle was hardly the first gun barrel he stared down from the wrong end. Mentally he added pointing a gun at the wrong man to the list of her faults.

"I'm no fool," Sis vowed, backing even farther away from him, beyond his reach. The boy made no move, plainly waiting for orders from his sister.

"Then I hope you're smart enough to know that if I'd intended to hurt you, you wouldn't be holding that rifle right now," Sam said, taking in the confidence with which she handled the gun. She knew how to use it, all right.

The voice called from the road again. "Well there you are, pretty lady."

Sam hoped the girl heard the slurred, mocking tone in the rider's voice. Sanders couldn't say anything without sounding like a snide son of a bitch.

Sam tipped his head toward the road. "As long as you've got their attention, make sure those *hombres* get a good look at you carrying that gun."

Uncertainty flickered in her eyes.

Slowly Sam turned to the road and gambled away the last advantage he had over the outlaws he'd been trailing for the last two weeks. They wouldn't recognize him this time, but after he faced them across the ravine, he would never have that edge again. Sanders was too cagey.

"Hi there." Sam waved to the three horsemen gathered around the wagon. From the corner of his eye he could see the confidence on the girl's face fall away. "Merry Christmas."

The three riders were standing up in their stirrups now, and Sam could see their faces over the treetops. Sanders wore the black hat with the snakeskin hatband, pulled low on his head. Cowan was huddled in a sheepskin coat, and Pearce sat astride a brown and white paint pony. Sam figured if he looked as dirty, road weary, and unshaven as they did, he couldn't blame the girl for her suspicions.

"Sure, Merry Christmas." Pearce and his *compadres* laughed unpleasantly as if the season's greeting was some kind of dirty joke. "What brings you out here on a cold day?"

"Cutting a Christmas tree," Sam answered, relieved that Sis seemed satisfied to let him do the talking. She was a proud thing, willowy and prim, with a head of thick, chestnut hair and eyes as golden as fine whiskey. Eyes big and round and sharp and quick. And her nose—turned up in the air. Even her threadbare coat and plain gray skirt didn't keep her from holding her head—and nose—as high as the queen of England's. Just how far would she go along with him? he wondered.

"Sounds like a lot of trouble for one day of the year," Cowan said, his face barely visible between the brim of his stained brown hat and the upturned collar of his sheepskin coat.

"You know how it is when you got family," Sam said with a shrug as if he were a hapless victim. Slowly, but not so slowly as to escape the riders' notice, he rested his right hand on the butt of his six-shooter. "What about yourself? Is there something me and the missus can do for you fellers?"

From the corner of his eye he saw Sis start, then glance at him, questions flickering in her eyes. Her moves were quick, decisive, her mouth set in a thin, grim line. For a moment Sam wondered whether she would turn the rifle on him. But, thankfully, like a good frontier wife, she raised the long barrel, resting it across one arm and over her shoulder in plain view, ready to use. If he were a man given to wild displays, which he wasn't, Sam could have kissed her.

"Danny, step out from behind that tree," he ordered softly without taking his eyes off the men on the road. It was risky, but Sanders didn't like even odds. "Show yourself."

Danny did as told, his legs braced, standing tall and sturdy.

At the sight of all three of them, the mounted men became silent.

Sam watched Sanders' eyes narrow. If Sanders decided to make trouble, things would get real nasty. Sam gathered himself for an attack, figuring he'd throw himself at the girl, take the rifle, and shove her out of the line of fire and do his damnedest to drop the outlaw leader. It was risky, but he could do it if he had to. Only if he had to.

"We just wanted to ask if this is the road to Denver," Sanders said finally.

"Yeah, Cowan here wants to see his girl in Denver," Pearce said, elbowing the rider huddled deep in a sheep-skin coat. Then he cackled. "He made a promise to see her for Christmas, didn't you, Jed?"

"Shut up," Jed said, pulling the sheep wool up around his ears.

"Well, you're headed right," Sam said, nodding toward the west nonchalantly, but knowing that the worst had not necessarily passed. "Abilene is a couple of days' ride from here and Denver another week at least."

"We was afraid of that," said Cowan from the depths of his coat. "Let's ride, boys."

"Yeah, we'll ride on," said Sanders, laying his reins across his horse's neck.

"So long," Sam called as the men rode out of sight. He fought back the urge to throw himself on his horse and follow them. Those bastards had robbed and killed too many innocent folks to be allowed to ride the roads like free men. Besides that, every one of them—Cowan, Pearce and Sanders—was worth five hundred dollars, dead or alive.

Sam glanced at Sis and her brother who should have stayed safe at home, pulling taffy by the fire. If it weren't for them and their Christmas-tree hunt, he'd be a whole lot closer to collecting his reward. He still intended to collect it, just as soon as he could safely get rid of the girl and Danny.

The breath Tessa had unknowingly held whispered between her lips as she watched the three riders disappear around the bend in the road. Their dust rose like a long plume, whipped southward by the wind. Tessa thought she heard a slow whistle escape softly from Harper's lips.

"Dammit," he muttered, glaring at her as if she'd just committed an unforgivable sin. "You and your damned Christmas tree just cost me a whole lot of money."

"I beg your pardon?" Tessa blinked and glanced in Danny's direction. She wondered if she'd done the right thing by staying silent during their encounter with the three men on the road. "I'll ask you to watch your language in the presence of children."

The cowboy's glare softened as his gaze flickered toward her brother. "Gosh darn it, Sis, you just cost me a lotta *pesos.*"

Tessa wanted to snap back something withering and righteous, but she guessed it would be useless. Besides, her journalist's instinct clamored for something more important. "Why? Who are they?"

"Dang, they looked mean," Danny muttered, still watching the riders' dust. "I bet they're from some famous outlaw gang."

"Are they outlaws?" Tessa searched the cowboy's face for a clue to the riders' identity—and to his. She had little doubt that they'd just encountered men—or *hombres* as Harper called them—whose deeds must have been recorded in newsprint. Deeds she'd probably read of. She read every newspaper her father had sent to them. It mattered little to her that the news was often weeks or months old. A story was a story, old or new. "Have we heard of them?"

"Are you a lawman on their trail?" Danny asked, the beginnings of hero worship gleaming in his eyes.

But Harper only turned his back to them and reached for the saw. "That's not real important now. Let's get this damned tree cut down so you can be on your way."

"After a scare like that, we deserve to know who those men were," Tessa insisted, unaccustomed to being refused.

Harper straightened. When he turned to her, his face was so stony cold she stepped back from him.

"After being fool enough to come out here to cut a Christmas tree and to leave your gun on the wagon, you don't deserve any more than you got."

"I probably shouldn't have left the gun in the wagon," she conceded, "but—"

"Do you want this damned tree or not? Make up your mind. I wouldn't put it past those bastards to change their minds and come back just for the sport."

The suggestion that the outlaws might return stole Tessa's words right out of her mouth. Humiliated and a bit daunted by the harsh set of Harper's mouth and by his language, Tessa decided not to persist with questions. She had little doubt now that she and Danny had just escaped unpleasant treatment at the hands of the three riders, thanks to Harper's fast thinking. "Yes, you're right, of course. We want the tree. What can I do to help?"

"Just stay out of the way and keep your eyes peeled for any more riders," Harper said from under the tree he'd resumed sawing.

"I'll watch," Tessa said, picking her way farther up the hillside so she could get a better view of the road. The cowboy's intentions seemed as honest as anyone's at the moment. And she had the rifle now.

For some time Harper and Danny worked together in near silence, exchanging only a few words as the saw whined and sighed through the soft sweet wood. When Harper did speak to Danny he addressed her brother as if they were equals—man to man bound together in labor no woman could manage. Danny scrambled to do whatever the cowboy asked of him. Whoever he was, whatever he was, Tessa liked that, the way Harper treated Danny like another man. Soon the tree began to wobble. Wood creaked. Then the tree swayed and crashed to the ground with an earth-shaking thud that surprised Tessa. It sounded far heavier than she had dreamed it would be.

Doubts assailed her. "Are we going to be able to get this cedar into the wagon? If we do, will it fit through the doorway to the schoolhouse?"

"Sure, we can get it to the wagon," Danny said, enthusiasm having returned to his voice. "It's got to get through the schoolhouse door. It just has to. It's a great tree."

"We can do it," Harper agreed with the arrogant shadow of male invincibility passing across his face. She'd seen the same expression on her father's. Now Danny was learning it too. We can do anything, the look said. Just ask us. Move a mountain or drag a two-ton Christmas tree across the prairie. Just ask us, woman. We are strong. We are immortal.

"I'll help you get it into the wagon," Harper offered. "There'll be men at the schoolhouse to help with carrying it in, right?"

"Yes, of course," Tessa said, well aware that he was eager to be on his way. She'd caught him glancing after the riders a couple of times as he and Danny worked.

Harper handed her the saw. "You take the top of the tree, Danny, and I'll bring up the rear."

"I'll make certain the wagon is ready." Tessa scurried ahead of them, leaping over the frozen creek and scrambling across the rocky ground toward the road.

Once she had the wagon tailgate down, she apprehensively watched Danny and Harper make their way down the slope, the tree resting on their shoulders. Harper obviously labored under the heavier end of the load, Tessa noted.

Despite herself, despite the fact that she didn't know who he was, she couldn't help but admire him for taking the weightier burden onto his broad shoulders.

Her brother paused at the creek, studying the rocks and the frozen stream. The crossing was narrow, no more than three feet wide at the most, Tessa thought. Still, the ice could be slippery. "Wait," she called out, starting back toward the creek. "Let me give you a hand."

"Naw, we can get it," Danny said, stepping out onto the ice. "This is nothing."

"Don't rush," Harper warned from behind the bouncing evergreen branches.

Danny's first step was solid, no slipping. A confident smile lighting his face, he placed his other foot forward and it seemed steady.

"Wait, Danny, I'm almost there," Tessa warned, hurrying down to the creek bank to give her brother a hand.

"It'll be all right." Danny swung his left foot forward again, but he slipped on the ice and went down, disappearing behind the tree.

Tessa screamed and lurched toward her brother. "Danny? Mr. Harper?"

From behind the crashing tree, she heard Harper curse.

Danny's howl rent the air. When Tessa reached him on the ice, he was writhing in pain and holding his right leg out in front of him.

Tessa slid to her knees and reached for Danny's right limb. Before she could touch it, he pulled it beyond her reach and clamped his mouth shut.

"What hurts?" Harper demanded from behind the tree trunk he lowered to ice.

"Danny slipped on the ice," Tessa said. "I think he's hurt his leg badly."

"Let me see." The tree had pushed back Harper's hat

and scratched his left cheek. She could see his entire face—the strong broad brow, the straight nose and those amazing blue eyes.

"Oh, your face." Tessa reached out to touch his abraded cheek.

He met her gaze with a forbidding frown. She pulled her hand back. What was she thinking? He was a stranger.

"I'm all right," Harper said, feeling his jaw as if he had no idea that he'd been injured. "It's nothing. Let's see, kid. What have you done?"

Pulling off his gloves, he knelt beside Danny who, white-faced and purple-lipped, suddenly seemed willing to allow Harper to touch his injured leg when earlier he'd pulled away from Tessa.

Tessa sat back on her heels, feeling inadequate and left out, yet glad of Harper's willingness to help.

"How bad is it?" she asked as she watched the cowboy examine her brother's leg.

Danny winced twice under Harper's examination, but made no sound. His manly silence was unusual. Danny often howled like a banshee at the slightest injury, seeking Tessa's attention or so she'd always thought. Now, with pain-filled but worshipful eyes, he allowed Harper to touch his leg rather than his sister.

"I'm afraid it's broken right here," the cowboy said, gingerly running his hand up and down Danny's calf. "It's not bad, but it needs attention. And he isn't going to be walking anywhere soon, let alone lugging around a Christmas tree."

"But we've got to have the tree," Danny wailed, his childishness suddenly surfacing. "Promise me we won't go back to Prairie City without the Christmas tree."

"We'll take a Christmas tree back to Prairie City," Tessa reassured her brother, surprised and gladdened by his determination in the face of pain. She had her own secret

reasons for wanting to provide the Christmas tree for the
Prairie City schoolhouse. She didn't want Danny to suffer,
but she wanted that perfect Christmas tree, too. "I promise
we will, won't we, Mr. Harper?"

Chapter Three

Tessa and Danny turned hopeful gazes on Harper, the man she'd held at gunpoint only an hour ago. "I'm sorry to have to prevail upon you like this, Mr. Harper. I know you want to be on your way to capture those outlaws, but if you could give us a hand . . ."

Harper glared at her for a moment, then released a slow, beleaguered sigh, as if, once more, somehow this muddle was all her fault. Tessa bit back a sharp comment. She did not like asking for help, especially from a stranger. And she knew he wanted to be on his way. She'd be glad to let him go—except she needed his assistance now more than ever. "I'll help you to the wagon, Danny. Then Mr. Harper and I will decide what to do about the tree."

"I'll carry him to the wagon," Harper offered. "Can't have him making the break worse."

"I can walk that far, honest I can." Danny gazed up into Harper's face with longing and hope. "I just need a shoulder to lean on, but promise me we'll take the tree too."

But the cowboy's jaw remained set, hard and unmoving. "I promise you'll have your tree on one condition."

Tessa glanced at Danny and he looked to her. They both held their breath. Could they agree to a condition?

"What is that?" she asked, finally.

"Danny has to do what I say."

"Oh, yes, whatever you say, Mr. Harper," Danny agreed, nodding his head eagerly.

"Danny keeps his promises," Tessa said, relieved by the cowboy's willingness to help them, yet apprehensive. For all she knew, he might be an outlaw himself.

"All right then, Danny. First you have to let me carry you to the wagon," Harper said, the harshness of his jaw never softening. "You're a big fellow, so I'll have to handle you like a sack of grain, over my shoulder."

"Whatever you say," Danny said.

"Let's go," the cowboy said, pulling Danny's right arm over his shoulder and leaning into the boy.

Under Danny's lanky frame, Harper trudged carefully over the ice and up the rocky slope toward the wagon. Tessa followed, wondering what she could do to help. Soon Harper reached the road and bent over to set Danny on the tailgate of the wagon. Together they moved him toward the front of the wagon bed with his leg extended and wrapped in a canvas tarp.

Rummaging through the basket of food and supplies that she'd brought along, Tessa pulled out a napkin full of cornbread muffins. She urged Danny to eat one and to drink some water. "You've got to keep your strength up."

Danny ate a muffin, but Harper refused the food.

Tessa frowned, miffed at having her hospitality declined.

"Well then, at least let me put some of Grandma's Grease on those scratches on your face," Tessa insisted, turning back to retrieve the medicine jar out of her basket.

"Grandma's Grease?" Harper repeated with a laugh.

"It's good stuff," Danny said with his mouth full of food. "It'll take the sting out of those scratches and make them heal faster." Tessa unscrewed the lid from the jar and let the cowboy look into it.

"What's in it?" Harper asked, sniffing at the concoction suspiciously.

"That's a secret," Tessa said, knowing if she told him, he'd refuse it just as everyone else always did—the first time. She scooped a little onto her finger and held it out toward him. "Don't let the smell fool you. Here, try just a little bit on this scratch."

The stubble of several days' growth of beard grazed her finger, but his skin was warm to her touch. Like a wary animal, he tensed when her finger touched his cheek.

"Does it burn?" she asked, surprised by his reaction.

"No, it's just cold," he explained, looking a bit sheepish. He turned his cheek toward her once more. "It's all right."

Tessa tried again. He allowed her to smear the medication across one particularly deep scratch. His acceptance of her touch made her heart beat a little faster. She drew away quickly, gazing up at him, surprised and breathless at her own reaction.

"There, isn't that better?" she stammered.

A slow smile spread across his face, a much nicer expression than the leer he'd given her earlier. "Yeah, that is better."

Tessa's heart warmed. "More?"

"Yeah," he said, leaning toward her once more.

Tessa froze, her heart still beating rapidly. Did he really expect her to put more medicine on him? The thought of feeling his rough warmth against her fingertips once more flustered her. She thrust the jar at him. "Here. Help yourself."

Plainly disappointed, he took the jar and slowly began to smooth the medicine across his abraded cheek.

Tessa watched shamelessly, fascinated by his fingers stroking the hard plane of his jaw. She licked her lips.

"A little more over here." She gestured, using her own face to direct him. "Yes, closer to your mouth. No, here."

Spontaneously, she reached out once more and touched the corner of his mouth smearing a bit of the grease over a small scratch. At the same moment he turned. Her finger brushed his bottom lip. Warm firmness greeted her senses and sent a strange thrill from the tip of her finger clear down through her insides.

At her touch he stilled instantly. Tessa snatched her hand away from his face.

"Did you get it?" he asked, unmoving as if he were afraid any action would disturb her.

"Yes." Tessa nodded frantically, praying that a blush wasn't rising in her cheeks. But the heat in her face told her it was. She busied herself with screwing on the metal cap. Then she offered the jar to him. "You can take this with you. I have more at home."

He looked at her, surprise on his face.

"It's the least I can do," Tessa said lamely. "Merry Christmas."

"Thanks," he said, accepting the jar, then pulling his hat down over his brow. "I don't usually get Christmas gifts."

He went to his horse and put the jar in the saddlebags. "Now, about the tree."

"Yes, the tree," Danny called to Harper. Her brother's face was still pale, but he seemed to have recovered some of his spirit. "You promised we'd get the tree."

"I know, I promised," the cowboy said, starting back down into the ravine. Tessa listened for impatience, but his voice was even and unreadable.

"Wait, Mr. Harper," Tessa called, following him with

the rope they'd brought looped over her shoulder. "I can help."

Harper stopped long enough to cast her a look of disbelief, then continued on down the rocky slope. Tessa followed unaided. When they reached Danny's tree still spanning the frozen stream, he regarded it for a long moment before he turned to her.

"I don't suppose you'd agree to a smaller tree?" he asked, eyeing her with a gleam of hope in his eye. "Cutting one of those closer to the road would be faster and easier than getting this huge thing across the creek and into the wagon."

"How are you going to explain that to Danny?" Tessa replied, holding her breath. What he suggested about a smaller tree made a lot of sense. But this big tree was so perfect, exactly what she had envisioned inspiring oohs and aahs from the citizens of Prairie City. She wanted this tree. Oh, yes, she wanted to get Danny home safe, too. But she wanted a tree tall enough and full enough to dazzle everyone in Prairie City. "It is such a nice tree, and you know what an important symbol of the season a Christmas tree is."

He pushed his hat back from his face and put his hands on his hips. "No, as a matter of fact I don't. Tell me."

"Well"—Tessa drew a deep breath, marshaling together all her skills of persuasion—"a Christmas tree, an evergreen tree, represents life through the darkness of winter. It reminds us of the tree of life that began with Adam and Eve and continued throughout the ages. An evergreen symbolizes life everlasting and eternal hope. In the Christmas tree—"

Harper held up his right hand to silence her torrent of words. He eyed her without the least bit of empathy in his hard blue eyes. "You really want *this* tree, don't you?"

Briefly Tessa considered making up a story as to why a

big tree was required, but one look into those penetrating blue eyes made her decide against it. They could read a lie on anyone's lips. "Yes," she admitted then she added, "and you made Danny a promise about the tree, Mr. Harper."

Harper frowned as he looked at the sky above. "Yeah, I made a promise to your brother. But with his leg needing medical attention and a storm coming, we've got to work fast. Throw me the rope."

Encouraged, Tessa did as he asked, then glanced at the sky above. The threatening cloud bank that had hovered on the horizon now stretched across the sky, heavy gray clouds hanging above them. Hope and fear fluttered in her heart. Harper jumped the creek and went to work on the tree. Without delay, Tessa joined him.

First, they turned the tree. Then they trussed it up so the branches would not be ripped off as they dragged it up the hillside. Working side by side Tessa became aware of Harper's strong hands and deft fingers on the rope.

"Hold this knot for me." He gestured to the tangle of rope he held in his hand. Though she knew he had other places he'd rather be, he worked swiftly and without complaint. "I'm going to have to cut the rope."

Tessa eagerly reached in front of him. "Here?"

"Yes." He pulled the rope tight, released the knot, and caught another. He stretched down with his free hand and suddenly a knife blade gleamed in the dull winter light. Caught in an embrace Tessa had not anticipated, she became very still. The warmth of his breath on her cheek and the pressure of his body against her back made her gulp.

"Don't let go," he warned, seemingly intent on his work.

"I won't." An uncomfortable warmth flooded through her as he moved to cut one end of the rope she held. If she relaxed one tiny bit they would be pressed together so intimately that—well, it didn't even bear thought.

"Steady," he said, his voice surprisingly low and soothing. "I'm almost finished."

The blade moved back and forth endlessly it seemed. Tessa forced herself to remain still, but they were so close—as close or closer than she'd ever been to Nathan. She could even see the dark stubble of his beard and smell the scent of him, the fragrance of leather and horse.

Suddenly, he released her. "There. A couple more loops and we'll be ready to drag it up to the wagon."

"Good." Tessa hurriedly stepped away from him, her breath coming more rapidly than normal. She hoped that he would not ask her to hold the rope for him again. And he did not.

Once the tree was secure, they began the long journey up the hillside, Harper pulling the heavy cedar and Tessa scouting their path, kicking aside large rocks and steering him clear of tree stumps. After about an hour of hard work they had managed to get the cedar up to the wagon.

Danny was awake and excited. He urged them on, making it impossible for either of them to quit or even mention the thought of a smaller, easier-to-handle Christmas tree. With more heaving, lifting, pushing and shoving, the tree finally rested diagonally across the wagon bed next to Danny. It was so big the top extended beyond the right corner of the wagon. The waving of the top made Duke and Duchess skittish. Duke in particular did not like anything that hung over the edge of the wagon he pulled. The horses nickered and pranced in their traces.

"Whoa," Danny called to the team. "It's going to be the best tree ever, you'll see, Tessa." He grinned, a weak, white-faced expression of pleasure.

She thought so too and grinned back at him, suddenly concerned for Danny. She and Harper had taken too long to get the tree into the wagon. But Danny's praise and genuine smile, even in the face of pain, was enough to make her glad she and the cowboy had persisted.

Harper closed the wagon's tailgate and double-checked the latches. "Tessa? So, that's your name, Sis?"

"Yes, Mr. Harper, that is my name," Tessa snapped, aware that the amenities had never been properly observed. "I am Tessa Jennings, and this is my brother Danny. Under the unusual circumstances, it seems we failed to properly introduce ourselves. And your full name?"

"Sam Harper," he said, without offering his hand or tipping his hat.

"Sam?" Tessa repeated. A strong, plain name, far too simple for a man who'd already demonstrated that he might be more complicated than he seemed.

"So, I should be calling you Miss Jennings instead of Sis," he said, walking to her side, but seemingly intent on picking the cedar spines out of the leather of his doeskin gloves.

"Yes, miss, not missus anybody," she quipped, feeling illogically that she must make that point.

"No offense intended." He dropped his hands to his sides and cast her a look of exasperation. "I was only trying to—"

"I know what you were trying to do," Tessa said, suddenly annoyed with her own ingratitude.

"Sis, my leg is starting to hurt more," Danny called softly, sounding very much like a boy.

"We're heading for home right now." Tessa turned her back on Harper and headed for the front of the wagon, sorry that she couldn't do more for her brother until they reached home.

"Hey, Sis, aren't we going to ask Mr. Harper home for

supper?" Danny asked as she climbed up on the wagon seat. "We owe him that much."

Tessa cast a quick glance in Sam Harper's direction, thinking the same thing. They owed Harper a hot meal. It was the kind of hospitality one prairie neighbor offered another who'd been helpful. From the way he met her gaze, she knew he'd overheard Danny. But Harper wasn't a prairie neighbor.

"I think Mr. Harper has business on down the road," Tessa said, reluctant to take a stranger like this cowboy into her home. She knew so little about him and what she did know—or guess—wasn't exactly reassuring.

"That's right," Harper agreed, catching her eye. "I've got to hit the road."

She realized that he knew exactly why she didn't want to issue an invitation. Despite his help, she considered him too suspect to be offered hospitality. Embarrassment flamed in her cheeks. If he said nothing, she knew it was for Danny's sake, not hers.

Harper began to untie his horse from the wagon wheel.

"But it's snowing," Danny said, struggling to sit up enough to see Harper over the wagon's sideboards.

The small stray flakes that Tessa had glimpsed and denied earlier were coming down steadily now, obscuring the road ahead and behind them. She smelled the snow, too, the clean raw scent that drifted on the wind just before a snowstorm. It hovered, riding lightly on the air, the fresh sharp smell of a blizzard to come. It was such an innocent, delightful smell when at home, the harbinger of snowball fights and snowman building. But on the open prairie it could be the prophecy of an icy death. She and Danny most definitely would be enveloped in white before they reached home.

"Where are you going from here that's closer than Prairie City?" Danny asked.

Tessa plunked herself down on the wagon seat and took up the reins, eager to be away from the cowboy now.

"How long back to Prairie City?" Harper asked, checking the cinch on his saddle.

"Only three hours," Tessa said, struggling with the wagon brake.

"It's going to be dark in two hours," he said without looking up from his saddle.

"I brought a lantern," Tessa said. She finally managed to release the brake and urged the horses on. The sooner they got started, the better, she told herself. She definitely didn't want to be obliged to Sam Harper for any more help. They'd accepted enough from him as it was. "We don't want to keep you from your business. Thank you for your help, and we wish you well, Mr. Harper."

As she drove the wagon away, she heard Harper's horse come up beside her. She was peering ahead and wondering where to turn around the wagon so she could get headed straight for home.

He sat tall and straight in the saddle as he rode alongside her. "There's a wide spot in the road ahead where you can turn the wagon around," he called over the growing wind. "I saw it from above. Follow me and I'll show you."

"I can manage, thank you." Tessa squinted into the distance already shrouded in drifting white, flurrying snowflakes drawing a downy curtain across the endless prairie. She tugged on the reins and followed Harper against her better judgment. When she reached the wide place in the road, she even followed his instructions, doing everything with the horses exactly as he told her. She was a fair hand with the wagon, most of the time. But in the snow, the wagon became stuck anyway.

Chapter Four

Sam pulled his coat collar up around his ears and urged Duke and Duchess onward through the blowing snow. He hunched over the reins, comforting himself with the thought that Sanders and his *compadres* were probably no better off than he was. But he was reasonably certain they hadn't gotten themselves roped into something stupid like delivering a Christmas tree to some prairie schoolhouse.

At first after he'd managed to get the wagon unstuck, he'd found himself volunteering to drive the girl and the kid home. All the while in the back of his mind he'd been fool enough to envision the gang galloping through the snow, putting mile after mile between them. But that couldn't be so, not in this storm. He could hardly see beyond Duke and Duchess' heads. The Sanders gang couldn't be any better off than he was. He glanced back at Tessa Jennings and her brother sitting in the back of the wagon. Or maybe they were.

He had to hand it to her. Tessa Jennings had only asked

for his help once after her brother had broken his leg. She'd hated doing it then. He'd seen that right away in her face. Yes, sir, she was too proud to ask. And how she wanted that tree—a cedar damned near as tall as a telegraph pole. He could see the desire in her eyes, in the wishful way she'd stared at it the moment he'd mentioned they should cut a smaller one. She wanted to take that tree home, but she'd had no desire to invite him along. The respectable ones never did.

She'd never admitted to being afraid to drive alone in the snow, but he'd seen the uncertainty in her eyes as she'd turned the wagon. It would be a thankless task, but he'd offered himself, anyway. It wasn't like he could leave a woman and a kid with a broken leg stuck alone on the prairie in the first blizzard of the season—even if Sanders was getting away.

Which wasn't likely, he realized as the storm worsened. The gang was probably holed up somewhere along the road. In fact they were probably sitting pretty around a red-hot tavern stove, with a bottle of whiskey, a deck of cards and a friendly sporting lady taking turns on their laps.

What was he doing? Playing do-gooder to a girl and driving a team through a storm to deliver a Christmas tree. He'd even given up his bottle of best whiskey, for medicinal purposes, of course. The boys back at Fort Smith would get a laugh out of this.

"Danny's fallen asleep," Tessa called from behind him in the wagon. She climbed onto the wagon seat with him, her face nearly hidden by the blue wool scarf she had donned. "Thank you for sharing your bottle. It did ease the pain for him, though I don't normally approve of ardent spirits. Anyway, can I spell you? We should be close to town now."

"I'm doing fine," he said, thinking he'd be doing better

if he were still on Sanders' trail. But things had changed now—thanks to the girl and her brother. He'd have to be doubly careful to stay out of sight. Jake Sanders never forgot a face. Up until now Sam had had the advantage. The gang's likeness had been posted across three states and Indian territory besides. They might know Sam Harper was on their trail, yet they'd never seen him until today.

But he'd had no choice, Sam reminded himself. Tessa and Danny had pulled up their wagon in the best ambush spot on Little Kitten Creek in the Flint Hills between Alma and Abilene. Sanders and his boys were criminals and fair game—worth a lot of money to boot—but Sam couldn't in good conscience start a ruckus that endangered bystanders.

"I could lead the horses, if that would help," Tessa offered, pulling her wool scarf closer and peering into the snow.

"What?" Sam said, jarred from the fantasy of how near he'd come to capturing his quarry. "Lead the horses? No need."

He could see the road despite the blowing snow. Even if he couldn't, he wasn't going to send a woman to lead the horses while he rode in the wagon. Maybe he wasn't respectable, but he had his own principles.

They'd been on the road almost three hours now. Tessa had spent most of the time in the back of the wagon, under the cover they had rigged to keep the snow off her brother. She had comforted Danny, pillowing his head in her lap and making certain that he was warmly wrapped in the old buffalo robe.

Sam had found himself envying the kid, warm and safe and coddled by his pretty sister. He glanced at Tessa now riding at his side and found himself strangely glad of her chattering company. "We can go straight to the doc's as soon as we get there, if you'll tell me where."

"It's not far, right on Main Street," she said. "And I want to thank you, Mr. Harper, for helping us. As soon as Danny is taken care of you must come to the house and stay for supper. Tina was going to simmer a stew while we were gone."

"Tina?" Sam repeated.

"My little sister," Tessa explained. "She stayed home to take care of Papa. She's learning to cook. Don't look so doubtful. It will be good—my own recipe."

Anything hot and cooked by someone who could do more than roast a skinned critter over a fire sounded delicious to Sam. But he wasn't entirely comfortable with the idea of sitting down at the table with Tessa, Danny, Tina and their papa. He wasn't the kind of man decent families took a liking to. "Look, as soon as Danny is at the doc's, I'll just take off."

"In this weather?" Tessa turned toward him. "Oh, you must stay so Papa can thank you for your help. We can even put you up for the night. There's an attic room—"

"Your thanks is enough." Sam shook his head. "I'll find a room if I need one."

She touched his arm, clearly imploring him to look at her. "But all of us owe you our gratitude. Prairie City wouldn't have a tree if you hadn't stopped to help. Why not stay? There's going to be a tree-trimming party. And lots of food, games and dancing."

Sam would have thought Tessa's request some sort of amorous trap if she'd been less reluctant to accept his help in the beginning. The invitation was sincere. She was a nice girl, and he didn't get himself obliged to nice girls.

"Look, I helped you with the Christmas tree because Danny reminds me of my little brother," Sam said, uncomfortable with her gratitude. "You don't owe me anything."

Tessa brightened. "You have a little brother?"

Sam wished he'd kept his mouth shut. She was full of

lady-do-gooder questions now; he could see it in the gleam of those whiskey eyes.

"What is his name?"

"Noah is dead." That should stop her questions, Sam mused.

"Oh, I'm sorry." Her voice was full of a sympathy he didn't want to hear. "What happened?"

"The war," Sam replied grudgingly, suddenly aware of his long-buried, aching grief for the brother he'd talked into running away with him to join the army so long ago. The Civil War was over and he'd been a lot of places and done a lot of things since then. Why did this pain suddenly seem so fresh? He shook his head, trying to free himself from long-suppressed feelings. "That was over ten years back."

"So long ago." She leaned forward attempting to look into his face, but he refused to meet her gaze. "You must have loved him very much."

"We were brothers," Sam said with a shrug. He and Noah had been all the family they ever remembered having after their ma and pa had died in the typhoid epidemic. Uncle Marley and Aunt Hester, unhappy people who'd taken them in, gave them food, shelter, work, whippings and little else. Running away to join the army had seemed like a great adventure and the perfect way to escape the sour couple's tyranny.

"Was your brother all energy and enthusiasm like Danny?" Tessa asked, obviously missing the hint that he didn't want to talk about his brother.

"Noah was a great kid," Sam admitted, thinking how alike the boys' smiles were. "Like Danny."

"Danny certainly seems to admire you." Suddenly Tessa stood up in the wagon box and pointed toward a square shadow looming ahead in the swirling white snow.

"There's Prairie City. See it? That's the corner of Mr. Russell's store. Drive past it, then turn down the street."

"I see it. We'll have Danny in safe hands soon." Sam said, understanding her sigh of relief. The storm could do its worst now. They'd reached safety without being blinded and lost, to drive in a whiteout for hours—or worse.

They took Danny home first so they wouldn't have to move him again in the storm. Then Sam volunteered to go after Doc Jones who was in his office.

"It's a clean break," the balding doctor announced a half-hour later, sitting on the edge of Danny's bed and assessing the injury with expert hands. "The swelling is not bad. The cold weather probably can be thanked for that. Good timing, my boy."

Everyone laughed at the doctor's attempts to keep his diagnosis light. The whole family was gathered round: Tessa, Hiram Jennings, and little sister Tina, a quiet child with brown hair and big brown eyes. Hasty introductions had been made, then Sam had edged himself into a corner out of the way while big sister and little sister fussed over Danny. The boy's color had returned, and though he looked uncomfortable in the midst of his sisters' tender mercies, he obviously wasn't suffering too greatly.

"The bone is just a bit out of line. I'll need your sister's help to set it and put a good splint on your leg." Doc Jones said, glancing up at Tessa.

She paled immediately and clutched a fold of her skirt. Sam knew enough about broken limbs to understand that Tessa would find the pulling of muscles and scraping of bones a very unpleasant task.

"Will it hurt?" Danny asked in a small voice, his bravado clearly fading in the face of renewed pain.

"I'm afraid it does," the doctor said with a grim nod. "Not much I can do about that."

"I'll help, Doc," Sam said, stepping forward. Coming to the rescue again like some kind of damned hero, he berated himself. He smiled reassuringly at Danny. "I've helped set bones before. We'll make a short, sweet job of it."

"By all means, let's get a man with experience to do it," Hiram Jennings said.

Relief washed across Danny's face, and he smiled up at Sam. "Yes, Mr. Harper, would you help?"

"Sure." Sam nodded, glancing quickly in Tessa's direction. Her soft, restrained smile of gratitude made him doubly glad he'd volunteered.

Danny was brave throughout the whole ordeal. When the splint was in place, Doc Jones sentenced the boy to a couple of days in bed before he could get up and get around.

"But what about the Christmas tree–trimming party tomorrow?" he wailed. "I can't miss the party. No one can miss the party."

"Can he get around with crutches, Doc?" Sam asked, reluctant to see Danny disappointed.

Doc Jones nodded as he gathered up his instruments and put them back in his black bag. "If the swelling stays down and you feel up to it. I have a pair of crutches I can loan you."

"See, you'll get to help decorate the tree," Tina exclaimed, a broad grin spreading across her little face. She danced around the room clapping her hands.

The exhilaration in the boy's eyes brought a smile to Sam's face. The Jenningses' enthusiasm was contagious.

Try as he might Sam didn't ever remember himself or his brother being so excited about Christmas. On their uncle's farm, the holiday had been as grim as the other days of the year. The horses still needed to be fed, the cows milked, the eggs gathered, as Uncle Marley always reminded Sam and Noah. The only thing special about Christmas Day had been a trip to church in the middle of the week and a fresh apple at supper time. Something to look forward to, but nothing to get excited about.

Doc Jones left. While Tessa and her sister went into a flurry of getting out blankets, preparing warm milk and warming bricks for the bed, Sam took the time to make a quick assessment of the family and the home.

The Jenningses' abode was a modest arrangement of rooms at the back of the newspaper print shop facing Main Street. In the furnishings he saw tradition and comfort: family photographs on the walls, more books and newspapers than he'd ever seen in one room stacked on shelves, on the floor a thick braided rug, well-worn chairs set about, scuffed footstools, a big table with a large reading lamp stationed in the center. Warm and cozy.

No surprise there, but one thing did catch him unprepared. Upon first meeting and shaking Hiram Jennings' swollen hand, Sam had liked him immediately. He'd had to reconsider his irritation with a man who sent his daughter and twelve-year-old son out alone to cut the Christmas tree. The editor in chief of the *Prairie City Spirit* was confined to a wheelchair.

"So who in town is supposed to help with the Christmas tree?" Sam Harper demanded from the doorway of the kitchen, where Tessa had gone to warm more milk for Danny. The gruff sound of his deep voice startled her and she jumped, turning toward him. Even without his hat and coat he took up the doorway, seeming to occupy more than his share of space in the house.

"The tree! I almost forgot about the Christmas tree,"

she said, rubbing the tingle at the back of her neck. This time she was certain he'd been watching her backside before he spoke. Suddenly she was aware of how unkempt she must look: her face windburned, her hair falling loose from the bun at the back of her neck, her workaday shirt-waist wrinkled and frayed. With a free hand, she tried to smooth her hair away from her face. She might have forgotten about the tree, but she had not forgotten Sam Harper. She should have taken a moment to freshen up, but there'd been so many things to do for Danny.

"Well, the horses are mighty worn out," Sam said, leaning against the door frame. He was watching her again with those clear blue, unreadable eyes. "I'd like to get them settled for the night."

The horses. She'd forgotten about the horses, too. They were usually Danny's responsibility. "If you would be so kind as to take care of Duke and Duchess, tomorrow I'll see to it that some of the school board members or Mr. Russell help get the tree out of the wagon and into the school in time for the party."

"I'll unload the tree at the schoolhouse door, then take care of horses," Sam said, crossing the kitchen to the peg by the door where his coat and hat hung. "The school is that building at the end of the street, isn't it?"

"Yes, but it is so late and I know you wanted to be on your way," Tessa protested, oddly flustered and uncertain as to whether she wanted him to stay or go.

"Unloading the tree and unharnessing the horses won't take long," Sam said. "I'll get a room at the boarding house we passed on the way into town if I need to. So I'll say goodbye now."

"Wait," Tessa blurted out, her good sense telling her it wasn't wise to have a stranger—one who wore his gun tied to his thigh—sleeping under her roof. Yet little pangs of disappointment needled her. She might never see Sam

Harper again. She couldn't just let him walk out the door after he'd done so much for her and the family. "Your bottle of spirits. I have it here somewhere."

"The whiskey is right there on the table," said Papa from the doorway. "We certainly do appreciate your help, Mr. Harper. What's this nonsense I hear about a boarding house?"

Papa rolled his chair into the kitchen. "Sam, isn't it? May I call you Sam? We have a room in the attic. Stovepipe goes right through it and makes the place as cozy as any room in the boarding house, though it's not as big. And a night like this isn't fit for any man to be out, especially not a man who has done the Jenningses a good turn. You must stay and join us at the supper table."

"Danny is awfully disappointed that you won't stay," Tina said, appearing at Papa's side.

"I already said my goodbye to Danny," Sam said gruffly.

Tessa carried the whiskey bottle to Sam. As she handed it to him, she stared up into his face, wondering why he was so determined to refuse their gratitude. On the other hand, if he wanted to leave, who were they to keep him? "Papa, I think Mr. Harper has business to tend to elsewhere."

"Not in this weather," Papa said, always so sure of himself. "Buffalo hunters have already been through here, saying this is a big storm come in from the Rockies. It's liable to blow for days. No, you'll want to stay here, Sam."

"I appreciate your hospitality," the cowboy said, shoving his hat down on his head and pulling on his coat. "But I'll get a room at the boarding house so I can be up and out early tomorrow morning. Don't want to trouble you folks, what with you having Danny to take care of and all."

Tessa felt Sam's gaze fall on her, and she looked up at him again, sensing for the first time a strange reluctance warring with his desire to leave. Maybe Danny really did remind him of his brother. Danny certainly seemed to like Sam.

"Well, the invitation is open," Tessa said, realizing she hadn't released the whiskey bottle into his hands yet. She let go of it, slowly. As she gazed up at the cowboy, she realized that she really wanted him to stay, for Danny's sake—and for his own too.

"Thanks. I'll remember that," Sam said, touching his hat as he turned toward the door. "Goodbye."

Icy wind whipped through the kitchen and the fire in the stove roared in the rush of air as the cowboy went out the door.

After the door closed, peace settled on the kitchen again, and Tessa, feeling strangely bereft, stared at the place where Sam had stood. He was gone and she'd probably never see him again, never find out who he was and what he did. Dangerous as it seemed, whatever he did couldn't be that bad. She regretted that she'd never have the chance to know more about him.

"Go put on your second-best shirtwaist and comb your hair, Tessa," Papa said, rolling himself with Tina's help back toward Danny's room. "Unlike certain local gents, this man has some substance to him. He's worth the trouble."

"Papa, stop your matchmaking. He's gone. Sam Harper just said goodbye," Tessa huffed as she stirred the stew. Sam's farewell had left her in a perplexing jumble of relief and despair.

"He'll be back," Papa said over his shoulder. "The wind is up. And remember those buffalo hunters I told you about? I happen to know they took the last vacant room at the boarding house."

Chapter Five

When Sam returned to the Jenningses' place, Tessa met him at the door, looking just as pretty as he'd remembered her. She'd taken the time to smooth her chestnut hair back into a bun and she'd changed into a soft yellow threadbare shirtwaist that hugged her breasts in a tempting way. But caution filled her whiskey eyes as he began to explain about the boarding house. Without a smile, she gestured for him to come in before he could finish as though she already knew the ending of his story.

With trepidation, Sam stepped into the very warmth that he'd been determined to avoid. Coming back to the Jenningses with his hat in his hand was one of the hardest things he'd ever done. Not because he disliked the family, but because he was afraid he did like them—especially Danny.

He'd been welcomed warmly by all, even Tessa if you counted that tight smile she gave him. Hiram had pumped his arm energetically. Little Tina had pulled a chair up to the kitchen table for him. Danny's eyes, full of the hero worship that made Sam damned uneasy, had followed his every move.

Only hanging his gun with his coat, hat and saddlebags on the pegs by the door won a softened smile from Tessa. Hiram had asked blessedly few questions during the meal and had filled the occasional quiet at the table with monologues.

Sam knew the food would be good. One sniff of the stew pot sitting on the stove when he'd carried Danny through the kitchen earlier had told him that. He'd known the bed in the attic, no matter how makeshift, would be soft. And it had been, the mattress stuffed with feathers just like Danny's and the sheets smelling of sunshine and good soap.

He'd passed the first night in the attic sleeping soundly and had awakened to find the storm outside blowing more fiercely that before. Riding out to an unknown destination in this kind of raging weather would be foolhardy. The only thing to do was stay and make himself useful.

"Golly, I'm glad you decided to stay," Danny said as he picked up the playing cards Sam had just dealt onto the checkerboard on the sofa between him and Tina. The boy sat, his injured leg propped up on a stool, wrapped in a blanket. His sister sat beside him. Outside, beyond the Jenningses' frost-covered parlor window, the blizzard howled. Earlier Sam had helped Tessa hang a quilt over the glass to keep out the cold. Inside, the giant kerosene reading lamp glowed on the table, and a fire crackled in the potbellied stove. They were snug as bugs in a rug, Sam thought.

"I'm glad I stayed too," Sam said, sorting out his cards and thinking a man could get pretty comfortable with a life like this.

"Now, what is a full house?" Danny began. "Is it when you have two of one kind and three of another?"

"That's it," Sam said, appraising his cards once more.

"Are they going to get away from you?" Danny asked, still studying his cards.

Sam looked at the cards he held. "Get away?"

Danny leaned forward as if he didn't want anyone else in the house to hear him. "That gang. The men who stopped to talk to us on the road to Abilene. Are they getting away in the snow?"

Sam drew in a deep breath. He hadn't forgotten about Sanders, but he'd had no intention of discussing the gang with Danny Jennings. "I don't think they are going any farther in this weather than I am."

"Are you a lawman?" Tina asked, in a childish whisper.

"Not exactly," Sam said, reluctant to reveal his trade. Bounty hunters weren't usually invited to sleep or dine in the homes of respectable families. "Are you two going to ante up?"

"Oh, yeah, and here's a red checker," Danny said, tossing the token wager onto the checkerboard.

"Tough wager, I'd better think about this," Sam said, amused by Danny's interest in the betting. All the while his ear was trained on the sounds coming from the kitchen. Tessa was in there, having her bath before the Christmas tree–trimming party. She was singing a Christmas carol, one he hadn't heard in years. He wondered if there would be singing at the party. He couldn't make out her words, but he could hear her voice, light and happy in anticipation of the festivities. He couldn't dismiss a certain curiosity about what girls did before a party: brushing their hair, smoothing creams on their skin and primping in the mirror he'd found tacked on the kitchen wall over the wash basin—which was way too low for him. He couldn't get out of his mind the image of Tessa going into the kitchen for her bath, her chestnut hair swinging across her back. Thick and silky. Touchable.

"Ante up," Sam instructed, still fighting that image.

"We did that already," Danny said, tossing the round game tokens onto the checkerboard. "And I'll throw in one more."

"Right, I'll see your two red checkers, and I'll up you one black checker." Might as well keep the game interesting, Sam thought, thankful that Hiram Jennings had gone to the print shop to work on the next edition of the paper. "Has your sister got a beau to primp for at this party?"

"Naw," Danny said. "Not since Nathan Purvis asked Nellie Russell to marry him."

"Dealer takes a card." Sam frowned at the thought of a man in Tessa's life and dealt himself two more cards from the deck. "Who is this Nathan? Is she sweet on him?"

"I'll take one card," Danny said, discarding one and reaching for the card Sam dealt. "And I'll see your black checker and put in one more myself. I don't think she was all that sweet on Nathan Purvis. But he is the schoolmaster, and he was the most eligible bachelor in Prairie City, at least that's what Pa said. Nathan came to call pretty often last summer. But Pa's wheelchair seemed to make him nervous."

"Schoolmaster and the most eligible bachelor, huh?" Sam pried, realizing in his distraction that he'd assumed he had a full house when he really only had three of a kind. He'd let the thought that a bounty hunter was pretty much outclassed by a schoolmaster distract him. "So what does your sister think about this Nathan What's-his-name marrying Nellie Whoever?"

"I think she was mostly mad," Danny said, waving his hand of cards around in the air. "Nathan and Nellie just up and said they were engaged at the harvest dance."

"But I saw Tessa crying once," Tina said, with a wide-eyed bob of her head. "Least, I think she was crying."

"Naw, not Tessa," Danny said. "She said Nathan was too self-centered for her. Pa said that's nonsense. He's afraid she won't ever get married, even though there are plenty of men who would be glad to have her."

"Why wouldn't she marry one of them?" Sam asked, suspecting there were more than a few frustrated suitors around where Tessa Jennings was concerned. She was pretty enough for any man.

"She's just too picky," Danny said, studying his cards. "She always has one reason or another why a man who has come calling isn't good enough for her. But Pa thinks it's because of us."

"Yes," Tina said. "That's right."

"Because of you?" Sam glanced across at Danny, surprised to catch a look of sadness on the boy's face. "Why would Tessa turn down a man because of you?"

"She's looking for someone to take care of us," Tina interjected, still seemingly intent on the cards in her hand.

"Least that's what Pa thinks," Danny said.

"Your play," Sam said, mulling over what the boy had revealed. When he tried to envision Tessa in this Nathan's arms, the only image that popped into his mind was that of Tessa in the ravine with her rifle aimed at him. Picky didn't have anything to do with it. Tessa Jennings would either find a man to help her take care of her family, or she'd do it herself.

"I'll match your bet and call," Danny said, with such casualness that Sam wondered if this really was first time the boy had played poker.

The kitchen door hinges squeaked.

"Well, I'm finished." Tessa's voice came from the doorway. "You're next, Danny."

Sam, Danny and Tina looked up from their card game

to see Tessa padding into the parlor. Her hair shone, burnished, in the lamplight. The hot bathwater had left her face flushed and her eyes bright and dark. The way her prim calico wrapper hugged her waist stirred unexpected desire in Sam. He couldn't drag his gaze off her shapely figure.

Staring at the checkerboard, Tessa moved closer to the sofa on which they sat. "What sort of checkers game is this?"

"It's five-card checkers," Sam said, making light of what he knew was bound to make her angry.

"We're playing poker," Tina sang out. "Just like they play at the Corners Saloon."

"Poker?" Tessa's eyes widened. Outrage reverberated in her voice. "You are teaching my little brother and sister poker?"

"We were tired of checkers," Danny piped up. "And Tina wanted to play and you can't play checkers with three people."

"Every man—and lady—needs to learn poker," Sam said with conviction. "Danny needs to know the fine art of bluffing. Your bluffing skills could use a little polishing, too."

"Fine art?" Tessa grabbed Sam's shirtsleeve, pulling him out of his chair, and drawing him away from Danny. She spoke in a soft but heated tone. "You would tell me that gambling is a fine art my brother needs to know?"

"Yes, and we were using the checkers for wagers," Sam said, certain his explanation was useless in the face of such righteous wrath. He remembered now why he'd been hesitant to return to the Jenningses' house. It was just too cussed hard to be respectable all the time.

"Mr. Harper, Danny and Tina like you very much," Tessa said, seeming to gather her strained patience about her like a mother's protective cloak. "In fact, your worldliness makes them think of you as something of a hero. But I'll have to ask you to refrain from teaching them corrupting games and sinful habits."

"Corrupting? Sinful?" Sam stared at her, his indignation growing. "It's only a damned game."

Her frowned deepened, and her lips became a thin, angry line across her face.

"It's a danged game," Sam repeated. "Poker isn't any more corrupting than other card games."

"I'll have no gambling of any kind in my house, please," Tessa said, bracing her hands on her hips so that her hastily buttoned wrapper gaped, exposing a delicious "V" of flushed, fresh-bathed skin at her throat.

Sam tried not to stare, but he lost the battle.

When the object of his stare became obvious to Tessa, she clutched her wrapper closed. "Honestly, Mr. Harper. Don't you know how to behave in a respectable home?"

"I can mind my manners," he muttered, offended that she would hint he didn't know right from wrong. It wasn't his fault that she was standing there in front of him only half dressed. He was only human after all.

"Then I must ask you to teach Danny and Tina some other card game."

"Solitaire?" Sam said, making sure she knew how little he thought of that pastime.

"Fine," Tessa said, clutching her gown closer. "And the bath is all yours."

When she left the room, the only sound to break the silence was the wailing of the wind, a reminder that Sam wasn't going anywhere. Swallowing his annoyance with Tessa, he walked back to the sofa and reached down to help Danny up. "Let's have a go at that bathwater before it gets cold."

"You're not bothered by her scolding, are you?" Tina asked, her eyes larger than ever and her gaze questioning.

"I know Tessa can be sort of aggravating, but she's really very nice." Danny's face was solemn, his eyes full of hope as he searched Sam's face. "You like her, don't you?"

Sam pulled the boy's arm around his neck and helped him to his feet. "No offense kids, but honestly I don't like your sister all that well."

"Danny has taken quiet a shine to Sam, hasn't he?" Papa said to Tessa when she dashed into the print shop. Tessa had been so upset about discovering the poker game she hadn't considered that Papa might be in the newspaper office. He was sitting at his desk, scribbling away in the pool of light from his desk lamp.

"Yes, he has," Tessa said, slowing down her hurried movements to make them seem normal. The shock and the outrage of finding Danny and Tina playing poker made her more determined than ever to find out what she could about Sam Harper. The memory of seeing something in the mail that might be enlightening had brought her rushing into the print shop. But there was no need to alarm her father. "What are you doing in here, Papa? I thought you'd be getting ready for the party."

"I just wanted to finish up this Christmas editorial," Papa said, dipping his pen in the ink bottle. "We can get it set and start printing tomorrow. What are you doing in here when you should be dressing for the party?"

"I just wanted to take a look at something that came in the mail." Hoping that answer would satisfy him, Tessa went straight to her desk. Without lighting her lamp or sitting down, she swiftly sifted through the stack of newspapers, a sheaf of announcements and the posters that arrived with every mail delivery. With her heart in her throat she cast aside first one then two, then several more WANTED posters certain that the faces she saw in the drawings didn't represent any of the men she and Danny had seen in the ravine near their wagon.

Then a picture on the front page of a Ft. Smith, Arkansas, newspaper caught her eye. She drew it from the untidy stack and held it up to the light from her father's lamp. Her mouth went dry. She recognized the one man as the rider with the snakeskin hatband. Quickly she scanned the newspaper article. His name was Jake Sanders, thief and bank robber, sought for assault of a lady and robbery. Even at the tender age of eighteen Tessa recognized journalism's euphemism for rape. She dropped the paper to the desk. Sam Harper, whoever he was, had probably saved her and Danny from a life-threatening encounter with wanted outlaws.

The tightness in Tessa's chest eased a bit; she picked up the paper and read on. A reward was offered for the capture, dead or alive, of Sanders and his gang members the article reported. Several known bounty hunters and a U.S. Marshal were supposed to be on the gang's trail. Sanders' men were thought to be armed and dangerous.

Knees weak, Tessa eased herself into the desk chair, her heart pounding with the suspicion she didn't want to accept. She tried to recall everything she could remember about Sam, his appearance, and what he'd told her about himself. She didn't think he'd exactly lied to her, yet he'd been evasive. Surely if he were a U.S. Marshall, he would have identified himself as such to her or her father. There would be no reason for him to be evasive about his identity. Unless he was one of the bounty hunters . . . Tessa didn't like that thought. But it made sense. If he was a bounty hunter, he'd be in a big hurry to catch up to this Sanders and his men. Sam was definitely in a hurry to leave. Maybe she should be thankful for that.

Everyone knew what bounty hunters were: men who hunted down other men for the reward, for money. Little better than Judas. A surprising pang of disappointment stung Tessa's heart. She wanted to think better of Sam, their rescuer. Danny and Tina's hero. But bounty hunting would account for the fact that he was traveling so close to Sanders and his men. He must have known they were right behind him. Why was he in front of them?

Cold realization dawned. That's what Sam had meant when he'd said she and Danny had cost him a lot of money. Tessa sucked in a breath. Sam had known the Sanders gang was coming. That was why he'd stopped to help her and Danny. He'd known all the time. That was why he'd been so gruff, so intent on hurrying. Their meeting had been more than a fortunate accident. He'd known about Sanders, and he'd been trying to get her and Danny out of the way. Maybe he'd been planning to do something to the gang at that place in the ravine.

"Did you find what you wanted, dear?" Papa asked, looking up from his writing.

"No." Tessa quickly folded up the newspaper with trembling hands. How close had she and Danny come to being caught in the crossfire of a bounty hunter ambushing outlaws? How could she have let a cold-blooded man like that stay under her roof? "I mean yes. Well, I found the paper, but it doesn't say what I thought it would."

She tucked the Arkansas newspaper under her arm so Papa would never catch sight of the Sanders gang story. Then, moving casually as if she lived with a bounty hunter under her roof all the time, Tessa left her desk and went in search of Sam.

She found him in the kitchen bending over the wash basin to peer into the mirror. He was shaving and Tina was talking to him, holding his towel and watching him with adoring eyes.

"Look, Tessa," Tina said. Sam seemed to have captured

another Jennings' heart. "Sam has shaved off his mustache."

"So I see," Tessa said, more fascinated by the shaving process than she cared to admit. She and Tina had watched their father shave hundreds of times and thought nothing of it. But Tessa had to swallow the lump that formed in her throat at the sight of Sam Harper with soap on his face and wearing a fresh shirt not yet buttoned over his chest. Her gaze lingered on the dusting of dark curly hair across his chest. She couldn't help but stare at the bare solidness and strength of his body. Barefoot, freshly washed, with water dripping from his dark hair, his shirt open and no gun strapped to his thigh, Sam Harper looked younger, gentler, almost vulnerable.

He turned to her and grinned. "Yep, no mustache. What do you think?"

"You look very nice," Tessa conceded as a blush warmed her cheeks. Her angry determination to have the truth from him softened. She liked the new clean-shaven look. She'd watched her father wash and shave a thousand times, but she'd never watched a stranger. Embarrassed, but disarmed by his nakedness, she held her ground and inwardly grappled to retrieve the indignation that had brought her marching into the kitchen in the first place.

"Hey, Tessa," Danny called, swinging around the kitchen table on the crutches Doc Jones had sent over. "I'm going to dance at the party, too."

"So I see," Tessa said, much less interested in the crutches than she normally would have been. "Mr. Harper and I have something to discuss. Danny and Tina, would you go see how Papa is doing with his editorial? Maybe you can start setting the headline."

Tina obeyed immediately. But Danny paused, his gaze shifting from Sam to Tessa. "Sure, Sis. We're going to have to get to work on the Christmas edition, aren't we?"

"That's right," Tessa said. She remained silent as Danny proficiently maneuvered his crutches, heading off to the print shop. Sam was wiping the soap from his face.

Tessa was suddenly reminded of the scratches on Sam's face. She turned to him. "Is your face better? Did Grandma's Grease help?"

"Yes," Sam said, continuing to look into the mirror. "Listen, if this is about the poker game—"

"No, it's about this," Tessa said, opening up the Arkansas newspaper to show him the story about the Sanders gang. She pointed to the drawings. "That's them, isn't it?"

Sam glanced at the newspaper briefly, nodded, then returned to his shaving. "That's them."

"And you're one of the bounty hunters that're after them, aren't you?" Tessa demanded.

Sam straightened, staring at the wall before him. "Maybe. What of it?"

"What—?" Tessa stammered. "There are innocent children in this house."

"I'm aware of that," Sam said, finally deigning to look at Tessa. "What's your point?"

"I'll tell you my point," Tessa said, then proceeded to stutter over it because she didn't want to have to put it to him. "Have you . . . ? I mean, did you ever—how many men have you killed?"

He blinked, then bent down to look into the mirror again and reached for the comb. "Haven't you counted the notches on my gun?"

Tessa's gaze darted to the gun in the holster hanging from the peg next to the door. "You know there are no notches on your gun. I don't for a minute believe that means you've never shot anybody. Not a man in your business."

"You know a lot about my business?" he asked, without looking at her.

"I don't just write for the newspaper, I read a lot of them, too." Tessa folded her arms across her breasts. "I'm informed."

Sam studied himself in the mirror once more. "Three."

Tessa dropped her arms to her sides, afraid to believe what she was hearing. "What? Three what?"

Sam turned to her, caught her gaze with those blue inscrutable eyes and held it. "I've killed three men that I know of. Isn't that what you wanted to know? I've killed three men."

Chapter Six

Stunned silence hung between them.

"Three?" Tessa whispered, trying to take in the reality of what he'd just said. The handsome dark-haired man standing before her who smelled of fresh shaving soap and leather, a man who'd eaten at her table and slept under her roof, had taken three lives. What kind of a man had she brought home and sheltered under her family's roof? A killer.

He scrutinized her, his gaze calm and unblinking. "I'm not proud of it. I did what I had to do to survive and get the reward. It was all legal."

"But that doesn't make it right," Tessa said, longing for him to laugh suddenly and tell her that he was just teasing and there would been no truth in his words, no dead bodies lying in the dust of his trail.

"No, you're right," Sam said, looking into the mirror again and beginning to button his shirt. His fingers moved deftly over the buttons, inserting each easily through the buttonhole, covering his muscular chest from Tessa's view. Her mouth went dry. A chill swept over Tessa. "So, now that you know what an evil man I am, are you going to kick me out?"

A gust of wind rattled the window panes and sucked viciously at the flames in the kitchen stove.

She leaned against the wall because her knees had gone weak. "No, of course not. I can't do that, not in this weather."

"And not in this merry season," Sam added with a mocking smile on his lips. "To turn me out would be very uncharitable at Christmas time, during a blizzard. It would be too hard to explain to Danny and Tina, right?"

Despite his lazy smile, Tessa sensed anger in him and she stepped back. "I have the children to think of."

"I promise not to draw on the kids, if they don't draw on me first." A lazy smirk spread across Sam's face. He slapped his thigh and pointed his finger at her as if it were a gun.

"This is no joking matter," Tessa protested, becoming a little angry herself. "Look at the influence you've brought into the house. You've already started Danny on poker."

"I doubt his soul is in jeopardy yet," Sam snapped, returning to the mirror. "From what I've seen it takes a whole lot more than a card game or two to condemn a man for eternity."

Tessa shook her head, truly fearful of him now. When she spoke she was surprised by the smallness of her voice. "Promise me you'll leave as soon as the weather breaks."

"As soon as the weather breaks, I'll be out of here," Sam said with a rueful laugh. "I've got places to go, business to do, outlaws to kill."

"Don't mock me like that," Tessa said, then felt compelled to add in a whisper, "Don't mock yourself."

"Why not? It's what you're thinking, isn't it?" Sam's

smile vanished and his face turned hard and uncompromising. All groomed and dressed in a blue shirt that matched his hard, blue eyes and wearing a black string tie, he suddenly looked grim and forbidding.

Tessa felt weak and hollow inside. "It's bad luck."

"I don't believe in luck." Sam shook his head. "The storm should let up tomorrow and I'll be out of here then. And I think you should be worrying about what you're going to wear to the party?"

Tessa looked down to see that she was still wearing her wrapper and hadn't even begun to curl her hair. She remembered that the curling iron was overheating on the stove. "We're supposed to get there early to set up the tree."

"I did that last night," Sam said. "But you'd still better get dressed so we can get over there. Don't you want to impress Nathan Purvis and make his girl jealous?"

Tessa gasped. "How do you know about Nathan?"

"Danny and Tina are real little chatter boxes," Sam said with an ironic laugh.

Tessa got the distinct impression that he was enjoying her dismay.

"I am not in the least concerned about impressing Nathan Purvis," Tessa said, without meeting Sam's gaze. Everyone in Prairie City, absolutely everyone, including herself, had thought that Nathan was going to propose to her last summer. She'd been mortified when Nathan and Nellie had announced their engagement at the harvest dance. Now even Sam Harper was laughing at her. She'd throttle Danny and Tina next time she corralled them alone, she thought, as heat flooded into her cheeks.

There was nothing for her to do now but hold her head high and go on as if she were truly happy for Nathan and Nellie. Wishing them well wasn't nearly as difficult as getting over the humiliation of losing the most eligible bachelor in Prairie City to the storekeeper's daughter. As ashamed of her petty feelings as she was, Tessa still wanted Nathan to regret turning away from her—just a little. Even more important, she wanted Prairie City to know that she didn't care.

The Jenningses and Sam were the first to arrive at the schoolhouse, save for the schoolmaster Mr. Nathan Purvis, who was busy building a fire in the stove when they entered.

Tessa had pushed her father in his wheelchair while Sam worked ahead of them, shoveling away the snow. Danny followed, surprisingly agile and carefree on his crutches. Tina trotted along at the rear, carrying the basket of Christmas ornaments, decorations and food.

"It's the most beautiful tree I've seen," Tessa gasped when she saw the giant cedar standing in the center of the schoolhouse floor where Sam had set it the night before. Secretly pleased by the wonder and surprise on Tessa's face as she walked around the bare tree, Sam smiled to himself.

She'd donned a blue dress, high at the throat, snug to the waist, with an apron of the same material draped across the front and drawn up into a sash at the back. Sam thought she looked pretty and stylish but he was glad that she had not misshapen her willowy figure with a bustle. He liked the backside she had turned to him just fine the way it was.

The school desks were pushed aside against the walls. The tree stood straight and full, with fragrant green branches lifted in anticipation of the decorations it would bear. Its regal top almost brushed the rafters of the schoolroom. The delight on Tessa's face was nearly enough to make Sam forget that she had invited him to leave her house as soon as the storm blew over. "It ought to be pretty. It's the tree you wouldn't give up."

She turned to him, apparently a little taken aback by his lack of enthusiasm. "I know you think it's silly, but it's even more beautiful than I remembered."

"It is a wonderful tree, Tessa, for a cedar tree," the schoolmaster agreed, clanking the metal stove door closed. "Coming from Vermont where we always enjoyed a long-needled pine for a Christmas tree, I can never quite get used to these spiny little cedars. But I think it is the tallest we've ever had. You and Danny have done yourselves proud."

Tessa turned to the schoolmaster; and to Sam's growing annoyance, she batted her eyelashes at the fellow. "Why, thank you, Nathan. Mr. Harper helped us," she was quick to add. Hastily she made introductions, explaining Sam's part in bringing the Christmas tree home and wisely omitting the encounter with the Sanders gang.

Sam shook Nathan Purvis' hand, noting the schoolmaster's cool and limp grip. Purvis was a slight man, dark haired with a high forehead, bushy eyebrows and soft, fleshy hands. Sam wondered what an attractive girl like Tessa could see in such a gent. Maybe it was the way the teacher was dressed, all dapper, in a suit with a waistcoat and a starched shirt collar. He was turned out damned near as pretty as an undertaker.

"How kind of you to lend a hand with the tree, Mr. Harper," Purvis said. "Just what kind of work are you in that brought you along that piece of Little Kitten Creek road in the dead of winter?"

"Cowpuncher," Sam said, falling back on his usual story. There was some truth in it, and any mention of his military service seemed to make people too curious. "On my way to Abilene looking for news of the spring cattle drives."

"I see," Purvis said, while his eyes followed Tessa who

was warming her hands by the fire. "Well, Prairie City is grateful you happened along to help. The tree is mighty fine."

"See, Sam, aren't you glad we didn't give it up, even in the face of the storm?" Tessa said.

"It's going to make the children so happy," Nathan said.

"Sure, I suppose it will," Sam said, staring at the cedar once more. A dim memory . . . vague and formless as a dream . . . assailed him, a dream of a Christmas with his mother and father when Noah was a baby. There had been a special meal and gifts tucked in his father's socks hung over a crude fireplace. The surprise, smiles, cries of delight and joy. But beyond that memory, where other Christmas recollections should dwell, a void gaped. Sam could recall no other time when anyone seemed especially concerned about whether he or Noah were happy.

"Do you think we will have enough candles?" Tessa asked as she and Nathan leaned over the teacher's desk, counting the candles and the holders carried in from the storage closet in the cloakroom. Their shoulders brushed as they bent over the candles. The sight of their hands occasionally touching annoyed Sam.

He frowned, suddenly irritated and impatient with the whole Christmas tree fuss. He glanced out the window, wishing for the storm to let up so he could head out soon.

"I never anticipated you'd bring back such a big tree," Nathan said.

"I didn't even think about the candles," Tessa admitted with a frown.

"Not to trouble yourself," Nathan said, smiling and reaching for his coat.

To Sam's exasperation, Tessa rushed to the schoolmaster's side to help him into the garment.

"Nellie said her father would donate whatever else we

might need. I'll go over to the store right now and see if they can spare us more candles and holders."

"How kind of Nellie and her father," Tessa said, her voice cool and her mouth pursed. Sam smiled to himself. Clearly the admission didn't come easily to her.

"Yes, it is generous," Hiram Jennings said, looking up from the box of decorations that he, Danny and Tina were unpacking.

"I'll be back as soon as I can," Nathan said at the door. "People will probably start arriving in about half an hour. A blizzard won't keep them away from a Christmas tree—trimming party. See to the fire, will you, Harper?"

"Sure," Sam said, a rush of unreasonable anger flooding over him. Nothing was too much trouble for Purvis, not even helping him with his coat. But to Sam, Tessa had issued an invitation to go away.

As soon as Purvis was out the door, Sam glanced at Hiram and the children to make certain they were occupied before he turned on Tessa who had moved behind the teacher's desk across from him. "So, will you help me put my coat on when I go? Will you flutter those lashes and offer me that coy little smile?"

Tessa looked up at him. The pensive look fell from her face. Her eyes widened in surprise, then narrowed in irritation. "I'm sorry if you found my request for you to leave offensive."

"You're damned right I did." Sam was surprised that she'd put into words exactly what he was feeling. "Invite me in to thank me, then turn me out the minute you find my line of work doesn't suit you. Not very Christmaslike."

"I'm hardly turning you out in the storm, now am I?" Tessa propped her hands on her hips and advanced toward him, her skirt swaying provocatively as she rounded the desk between them. "I seem to recall there was a time you were pretty anxious to be on your way. Something about Danny and I losing you a lot of money."

Sam remembered those words well enough to know better than try to deny them. "You and Danny wanted to know who they were and what had just happened, so I told you."

"And Danny worships you like a hero anyway," she said.

"You wish he didn't?" Sam challenged.

Tessa frowned at him, her pretty lips pursing together in an expression of frustration and regret. "Please don't think I'm not thankful for all your help with the tree and your protection from whatever else might have befallen us out there on the prairie. I know I sound terribly inhospitable and ungrateful. But I must think of my family."

Sam glared at her. He knew exactly why she wanted him out of her house. "You want me to leave because you're afraid Danny might end up like me. Isn't that the truth?"

"Danny is at a very impressionable age, and he's without a father who can do things with him. Do you blame me?"

"A poker game is hardly going to turn a kid like Danny into a trail bum."

"Maybe not," Tessa admitted solemnly, "but the possibility scares me to death."

The reply startled Sam. He looked away. Of course she wouldn't want her brother to end up like him. He shoved his hands into his pockets. He wouldn't wish his life on someone else, though it suited him well enough. "Well, now at least you're being honest."

She suddenly offered him a tremulous smile. "Would you mind helping me put the candles in the holders?"

Much as Sam wanted to say no, much as he wanted to walk out of that schoolhouse and ride out of Prairie City and never look back, he moved to the desk and began to help her. With the damned storm outside he couldn't leave. Not yet, anyway. "So these candles in the holders go on the tree first?"

"Heavens, no," Tessa said with a soft laugh. "The candles go on last."

Sam looked down at the candles and holders, feeling as though he were in a foreign country.

"See what my class made," Tina said, skipping away from the box of decorations that she, Danny and Hiram had been unpacking. She held up a long garland made of popcorn and buttons. "We'll put on the garland first, as soon as everyone is here. Garlands always go on first, Mr. Harper. Don't you know anything about trimming a Christmas tree?"

"I'm afraid not Tina," Sam said. His ignorance was somehow easier to admit to the younger Jenningses. He ignored Tessa's look of surprise. "I've never trimmed a Christmas tree."

"You've had Christmas stockings, haven't you?" Danny asked, disbelief in his voice.

"Sure," Sam said, remembering the stockings he and Noah had hung before their parents died.

"So this is your first Christmas tree," Tina said, clearly delighted with the prospect. "Wait till you see it with the candles all burning and all the decorations hanging from the limbs. It will be so beautiful. You're coming to the candle-lighting party on Christmas Eve, aren't you?"

"Sam has other places to be on Christmas Eve," Tessa put in.

"Yes," Sam agreed without looking at any of them. "I've got other places to be."

Without saying more, he went to work putting the candles in the holders.

*   *   *

Just as the schoolmaster had prophesied, families started arriving about a half-hour later. No sensible long-distance traveler would brave the road in the blizzard. Yet the howl of the wind and the sting of the blowing snow did little to keep friends and neighbors from driving to town to cele-brate the season together. Opportunities for socializing came along too seldom as it was. They could always spend the night in the schoolhouse if they had to. Families poured through the door: mothers, fathers, boys, girls, infants, grandmas and grandpas, aunts and uncles, spinsters and courting couples. Even the buffalo hunters blustered in, noisy, smelling slightly of green hides and red-faced from imbibing spirits.

Laughter rang out and cordial greetings were exchanged among the happy celebrants. The cold schoolroom was soon filled with warmth and noisy chatter. The mood was as foreign to Sam as that at a ladies' tea, but he found it agreeable. Newcomers shook his hand and welcomed him, thanked him for his help with the Christmas tree. Soon the word was passed among the men that liquid Christmas cheer was being served out in the shed where the horses were stabled—to make sure Ed Garvey didn't add whiskey to the punch and offend the ladies or the clergymen pres-ent. Sam thought Garvey looked harmless enough. He figured it was the rowdy buffalo hunters who would bear watching.

He chuckled to himself. Wouldn't the boys at Ft. Smith get a laugh out of this? Sam Harper playing peacekeeper among a crowd of sod busters.

Children scampered in all directions, playing hide-and-seek among the desks shoved against the walls and the coats hung in the cloakroom. The women fussed over the new babies. The men shared stories of livestock problems and crop yields. The food table was soon loaded with veni-son, pork, prairie chickens, potatoes, nuts, pumpkin pie, cornbread, cookies and even a plum pudding—made from buffalo suet contributed by the hunters.

Before long, organization grew out of the chaos and the little children were decorating the lower branches of the tree. The older children worked above them. Then the adults took over decking out the upper limbs.

The tree was so tall that reaching its highest limbs was indeed a challenge. Tessa soon prevailed upon Sam to place ornaments on the loftier branches.

Nathan Purvis had returned with a young woman, Nellie, Sam assumed. She was a pretty little thing with dark hair and rosy cheeks. She was decked out in a red and white store-bought dress amplified with a bustle. She clung to Purvis' sleeve.

"No, hang the little trumpet on the branch to the left," Tessa directed, leaning in so close to Sam that he could smell the scent of cinnamon on her.

Sam purposely reached for the wrong branch, hardly noticing the one she spoke of. He would hook the dang thing on six wrong branches if it kept her near.

"Isn't that disgusting, clinging to a man like that?" Tessa whispered, nodding in the direction of the schoolmaster. "She is rather shameless, isn't she?"

"Shameless?" Sam repeated. "No offense, but I've seen sporting ladies with more discretion."

"Sam!" Tessa scolded under her breath and blushed. A naughty smile twitched at the corner of her mouth.

Encouraged, Sam grinned.

"You are determined to make me ashamed of myself," Tessa said, but her eyes drifted in the direction of the schoolmaster again.

Sam nudged her shoulder with his elbow. "Now, where did you want this toy trumpet?"

"Just up there," Tessa said, pointing to the same branch that he'd been avoiding for some time.

"So the schoolmaster would rather marry the store-keeper's daughter than the newspaperman's daughter?" Sam asked, fishing for a reaction from her. "Is that such a disappointment? Somehow I don't think Nathan ever really captured your heart."

"What do you know about a girl's heart?" Tessa asked, glaring at him.

"Not much I suppose," Sam said indifferently, though he covertly watched every shift of her expression. "But it seems to me if you loved him, you'd be fighting for him. Seems like you'd be dragging him over there under that mistletoe the reverend's wife hung above the cloakroom door. Not dragging home some Christmas tree to impress the fine citizens of Prairie City."

"I don't fight over men, thank you," Tessa said, her back stiffening and her mouth pursing in that funny way it did when she was angry. "Mrs. Kirkland hangs up that silly dried-up piece of Christmas greenery every year. It doesn't mean anything. And I'm not trying to impress anyone. I'll have you know the Jennings family has nothing to be embarrassed about and still holds a respected place in town."

"Sure you do." Sam shrugged. "So then I guess you don't want me to take you over to the mistletoe for a kiss, just to prove to the town that you don't give a horse's feather about Nathan."

"Of course not," Tessa said, staring up at him as if he'd just spoken words of heresy. Her head turned slowly in the schoolmaster's direction again.

The couple was leaning toward each other, talking softly and nearly rubbing noses.

Tessa turned back to Sam, her eyes wide and searching. "Would you do that for me, under the mistletoe, I mean?"

Sam took a long slow breath as he promptly hooked the trumpet on the branch Tessa had designated earlier.

Seizing her hand before she could change her mind, he towed her across the crowded room. Under the dried remnants of greenery which many Christmases ago had probably been fresh mistletoe, he swung her around to face him.

"Only to prove that I don't care," Tessa continued, her head tipped back, inadvertently exposing her vulnerable throat to Sam's searching gaze. "You know, a polite kiss, just long enough for everyone to see and know—"

"I know what to do." Sam didn't even give her time to finish. Beneath the mistletoe, he grasped her by the shoulders, pulled her to him and lowered his face to hers.

He explored her warmth and sampled the texture of her lips with abandon. Gently he nipped her bottom lip.

Without seeking escape, she spread her hands against his chest, and made a small sound. Her lips never parted under his. But as his tongue slid along her lower lip one last time, he felt her fingers curl into fists, her nails scratching across the fabric of his shirt. The touch fired his blood. With great effort he managed to curb the urge to ravish her mouth before the respectable citizens of Prairie City.

She gasped when he released her and stared up at him, her eyes wide with confusion and her lips glistening from his kiss. She looked so young and, despite all her strength and determination, so vulnerable. For a moment Sam was sorry he'd taken advantage of her.

Murmurs ran through the party guests.

Slowly Tessa backed away from him, her gaze still locked on his face.

"Do that again, Harper, and Hiram will make you propose to her," someone called from amidst the tree trimmers. The crowd laughed.

Sam gathered his wits enough to turn and grin at them. He wished Tessa would smile too. "Is that the effect you wanted?"

She nodded without uttering a word. A blush had risen

in her cheeks, but her complexion had paled. Her confusion did not seem like a good sign. Sam began to think he'd overplayed his hand. It was always a mistake to fool around with nice girls.

"Move on, son," said an old gentleman with a white-haired lady on his arm. "Give an old man his chance. After that display, the missus demands her kiss."

Sam reached for Tessa, but she moved out of his reach, allowing the older couple to come between them.

Chapter Seven

Involuntarily Tessa licked her lower lip, half expecting to taste Sam's kiss still on her. To her disappointment, she found nothing but a certain tenderness that had not been there before.

She stepped aside for Mr. and Mrs. Asher who seemed so eager to try their luck under the mistletoe. When Tessa looked up for Sam, he had turned away. Hands tucked in his front jeans pockets, he'd strolled off across the room to speak to Papa and Danny. Tessa couldn't help but stare at the cowboy's retreating back.

She should never have agreed to his suggestion of a kiss under the mistletoe. In fact, she'd been surprised when he'd brought up the idea. Watching Nellie press herself against Nathan reminded Tessa that only last year the schoolmaster had kissed her chastely under the Christmas greenery. A harmless kiss exchanged with another man in the spirit of the season had seemed like an excellent way to demonstrate her indifference to Nellie and Nathan's engagement.

She hadn't counted on the heat and depth of Sam's kiss leaving her witless and weak-kneed. He'd wanted something from her in that kiss, and she hadn't given it to him. Who was this man who didn't know how to decorate a Christmas tree, who accepted Grandma's Grease as if it were a gift and who kissed with an expertise that had left her licking her lips for more.

Sam Harper was an enigma to her. Half a hero and half a scoundrel—or at least half a rascal—who had killed three men. That thought never failed to make her stomach queasy. What Sam had told her about himself and how he acted seemed at odds to Tessa.

Suddenly realizing that she'd completely forgotten about Nathan, she searched the room for him. She didn't have to look long. Tina was tripping across the floor in her direction, with Nathan following her.

"Look, look," Tina piped, holding up the big shiny tinfoil star that went on the top of the tree. The ornament had been made only a couple of years ago from bits and shreds of tinfoil gleaned from rare foil wrappers from tobacco and food products. Nearly everyone in or near town had contributed salvaged foil. The star's silvery points flashed in the light from the oil lamps. "Mr. Purvis drew names for who could put the star on top and I won."

Nathan Purvis followed Tina to Tessa's side.

"Congratulations." Delighted, Tessa clapped her hands. "That's wonderful."

Tina laughed and skipped off in the direction of Sam, Papa and Danny, chanting "Look, look."

"That was nice of you. Nathan," Tessa said. "Thank you for letting Tina top the tree."

"It seemed the least I could do for the trouble you and Danny and the cowboy took to bring us a tree," Nathan said, his mouth pinched in an expression of condemnation that Tessa did not understand. "I'm glad to see you are enjoying the party."

"Yes, it's very nice," Tessa said, suddenly aware that Nathan had a purpose other than socializing for leaving Nellie's side to chat with her.

Nathan cleared his throat. "I do think I should mention to you and your cowboy friend, if our good reverend won't, that there are children and families here. You should conduct yourselves accordingly," he added.

Tessa bristled. "What are you talking about?"

"The kiss under the mistletoe," Nathan said. "It was a little longer than proper in view of the other guests here."

"It was only a Christmas kiss," Tessa said, "bestowed in the good will of the season and in appreciation. Mr. Harper was very helpful with the tree. Danny and I could never have managed it on our own."

"Yes, but I'm surprised at you, Tessa," Nathan said, clasping his hands behind his back and rocking arrogantly on his heels. "He's a stranger, a ragtag cowboy. And you're usually so levelheaded."

Tessa stared in openmouthed astonishment at the schoolmaster. "What do you know of Mr. Harper? Or of me for that matter?"

He turned a tight, condescending smile on her. "I'm simply reminding you gently of your manners."

"You remind me of my manners?" Tessa looked Nathan up and down. Suddenly his discomfort in the presence of her father's wheelchair seemed a sign of weakness, his fine clothes evidence of vanity. And his righteous judgment revealed a narrow-mindedness that had no place in Tessa's life. Why had she never noticed these traits before? "Then I'll remind you of the same thing, sir. I've seen pea vines that didn't cling to a fence post as tightly as Nellie hangs on you."

Nathan's mouth dropped open. "We are engaged. Nellie is simply showing her affection. She's a very demonstrative girl."

"I can assure you, she's demonstrated more than enough of it for all of us," Tessa snapped, only too aware that she'd lost her temper and she didn't give a fig. "I'm surprised someone hasn't told you so before now."

"I simply thought to advise you since your father is ill and unable to counsel you." Nathan glared at her, but when he spoke again his voice was conciliatory. "And I thought you were generous and ladylike enough to be happy for Nellie and me."

"I am," Tessa lied, refusing to meet his gaze. "But my father is ill, not addled, and my generosity does not extend to allowing you to tell me how to behave."

He nodded. "Of course not. My mistake. Good evening, Tessa."

Nathan walked away.

Tessa waited for the turmoil and regret to descend on her. Was it possible? Had she ever been so foolishly fond of this man as to dream of walking down the aisle in the perfect wedding dress with Nathan at her side? A light-hearted sense of relief stole away Tessa's anger. It would never happen. She had enough responsibilities without adding the propriety of being a schoolmaster's wife to them. She glanced in Papa's direction. As she watched, Sam crouched down beside her father's wheelchair to listen to Tina's story about the star.

All Tessa could hear was Tina's small voice saying, "Will you help me? Please, Sam? Will you help me?"

With a slow grin spreading across his face, Sam rose easily and swung Tina up in his arms. Everyone turned and laughed as they watched him stretch, lifting her over his head and toward the Christmas tree.

Tina held the star out over the bare treetop. A hush fell over the party guests. Her little face solemn with concentration, she tenderly fit the crowning decoration down on the loftiest portion of the cedar tree. As soon as Sam set her down, the crowd applauded. Tina smiled shyly and reached up for Sam's hand, giving him her most beautiful smile of thanks.

How could such a man be a killer? Tessa wondered. He'd never said no to any of them when they'd asked for help. He'd never blinked at the sight of Papa in his wheelchair.

The thin reedy strains of the pump organ whistled forth, calling Tessa's attention to Nellie Russell whose dainty hands pressed the instrument's ivory keys. Nathan industriously worked the hand bellows.

Feeling more festive than she had in months, Tessa smiled. She was free. Laughter bubbled to her lips as she pulled her carol book from her pocket and moved toward Papa, Danny, Tina and Sam. She was free. She loved to sing Christmas carols. She'd sing as loudly and joyously as she wanted, and Nathan could just put his hands over his ears.

"This ramp needs to be fixed," Sam called above the howling wind as he bent over the crude, shaky incline someone had built into the house for Hiram Jennings' wheelchair. They had just returned from the party. He and Tessa had managed to get Hiram, Tina and Danny into the house. The ramp had been so unsteady that he'd returned to have a closer look at it. "This plank is loose here, and it needs another brace across this end."

"Danny and I aren't exactly carpenters," Tessa replied from the back porch.

"You did a fine job," Sam said, understanding the necessity for the ramp. It really wasn't a bad structure considering a twelve-year-old and a girl had built it. "It just needs an extra board or two."

"Come inside before you catch your death in this storm," she cried over the wail of the storm. "I'm going to make some hot cider."

Sam looked up to see her silhouetted in the yellow light shining through the kitchen doorway. After the warm camaraderie of the Christmas tree–trimming party, the sight was about as welcoming—and tempting—as any he'd encountered. He was beginning to understand why a man might give up his freedom and risk his heart for a wife. Being needed and welcomed had a certain undeniable appeal. Not that Tessa needed or welcomed him. Without hesitation, he leaped up on the porch and followed her into the house.

Inside she already had a fire roaring in the kitchen stove and was pouring cider into the tea kettle. Hiram Jennings was sitting in his chair in the kitchen doorway.

Sam pulled off his coat and hat and hung them up.

"I'm exhausted after that party," Hiram was saying. "But I just wanted to thank you, Sam, for speaking to those buffalo hunters at the party. They were getting awful rowdy there at the end."

"They just forgot their manners," Sam said, trying to play down his part in convincing the drunken hunters to refrain from dancing around the schoolhouse and firing their guns in celebration. "They didn't mean any harm."

"Well, somebody they could respect needed to settle them down," Hiram said, "and you seemed to be just the man. Ever think about becoming a sheriff?"

"Become a walking target for every town rowdy?" Sam asked. He'd been offered a lawman's job before. "I don't have the patience for that kind of work."

"We don't have many rowdies around here," Hiram said, rolling his chair out of the kitchen. "Think on it.

You'd be welcome here in Prairie City if you changed your mind. Sheriff Sam Harper. Sounds good, doesn't it?''

"Don't you want some cider, Papa?'' Tessa asked as her father disappeared from sight.

"You two go ahead without me,'' Hiram called back. "I think I'd like to finish up that editorial I started this afternoon. Tina and Danny are already in bed. Good night.''

As soon as they were alone, Tessa smiled at Sam uncertainly. "I hope you enjoyed the party too. I know going wasn't exactly what you wanted to be doing.''

"I kinda liked the singing,'' Sam admitted with a grin. "Haven't sung those songs in years.''

"But you've sung them before, and you were in good voice too,'' Tessa said, sending him long, curious look.

"Singing was the only part of churchgoing that I liked,'' Sam said with a shrug as he thumbed through the pocket carol book Tessa had left on the kitchen table. The thin tome was well used, but well cared for too. It obviously meant a lot to Tessa. "Singing hymns and listening to the long, windy sermons were a reprieve from fetching and carrying for Uncle Marley. Noah and I could raise our voices and sing to the rafters with all our hearts and nobody minded.'' Sam hesitated, just a little embarrassed by what he'd revealed. Tessa seemed busy with the cider, so he decided it was a good time to change the subject. "This is a nice songbook.''

"I love Christmas carols too,'' Tessa said, setting blue enameled mugs down on the table. "Always have. My mama gave me that book many Christmases back when I was just able to read the verses. She knew how much I liked to sing. It's always been special to me, but useful too. I can never remember Balthazar's verse of 'We Three Kings.' ''

" 'Myrrh is mine; its bitter perfume,' '' Sam sang,

" 'breathes a life of gath'ring gloom . . .' That's Balthazar's verse."

He was going to go on until Tessa turned to him with a strange, sad look.

" 'Gath'ring gloom.' I don't like that phrase; I guess that's why I can't remember it. Sit down and drink your cider."

"Maybe it's none of my business," Sam began, "but what did the schoolmaster have to say after our, uh, our trip to the mistletoe? I saw him talking to you."

"Enough for me to understand him better," Tessa said with a small smile of dismay on her face. "I don't think I would have made a very good schoolmaster's wife."

Sam had his own thoughts about what kind of wife she would make, and a secret satisfaction crept over him.

For a moment they sat at the table in silence, listening to the window moan and howl outside.

"The storm sounds worse," Tessa observed.

"You think so?" Sam set his cup down and studied her. "I thought it had let up some. I think the worst is over and I can clear out of here early tomorrow morning. Sanders and his gang are bound to be on the trail by that time. I'll have some ground to cover and time to make up."

"There's something I don't understand about Sanders and his gang," Tessa said, studying her cider cup.

"What about them?"

"Well, there are three of them and there's only one of you," Tessa said, looking across the table at him solemnly. "How are you going to capture three outlaws who don't want to be captured?"

Sam shrugged. "I'll surprise them someplace where I have the advantage, and I'll offer them the chance to surrender." It had all been very clear to him from the beginning. He'd talked to the victims of the gang's crimes, and he understood how they operated.

"And if they don t surrender?" Tessa asked, her voice low and unemotional and her whiskey eyes dark and soft.

"I eliminate Sanders. Cowan and Pearce won't know what to do. They depend on him to tell them every move to make. Without his orders, they'll either give up or run off. If I have to, I'll track them down one at a time."

"It's as simple as that?" she said, staring down at her cider mug again.

Impatient and annoyed, Sam shifted in his chair. He knew she didn't like what he'd said, and he wondered why she'd bothered to bring it up. "It's not a very complicated business."

"Just risky," she added, without looking up.

"You could say that." The good feelings that had made him feel warm and mellow after the party deserted him. Nothing had really changed. He was a bounty hunter, treading where he wasn't really wanted. She was a sheltered girl who couldn't understand how a man could drift along doing what he did. "Look, I don't think anything good is going to come of this conversation, so I'll just say good night now."

The chair scraped the floor as he rose from the table without thanking her for the cider. He saw no reason to thank Tessa for hospitality which had been withdrawn. "Storm will have broken by morning. I'll be up and out early just like you want. No need for you to trouble yourself."

He turned his back on her and her questions, and climbed the ladderlike steps to his attic room.

Tessa sat at the table alone. The fire in the stove died, and the night's cold seeped into the kitchen, creeping along the floor and up around her limbs. She stared unseeing into her cold cup of cider feeling like a silly, ungrateful child.

Sam had been nothing but generous to her and all of the Jenningses. Nothing in his behavior at the party had been in the least reprehensible. He'd been a fine example for Danny—maybe except for the kiss under the mistletoe. Tessa couldn't resist putting her fingers to her lips as she recalled the warmth of his mouth on hers.

Sam had even helped Tina top the tree. Then he'd saved the party from the boisterous violence of the buffalo hunters, venturing out to face them while Nathan quaked in his fancy shoes. Maybe Sam had killed a few outlaws in the course of his job. Heaven knew there were plenty of them riding across the plains and through Indian territory. Their wanted posters crossed Tessa's desk every week. Someone had to keep order somehow. What kind of thanks had she offered Sam? She had asked him to leave their house in the dead of winter at the height of the most loving and giving season of the year. How thankless. How selfish. They owed Sam a lot, and the least she could do was let him know that whatever he'd done elsewhere, he was welcome under the Jenningses' roof.

Sleep evaded Sam even though his bed was soft and the room warmed by the fire in the kitchen stove below. He lit the small lamp Tessa had been given him the first night, pulled off his boots, then lay back on the narrow bed. Images from the party intruded, dancing across the rafters in the shadows cast by the lamplight. Many Prairie City folks had thanked him for helping bring in the tree. The children had been especially appreciative, delight and anticipation shining in their round eyes. Santy Claus is coming, they all reminded him. With the smiling images of the children and their parents came an unfamiliar sense of warmth and belonging.

Last Christmas he'd been in a Ft. Smith saloon with a bottle of whiskey, playing a poker game with acquaintances to pass the hours. One good fight had broken out and relieved the boredom. As Christmases went, it had been as good as any he remembered.

The strangeness of this new feeling in Prairie City troubled Sam. He wasn't certain whether he'd be glad to leave behind the town, its folks and the Jenningses with their feather beds and good food—their easy life was bad for a man on the move who lived by his wits—or whether he wanted to linger, to soak up the good will and well wishes from people who seemed willing to accept him for who he was and for his efforts on their behalf.

Tessa had asked him to leave, but maybe he could change her mind. Once she'd gotten over the shock of knowing what he did, she seemed less determined to be rid of him. And there had been that kiss under the mistletoe. If her lips did not lie, she definitely had responded to him. If he played his cards right, appealed to Danny and Tina and Hiram Jennings who certainly wasn't a man to judge another too quickly, Sam could probably get himself reinvited—if he wanted to stay.

Not that he really wanted to. He had Sanders and his gang to track down. But it would be nice to be the one doing the leaving and not the one who was being kicked out.

Sam drifted off to sleep.

A knocking startled him awake. Instinctively his reached for the gun under his pillow, but nothing was there. He'd left his holster hanging in the kitchen in deference to Tessa and her father. Alert, he sat up in bed and listened. The knocking came again from the trap door that led to his attic room. He must have fallen asleep shortly after the idea of staying longer with the Jenningses had occurred to him. His lamp was still burning, though it was beginning to sputter for lack of oil. The house was quiet save for the knocking at his door.

"Who's there?" he called, the fog of sleep promptly evaporating.

"Sam, it's Tessa." Her voice reached him through the door, its tone soft and strained. "I saw your light, and I want to talk to you."

Sam swung off the bed to pull open the door for her. "Is something wrong? Is your father all right?"

As soon as the door fell back, he stared down into a face framed by loose chestnut hair. Her calico wrapper was snugly buttoned at her throat, and her hands clutched the top step of the ladder stairs.

"It's no trouble like that," she said, shaking her head so that the lamplight shimmered off the gold and red of her tresses. "I just wanted to say something to you."

"Well, the open door makes a draft," he said, reaching for her hand. "Come on up so we can close it."

When Tessa was standing in the attic room where Sam had to duck his head, he closed the door.

He turned to her and gestured awkwardly toward the bed. "Have a seat?"

Uncertainly she lowered herself onto the edge of his bed, looking soft and innocent. Sam sat down cross-legged on the trap door because he knew if he sat down on the bed beside her, he would be unable to keep his hands off her. The memory of the kiss beneath the mistletoe was still too fresh. "So what is it?"

She drew a deep breath, as if something weighty was about to spill forth. "I want to say that I'm sorry for asking you to leave the house."

She paused and, when Sam started to tell her to forget it, held up a hand to silence him. "Let me finish. You've been nothing but kind and helpful, with the tree and Danny and Tina and Papa. And how do I repay you? By asking you to leave over something that was—well, it's not like you're an outlaw. Everything you've done while you've been here shows there is no reason not to trust you. I'm sorry, and I'd like you to stay as long as you need to, regardless of what the blizzard is doing. I want you to know that you're welcome here as long as you'd like to stay.''

Sam stared at her, more touched by her apology and her invitation than he cared to admit to himself—or to her. Tessa was a proud girl. Coming to tell him this would not have been easy for her.

Though the invitation to stay had been something he had thought he wanted, now that it had been offered, he was suddenly less certain that he should linger in Prairie City. ''I might consider staying if I could teach you poker,'' Sam said as offhandedly as he could manage.

Tessa smiled. ''Papa didn't think a few lessons in poker corrupted Danny or Tina too much, but no money wagers, you understand.''

The lamp on the floor near the stovepipe began to flicker again.

''Your lamp is low on oil,'' Tessa said, rising off the bed to adjust the unsteady flame.

Sam reached for it too, just as the flame sputtered and died.

They froze in the darkness. He found himself kneeling on the floor, shoulder to shoulder with Tessa. He couldn't see her face.

''If we wait a minute our eyes will adjust to the dark,'' Tessa whispered without moving away from him. ''Light will come in the gable window. Then I'll get us some oil.''

''Why bother after our eyes have adjusted?'' Sam said, turning his head so that stray strands of her hair tickled his face and he could catch the delicate cinnamon scent of her.

"True, and I really should leave you to get your sleep."

He could tell from the sound of her voice that she had turned toward him. He lowered his face to hers, the warmth of her cheek and her rapid breathing guiding him to her lips. Slipping his hands into her silky chestnut hair he settled his mouth on hers. She leaned into him. Her lips parted beneath his and a small sigh of gratification escaped her.

Greedily, his tongue slipped between her lips. She admitted him, slipping her arms around his waist and clinging to him. The inside of her mouth tasted as delicious as any Christmas delicacy.

She hardly seemed to notice when he unbuttoned her wrapper and slipped his hands inside. He couldn't resist the need to savor the soft suppleness of her body. She could have pushed him away, but she moaned and her mouth became his to explore, soft and hot. Through the flannel of her gown he reshaped her breasts to fit his hands, firm moldable tender flesh. When he drew his thumbs across their tips, they pearled beneath his touch. His body quickened.

Tessa pulled her mouth from his and panted, her breath hot and fast against his jaw. Sam was on his feet in a flash, drawing her up and across the short distance to the narrow bed. He placed her on it and lowered himself beside her, pushing aside the folds of her wrapper and finding her lips again.

As his hands slid down over her hips, smooth and bare beneath the flannel, he pulled her close against the length of him. He kissed her cheekbone, her nose, then her mouth. He moved down her throat, feathering kisses along her neck with his lips, then his tongue.

She whispered sighs of encouragement as her fingers raked through his hair.

When he reached her breasts, he took one taut bud into his mouth, suckling it hungrily through the cloth.

Reflexively she drew back. "Sam?"

"It's okay, darlin'," he soothed, stroking one breast while he brushed his lips against the other. He couldn't get enough of her. He nudged and nipped ever so gently, enjoying the small needful sounds she made.

Sam slipped a hand down her thigh once more and slid his hand beneath the hem of her nightgown. Satiny skin warmed his hands. At the touch of his fingers along her bare inner thighs, Tessa's back arched and she released a startled sigh of pleasure. She gave no resistance as he explored the abundance of textures he found at the top of her thighs.

In another time and in another place he had done all these things before—kissed and stroked a woman—but this experience with Tessa was unique. Holding her was familiar and novel all at once. Every reaction of hers stirred him: the soft sounds on her lips, the sensuous movement of her hips, the touch of her hand to his neck. And he wanted more from her. Yet, his own satisfaction was not going to be enough, not nearly. Burning though he was to bury himself in the moist hot folds of her that opened beneath his fingers, he had to know that he would not hurt her—her body or her brave, tender heart.

He paused, his body throbbing and his heart aching. Before he realized what she was doing, Tessa had risen on her elbow just enough to hastily untie the ribbons at the throat of her nightgown, slip it off her shoulder and bare one plump breast, pearled and swollen from the attention he'd already given it.

Sam sucked in a sharp breath. Desire flamed through him. It was all he could do to keep his hand from reaching out to cup her in his palm. He burned to take what was offered. He desired what he knew she had given to no other man.

But even in the heat of the moment, icy panic wormed its way into his gut. She was a nice girl. He couldn't take advantage of a nice girl, a girl who hardly knew what treasure she offered. He definitely couldn't do it under the same roof where her family slept. He might be a saddle bum, but he had that much decency.

"What the hell are you doing?" Sam rasped, yanking her nightgown down over Tessa's knees and shoving her away. He nearly fell off the narrow bed as he scrambled away from her.

His body protested the agony of separation—of loss. Cold pressed around him like a vise. But he forced himself to put as much distance between them as he could manage in the attic room.

"Cover yourself," he ordered, his gaze hungrily feasting on her bare breast. No matter the temptation, he wasn't about to get himself tied down like his uncle, sour and grim, spoiling to find fault, determined to impose his own dissatisfaction with life on everyone around him. Sam had vowed a long time ago as he and Noah plotted their escape to join the Union forces that he'd never get tied down like that. He'd never end up like his uncle and his aunt.

He would not risk his heart, and he sure wasn't going to gamble away his freedom.

Chapter Eight

Wide-eyed, Tessa looked up at him in confusion. So naive and pure. So tempting and desirable. Sam almost groaned aloud. A softer heart than his would have melted.

"Do it," he commanded, certain that her life and his future depended on her obedience.

Without arguing, she sat up on the bed and covered herself. She ducked her head as she hastily tied the ribbons. "I'm sorry. I don't know what I was . . . I don't know . . . I'm sorry."

Sam rubbed his hands on his jeans and forced himself to breathe evenly despite the throbbing in his loins. "We're not going to even talk about this. It never happened. You never came up to my room." He reached down and pulled open the trap door without looking in her direction. He couldn't bear to see the hurt and dismay on her face. "Just go back to your room. Go. Get before I—just get. Now. I'll be gone in the morning."

"You can't leave in the dark with the storm and all."

Slowly Tessa crawled off the bed, pulling her wrapper around her as she moved. Then she padded toward the door, her hand clutching the wrapper closed at her throat. At the door she turned to him. "Please don't let my presumptuousness send you away."

"You're not sending me away," Sam said, meeting her gaze at last. The painful yearning to take her returned. She seemed so genuinely confused and concerned about him that he longed to take her in his arms. The least he could do was reassure her that she had done nothing wrong and that he was far too tough to be frostbit in a storm. But he drew back from her as she neared him and the door. He didn't dare touch her again. "The storm has let up."

The night beyond the house was silent as they both listened, their gazes locked.

"I guess it has, but—" she began.

Sam gestured sharply toward the door. "Go to bed."

Tessa held his gaze a moment longer, her eyes full of a silent plea for him to change his mind; then she obeyed, climbing silently down the steps.

Sam closed the door, relieved to see her go, yet aching still to hold her. He closed his eyes. He'd known she was going to be trouble when he'd first spotted that pretty little backside by the road. Since that day he'd let her lead him a dance, and now he deserved what he'd gotten—or didn't get.

He dragged a hand through his hair in disbelief. Wouldn't the boys at Ft. Smith get a good laugh out of this? Sam Harper sending a half-naked girl out of his room without finishing the job. But they wouldn't laugh. Because he wouldn't tell them about Tessa. She was too special. They didn't need to know about her.

Hastily Sam reached for his boots. Leaning against the rafters, he started pulling on first one, then the other.

Tessa was very special. He knew better than to fall into any sentimental tangle with a girl like her, a good girl—a fatal trap for a man like him. If he knew what was good for him, if he was smart and used the brains the good Lord had given him, he'd be out of the Jenningses' house as quick as streak lightning.

With trembling hands, Tessa lit the kitchen-table lamp. What had she been thinking, going to Sam's room like that? she scolded herself. Nothing. That was the problem. She'd thought of nothing but what she wanted. She'd gone to his room to ask him to stay, because she truly wanted him to stay. And because he deserved the Jenningses' hospitality. And because she'd glimpsed something in his cool blue eyes—something that hinted he wanted to stay, for a while longer at least. Encouraged, she'd thrown herself at him and scared him off. Just as she'd scared off Nathan.

Tessa shook her head over her folly. She'd expected nobility from the schoolmaster—acceptance of her father's condition—and Nathan had run in the other direction. From Sam she'd expected too much commitment, and now he was running too. And why shouldn't he? He owed them nothing.

When they had touched in the dark, she'd yielded to the desire to have him touch her again. A strange compelling need that she'd never known with Nathan. Where had it come from? Had it grown out of that reckless kiss under the mistletoe? Whatever its source, it had felt good, his touch. How easy it has been to resist Nathan and fend off his advances as improper. How irresistible any contact with Sam was.

Tessa shook her head to dismiss the fresh memories of Sam's touch.

Purposefully she moved about the kitchen retrieving the

last of the bread from the bread box and a bit of bacon and venison from the pantry. She even had a few cookies left from the tree-trimming party. There was some honey butter she could wrap in paper and send along. She worked quickly as she listened to Sam's rapid movements in the attic room above her. He'd meant what he'd said about leaving. She tried to evade any more thoughts about their moments together by forcing herself to think of what Sam would need on the road. But her body, flush and frustrated, refused to allow her to forget the feel of his hands on her skin, of his lips warm and persuasive on her breasts.

He was leaving.

Tessa bit her lip, the pain momentarily clearing her head. What else would Sam need on the road? She could spare him some coffee and a bit of sugar. She'd noticed when sweets were around, like the cookies she had made or the candy at the tree-trimming party, that Sam helped himself to his share. He had a sweet tooth.

He also had a chest as hard as a rock and fingers as clever and masterful as a magician's. With his kiss and his touch he'd made her feel more feminine and womanly than she ever had. But she couldn't let herself think of that now. She would not lose her composure. She was simply sending off a man who had helped her family. In appreciation she would give him a bundle of food. It was the least she could do for him. Little did he know, but she was sending her heart with him as well.

"What's going on?"

Tessa turned to find Danny leaning on his crutch in the kitchen doorway. She realized that she forgotten about her task. The food she was packing for Sam lay scattered across the table. "Sam is leaving."

"This time of night?" Danny asked as he yawned.

"The storm broke and he wants to be on his way," Tessa said, numb with the prospect of never seeing Sam again.

Danny seemed to blink himself awake, suddenly understanding what she'd just told him. "He's really leaving now?"

"But I've got something to give him," Tina said, peeking around her brother in the doorway.

"Go get it," Tessa told her sister as she dismally lowered herself onto a kitchen chair. A sudden wave of guilt overwhelmed her. If she hadn't gone up to the attic to ask him to stay, maybe he wouldn't be packing his gear right now. Maybe if she'd said something different or offered him something else, he wouldn't be riding off into the cold night in search of outlaws who would be as determined to kill him as he was to capture them.

As soon as Tina left the kitchen, Tessa asked. "Is Papa awake?"

Danny shook his head and hobbled to the kitchen table. "No, he enjoyed the party, but it wore him out."

Tessa nodded. Let Papa sleep. His questions about why Sam was leaving would be too hard to answer right now. Quickly she rose from the table and went in search of the Christmas gift she'd decided to give Sam.

When she returned to the kitchen she could hear someone outside hammering on the porch. She looked to Danny, who was sitting at the table.

"Sam took the hammer and some nails and said something about the ramp," Danny explained without her asking.

Tessa went straight to the food bundle she'd packed and tucked her gift deep inside. Maybe he was leaving them behind, but she was determined to send a little something of her heart with him.

With a burst of icy wind, Sam came back into the kitchen and laid the tools on the bench by the door.

"That should hold that ramp steadier," he said without looking at her or Danny. He quickly unbuttoned his coat and reached for the gun belt that hung by the door. He began strapping the weapon onto his hip. The sight made the bottom drop out of Tessa's stomach. He'd armed himself as if it was the most natural thing in the world.

To cover her anxiety, she retied the bundle of food she'd prepared for him. Her hands shook as she worked, fighting back the tears and wondering when in the last two days—what moment precisely—had she come to care so much about Sam Harper. Was it when he'd helped her with the tree? With Danny? Or when he'd lifted Tina in his arms so she could top the tree? That was it. The memory of Sam and her sister brought a wistful smile to Tessa's lips.

"It's clear as a bell out," he said, turning to them at last. "If I lose the road, I can navigate by the stars."

"The road will be drifted in places," Tessa warned, knowing a drift of snow was not going to keep Sam from leaving them. "Take care with your horse."

"Wait, wait," Tina called, padding into the room with something clutched to her chest. "I have a Christmas gift for you, Sam."

Astonishment crossed his face, but he made no move to accept Tina's gift. Uncertainly he glanced at Tessa. She realized that he was embarrassed and wanted to refuse the present. She hoped that he wouldn't.

"I thought you'd be staying longer," Tina explained, "at least until the Christmas tree–lighting party, but since you're going now, I'll give it to you."

She thrust a small box at him.

Tessa, Danny and Sam stared at the box in silence. It was a paper and flour paste creation about the size of a deck of cards covered in black and white prints of horses and carriages cut from the newspaper.

"Please, I made it for you," Tina said, her small hopeful face tipped up to Sam.

"But I don't have anything for you," Sam said, genuine dismay rumbling in the timbre of his voice.

"But you gave me my gift already," Tina said without pause.

Sam appeared more confused than ever.

"You gave me wings to put the star on the tree," Tina said, her sweet narrow face filled with the light of a little girl's love.

"That's right," Danny said, the hint of a pout on his lips. "I didn't say anything, but I've never gotten to top the Christmas tree."

Sam stared at the box.

"Take it," Tessa urged. Sam's gaze met hers again and held for a moment. She willed him to know that she wanted him to have the gift for his sake and for Tina's too. His gaze dropped away as he accepted the box from Tina and opened it. Inside was the Jenningses' only deck of playing cards.

"I made the box myself," Tina said, her face solemn in its plea for approval. "But giving the cards was Danny's idea. We thought you should have the cards to play games with your friends or play solitaire. And maybe you'll remember us when you play."

"Solitaire," Sam repeatedly softly. Then he grinned bashfully at Tina and Danny. "Thank you. And the box is real nice, too."

"I only have this to offer," Tessa said, taking the bundle from the table and handing it to Sam. "It's some food."

"Look, I don' know what—" Sam began, accepting the bundle, but shifting uneasily from one foot to the other.

"We appreciate all the help you gave us," Tessa said, stepping back from him to prevent him from handing the food back to her. "You know, with the tree and all. Please allow us to repay you with a bite or two."

"Well, when you put it that way," he conceded, eyeing

the sizeable bundle. "Everything I've eaten under the Jenningses' roof has been a he—heck of a lot tastier than anything I might get along the trail."

The compliment brought a reluctant smile to Tessa's face.

"I'd better get going before the storm changes its mind and blows up again," Sam said. Danny rose from the table and hobbled toward the cowboy, his hand extended. "It's been right good knowing you, Sam. Hope you'll stop by if you're back this way again."

They shook hands. Tina danced up after her brother and threw open her arms for a hug.

Sam stooped down and took her up in his embrace, accepting a kiss on the cheek.

"Come back for the tree-lighting party on Christmas Eve," Tina said. "You have to see your tree all lit up."

"Maybe I'll do that," Sam said against the top of Tina's head.

No conviction rang in his voice. With a sick, sinking feeling in her belly, Tessa knew they'd never see him again. Even if he bested the Sanders gang and received the reward money, he wouldn't ever ride into Prairie City. He'd be off on another chase, never staying anywhere long enough to take on responsibilities. Giving to others, but hesitant to receive. Sam wasn't ready to surrender that much of himself. That was the gift Tessa wanted of him—himself. He could not give it.

And there was nothing she could do to change that.

Sam straightened to his full height and caught Tessa's gaze once more. "Thanks to all of you and your father, too, for the hospitality."

Tessa clasped her hands before her and inwardly pulled at the threads of her unraveling composure. She made no move to approach Sam. But she didn't trust herself. His voice sounded as raw as her heart. "It was the least we could do."

"Come on, Tina," Danny tapped his sister on the shoulder, prodding her toward the door. "Let's go make certain Pa is sleeping okay."

Tessa was too surprised by Danny's shrewd retreat to think of calling her sister and brother back.

As soon as the children were gone, Sam cast Tessa a grieved look. "Your sister was willing to give me a goodbye kiss."

"After what happened upstairs, I didn't know if you'd be . . ." Tessa shrugged, hopelessly confused.

Sam closed the distance between them. He took her chin in his hand and lifted her face his. "Promise me one thing."

Speechless, Tessa nodded.

"Never kiss anyone under the mistletoe without thinking of me."

Hot tears threatened, but Tessa fought to hold them back. "Oh, Sam, I could never forget you," she whispered.

"I'm glad to hear that," he said, his lips only inches from hers. "Because you're pretty damned unforgettable yourself."

He kissed her soundly, a salute and a farewell all wrapped up in one brief meeting of the lips; then he was gone.

Tessa never shed a tear, at least not until Sam was out the door and out of sight.

Chapter Nine

Ruthlessly Sam blanked thoughts of Tessa and that last kiss out of his mind and rode hard, picking up the Sanders gang's trail a whole lot sooner than he'd expected to—at the second homestead where he stopped. It turned out that the gang had ridden only a few miles beyond the ravine where he'd helped Tessa and Danny with their Christmas tree.

Sanders, Cowan and Pearce had come upon the place and made themselves comfortable during the blizzard. For two days they'd bedeviled the farmer and his family, drinking, eating up most of the provisions and boarding three horses without paying a penny. In fact, they'd stolen a new saddle. Upon hearing the farmer's tale of woe, Sam just shook his head. He figured the man had gotten off easy. He was still alive, and his wife hadn't been molested.

The couple he encountered farther down the road hadn't been quite so lucky.

It was late afternoon when Sam spotted the covered

wagon ahead on the trail. He'd been riding hard, as if he could outdistance the pesky thoughts of how warm and cozy Tessa's kitchen would be. It annoyed him that he couldn't put her out of his mind as easily as he had other women. The Jenningses' kind of domestic life wasn't for him. The longer he rode in the cold, the sorrier he was that he'd accepted the gift from the kids. He'd never be able to look at that deck of cards without thinking of Danny and Tina, their worshipful faces aglow with tender generosity. He hated accepting gifts. They were obligations, and he didn't like being obligated.

He shifted in the saddle, growing angrier and more uncomfortable with his thoughts by the mile. The fact was, he'd been a fool to let the Jennings family seduce him away from his goal in the first place. He had to forget Tessa, but thoughts of her refused to die. Purposely he turned his anger and frustration toward Sanders.

The snow clouds had disappeared from the sky, and the prairie lay white under its blanket. He knew something was terribly wrong as soon as he saw the covered wagon. The horses were down in their traces, legs folded under them and heads tucked liked great dead animals. But a hint of smoke rose like a string of gray yarn into the brittle blue sky.

As Sam rode closer a woman wrapped in a blanket squaw-style climbed out of the wagon. She stood by the wheel and watched him warily. When he drew nearer, she walked out toward him, her footsteps crunching in the snow. She seemed intent on preventing him from coming closer.

"Howdy," Sam greeted, pulling his horse to a halt and taking in the grim youthfulness of her face. Her lower lip was swollen and bruised, and her right eye was black. "Looks like you got some kind of trouble."

"My husband is in the wagon," she said as if to warn him she was not alone, but the husband made no appearance.

"What happened to your horses?" Sam asked, eyeing her more closely and realizing her bulk wasn't due to the blanket wrapped around her. She was with child. He glanced toward the wagon again and wondered what kind of fool would bring a pregnant woman out on the trail in this weather.

"Riders shot 'em," she said, a hint of defiance in her voice. "If you want anything, you're too late. They took it already."

Sam studied her with new interest. "Who? What did they look like? How long ago?"

"Last night," the young woman said, watching him more hopefully now. "Shot the horses, took our gun and ammunition and all our food."

"And did they put that bruise on your lip?" Sam asked. She nodded.

Fury grew slowly inside him. How much courage did it take to beat a pregnant woman? He swung down from his horse and opened his saddlebag to find the food Tessa had packed for him. "I have food. Where's that husband of yours?"

The light of hope disappeared from her face. She moved closer to Sam, speaking in a low voice as if she didn't want to be overheard. "He's in the wagon. A beam crushed his leg at home—we were building a dugout shed for the animals—and after a week, well, his leg wasn't healing. So I told him we just had to go to town to see the doctor. First the snowstorm hit; then those men came along. They beat Jim, too."

"You okay?" Sam asked, studying her more closely now that he'd dismounted. She looked too pale to be healthy.

"I had some odd pains a few hours ago," she admitted, avoiding his gaze as she rubbed her back. "But they went away. Please don't tell Jim. I don't want him to worry. He's hurt bad himself."

Her concern for her injured husband was justified. Inside the wagon Sam found that Jim Coker had been viciously beaten and his crushed leg was festered and swollen. The man didn't need to hear bad news about his pregnant wife. Sam handed the bundle of food over to Mrs. Coker, and he built up the fire in the stove to warm them all.

As he worked he listened to their account of their harrowing run-in with three men who had to be Sanders' gang judging from Mrs. Coker's description. One man with a rattlesnake skin hatband on his Stetson, a man in a sheepskin coat and a third on a paint pony. As she talked, she carefully unpacked Tessa's bundle of food, rationing out the items to her husband and to Sam.

Jim Coker said he wasn't hungry and handed his portion back to his wife. But Sam could see from the way the man's eyes followed the cornbread crumbs that dropped to the wagon floor that he was lying. Sam understood. Jim Coker wanted his pregnant wife to eat. Her consideration for him and his concern for her moved Sam. Their selfless, practical, loving care wasn't something he'd often seen between a man and a woman. He'd sure never seen anything like it between his Uncle Marley and Aunt Hester.

"Here," Mrs. Coker said, holding something out to Sam. "I think this is yours, Mr. Harper. Something special packed for you, I think. You'll want to keep it, I'm sure."

Sam started to refuse the item, thinking it was food that he planned to leave with them while he went for help, but when he glimpsed the small, flat book, his heart skipped a beat.

Mrs. Coker was offering him Tessa's pocket Christmas carol book.

A strange mixture of pleasure and dismay nearly overwhelmed him. He suppressed it with great effort and stared at the songbook until his heart began to beat normally again.

"It belongs to somebody I know," he explained, willing his voice to remain strong and even, no break in his words. What the hell was Tessa trying to do? Putting something of hers in his stuff was like reaching out to him—like touching him. He didn't want to be touched by her. That was why he'd left Prairie City.

Mrs. Coker smiled knowingly, the expression lopsided because of her swollen lip. With a hand wrapped in rags for warmth she tapped the book's cover. "Did you see the note she wrote you? Right there on the inside."

Under the woman's scrutiny, Sam had to open the songbook to read Tessa's graceful script. May all your Christmases be full of warmth and song, she'd written. Then she'd simply signed the note Tessa.

Sam's heart ached. He couldn't meet Mrs. Coker's shining eyes. If he was lucky, he'd spend this Christmas and all his future ones drinking in some barroom with a half-dozen other saddle bums who had nowhere to go. That was what he wanted he reminded himself.

"From your girl, I bet," Mrs. Coker added.

Sam nodded, unwilling to explain that he'd never had "a girl" in his life and he had no intention of starting now. But an odd thought wormed its way into his head. Jed Cowan in Sanders' gang had a sweetheart. Everybody knew. Cowan had a girl waiting for him in Denver, where the gang was headed. How could a no-account good-for-nothing like Cowan have a girl waiting for him? Sam Harper had no one.

No one who waited for him and cared what he thought or how he felt, like these two married people cared about each other. No one waited who would attempt to protect him from his fears, not that he had any.

That was the way he wanted it, Sam reminded himself.

"Put it in your pocket," Mrs. Cooker urged. "I know your girl wanted you to carry it close to your heart."

"Probably." Sam tucked the songbook inside his coat pocket without attempting to explain why Tessa's songbook threatened his freedom. He'd carry it in his pocket, next to his heart until he found a post office and could send it back. Then he would keep riding west.

Sam soon located a source of wood for the Coker's fire before he left them to summon help and a doctor. He knew that Abilene wasn't too far ahead and help would be available there.

Twenty-four hours later with Christmas still two days away Sam was ten miles west of Abilene, hot on the Sanders gang's trail and with Tessa's book still tucked inside his coat while thoughts of her were lodged in his mind. Damn the girl, her Christmas tree and her songbook. Sam wished she just left it the way he'd meant it to be. She owed him nothing, and he owed her the same. Gifts made obligations. He didn't want any obligations. He didn't need that kind of burden or encumbrance.

In those twenty-four hours Sam had watched a sheriff's deputy and a doctor head back down the road to aid the Cokers, and he'd discovered that Pearce had traded his horse in for a bay. The paint pony had gone lame, but that hadn't slowed the gang down. They'd apparently minded their manners while they were in Abilene. They'd hit the road after spending the night in the hotel, from what Sam could find out, and now they were back on their way toward Denver, on their way to see Cowan's girl.

Only a dusting of snow covered the prairie west of Abilene, but the wind blew just as cold as it had during the blizzard. Right after dark, Sam caught up with the outlaws in a deserted homestead.

Chapter Ten

Beneath the abandoned homestead's window Sam crouched in the cold and listened to the complaints of the men by the fireplace inside.

"It's your turn to get fuel for the fire, Jed," said Sanders as the gang huddled around the dying fire.

"I went last time," whined Cowan. "Make Pearce go."

"You liar," Pearce said. "I went last time. It's your turn, boss, unless you let us burn the newspapers."

"I don't feel like going, and I ain't burning the papers," Sanders snarled. "My name is in them and yours too. I'd show you if you could read. Go on. One of you find some fuel, or I'll start breaking up the benches you're sitting on."

Sam heard someone mumbling, then the door hinges creaked.

"And get enough this time to last all night," Sanders hollered after the man leaving the cabin.

Sam waited, watching as a tall man carrying a bucket—

Pearce, he guessed—walked across the thin blanket of snow toward the shed where the horses, including his own, were tied. The mound of buffalo chips piled against the shed wall was the outlaw's destination. By the time Pearce got there and figured out there were too many horses, it would be too late.

Sam knew his advantage lay in the gang's separation. Moving quickly, he crept across the open ground, around the back of the shed and up behind Pearce, who had started to shovel chips into the pail. Sam quickly overcame the outlaw before the man could make a sound to warn the others. Then he made quick work of gagging and tying Pearce and dragged him into the shed with the horses. One gun eliminated.

Sam tucked Pearce's six-shooter into his belt and sat down on the flipped bucket, out of sight just inside the shed door. Things would only get trickier from here on. He settled down to wait, imagining the conversation that was bound to go on in the cabin.

"Sure is taking Pearce a long time," Cowan would complain, rubbing his hands near the stove. "Fire is fading fast."

"Seems so," Sanders would agree.

"You think something is wrong?" Cowan would ask. "Him being gone so long. I mean how long does it take to shovel buffalo shit into a pail?"

"Hard to know," Sanders would say, taking out his gun to spin the cylinder and check the ammunition.

"Damn, it's cold," Cowan would snivel, waiting for Sanders to solve the problem.

Sanders was no fool. Finally, the outlaw leader would speak again. "Quit your belly achin' and get your frozen ass out there to see what's keeping Pearce."

Cowan would grumble, but he would go.

The question for Sam was, would Sanders follow Cowan, or wait to see what happened?

"Hey, Cal, what you doing out there?" It was Cowan's voice.

Hidden deep inside the shadows of the shed, Sam looked out to see Jed Cowan standing outside the cabin door, his hands cupped around his mouth as he shouted for Pearce.

Sam drew his gun and watched. He wanted Cowan to get farther from the cabin before he confronted the outlaw. At his feet Pearce struggled, but the gag and bindings held.

When their saddle buddy didn't answer, Sanders stepped out the door. He shoved Cowan toward the shed so hard the outlaw almost lost his hat.

"You a coward or something? Let's find him," Sanders ordered. "And stick together."

Cowan grabbed his hat, cast Sanders a look of annoyed confusion, but turned and stumbled toward the shed. "Pearce, where are you?"

Sanders followed Cowan closely.

Sam cursed his luck. He knew the outlaw leader was on to him and had decided that Cowan was going to be sacrificed. Whatever was going to happen, Sam couldn't allow them to find Pearce and return the odds to three to one.

Sam crouched down inside the shed and leveled his gun at Sanders. "Pearce isn't coming back. Throw down your guns and put your hands in the air."

Both men halted.

"Is that you, Harper?" Sanders called without making a move to do as he was told. "You're the one the marshal told the papers would be tracking us."

"It's me," Sam said, refusing to allow Sanders to seduce him into stepping out from the cover of the shadows.

"It was you on the road back there, with the girl and

the kid and Christmas tree?" Sanders asked with an ironic laugh.

"It was me," Sam admitted. "And you're going back with me alive so I can claim that reward on your head."

Cowan spouted a stream of curses.

Sanders laughed. "It ain't likely."

The outlaws' hands hovered over the guns they wore.

"Don't be fools," Sam warned. "I've got you in my sights. Just ease your guns out of their holsters. Drop them on the ground and put your hands in the air."

"Or you'll do what?" Sanders demanded. "Shoot us? You might get one of us, Harper, but you won't get both."

"Don't count on it." Sam was certain that they hadn't spotted exactly where he was yet.

Sanders began to step forward, keeping Cowan between him and the shed so that Sam couldn't get a clear shot. Cowan remained frozen.

In a flash Sanders went for his gun. A bullet splintered wood from the door frame above Sam's head. Unable to get a clear shot at the outlaw leader, Sam ducked deeper into the shadows.

"Come here, you jackass," Sanders shouted at Cowan. Sam heard the scuffle of boots in the snow. When he got a look out the door again, he saw Sanders clutching Cowan so that the outlaw's back was to Sam.

"Come on out, Harper," Sanders taunted. "Show yourself and take a shot at me now. A lot of good it will do you. Lawmen take a dim view of finding bullets in a wanted man's spine."

"It ain't goin' be my spine," Cowan cried, struggling to free himself from the outlaw leader. "You bastard."

"Let him go, Sanders," Sam called, coming out into the open in a desperate attempt to gain control of the situation. "Throw down your guns and give up. Don't turn this into a gunfight."

But the outlaws flailed at each other until Sanders threw Cowan away from him. Cowan stagged backward, his gun drawn at last and aimed at Sanders.

"Don't be a fool, Cowan," Sanders warned.

Cowan fired. Sanders winced as if he'd been winged, but his grip on his gun remained firm. Sanders fired back and Cowan staggered backward, his gun hand swinging wide. He got off a second shot, but it hit the ground sending up a plume of dirt and snow.

"You jackass," Sanders bellowed at Cowan who was sinking to the ground. "You shot me."

"God damn, I . . ." Cowan's knees buckled.

Another shot rang out. Cowan yelped, spun around and dropped.

Then Sanders whipped around in Sam's direction. A bullet whined past Sam's ear.

Without hesitation Sam took aim and fired. Heat and light flashed in his face. The gun bucked in his hand. Instinctively Sam threw his free arm across his face. He ducked, though he realized that the explosion was his own gun backfiring on him.

Sanders took immediate advantage of Sam being disarmed. The outlaw leader began to trudge across the open ground throwing rapid fire at Sam. A fiendish smile spread across Sanders' face as he squeezed the trigger as fast as he could. Sam stared at the flames shooting out of Sanders' gun barrel. Panic threatened. For the first time in his life he was scared. In that instant he knew it might be all over for him. He understood with gut-wrenching clarity that he wasn't ready for life to end this way in this place.

Fighting back the panic Sam coolly whipped out Pearce's gun from his belt and took aim. But before he could squeeze the trigger, a shot rang out.

"You bastard," Cowan hissed, and fell back in the snow.

The impact of the bullet sent Sanders staggering backward a few steps. He tottered for a moment, lifted his gun again as though he would fire off another shot. Abruptly he fell backward into the snow.

Sam waited for the gun smoke to drift away. Silence settled over the scene. When no one moved, Sam strode out of the shed straight to Sanders' body. The outlaw leader was dead. Sam didn't need to take the man's pulse to find out. Sam kicked Sanders' gun beyond his reach and strode past the outlaw's lifeless body to Cowan.

Cowan still breathed. Sam bent over the outlaw whose chest rose and fell rapidly. His eyes were closed, his face was white. But each rasping breath sent a plume of frost into the cold night air.

"Jed?" Sam said, pulling the man's coat aside to see how bad the wound was. Sanders' bullet had gone all the way through. Blood bubbled up through the wound, staining the outlaw's clothes and at his back the snow—a blossoming dark blotch against the white. There wasn't anything Sam could do for him. Sam shook his head and replaced the coat. "Jed? Can you hear me?"

The outlaw's eyes blinked open, and he turned his head toward Sam. His eyes were glazed, but Sam thought Cowan recognized him. The outlaw stretched out a hand as if in appeal. His lips moved, but no sound came out.

Sam shook his head again. "I can't hear you. What are you saying?"

Jed's lips moved once more. "Tessa . . . Tessa's going to be so mad at me."

Sam froze. The sound of Tessa's name was the last thing he'd expected to hear from the outlaw's lips. The hair on the back of Sam's neck tingled. What was Cowan doing muttering her name? The pounding of his heart thundering in his ears, Sam leaned closer. "What are you saying, Jed?"

"I told her I'd see her at Christmas time," Cowan murmured, a smile trembling on his lips as he looked directly at Sam. Sam fought back a shiver. The outlaw was dying and didn't know what he was saying. That was it. He realized it wasn't his face that Cowan saw.

"Bessie, Bessie, Bessie," Cowan repeated in a strange singsong that brought relief and pain to Sam's heart. Bessie was the name the outlaw had been saying. Not Tessa. "Bessie, I almost made it to Denver."

Coughing racked Cowan's body. Blood bubbled up into his mouth and trickled out the corner. Sam did what he could to ease the spasm.

This time when Cowan opened his eyes, Sam knew the outlaw saw him.

"I'm dying, ain't I?" Cowan managed to say. "Don't lie to me. Just promise that someone will tell Bessie, gentle like. Someone who won t make me out to be a good-for-nothing. I don't want her to think I was a good-for-nothing that bled to death in the snow 'cause I deserved no better."

"I promise someone will give the news easy to your Bessie." Sam nodded, suddenly knowing he would want no less himself.

"And tell her I was buried with her hankie in my coat pocket, close to my heart." A grimace that Sam took for an attempt to smile contorted the outlaw's face. "She'd like to know that."

"I'll see that she's told," Sam said.

Cowan moved his head as if Sam's words satisfied him. Then he began to cough again.

The fit was over quickly this time. Grateful for that small mercy, Sam closed Cowan's eyes with cold, shaking hands.

Slowly, he stood up and surveyed the carnage between the cabin and the shed. Pearce was still tied up in the shed. Sam would take care of him in good time. Sanders lay sprawled on the ground, and Cowan lay huddled on the snow, his life darkening the white blanket around him.

The outlaw wasn't the first man Sam had held a death watch over. But this was the first time in his years as a bounty hunter that he felt he'd truly stood in the shadow of death.

The knowledge knifed through him with a sharp, cold blade. In his heart Sam knew that but for the Grace of God he could have been lying in Jed's place, his life's blood spreading wider and wider in the snow, having died alone. And it could be him repeating his girl's name. Tessa's name. Would she care? Would anyone have told her if it had been him? If they had, would they have been gentle? Would they have portrayed his death with dignity? Would she weep for him? Would she mourn?

Sam looked down at the dead men at his feet. Was this the fate that awaited him? Death in the middle of nowhere with nobody to cry over him. No one to care.

If there wasn't caring in life for a man—and dignity in his death—then what was there?

The chill of the winter night settled across his shoulders, clearing his head. Suddenly he remembered Tessa's book in his coat pocket. He reached for it, patting the miniature tome to reassure himself that the little bit of herself she'd sent along with him was still there. He drew a deep breath of satisfaction.

He sure didn't feel like singing at the moment, but he knew what he had to do. He'd hauled dead bodies into the sheriff's office many a time in his bounty-hunting career. That would be easy. Once that was done, he had something more difficult to do: write a letter.

Chapter Eleven

"Ed Garvey, what are you doing?" Tessa fussed as she swatted at the drinker whose whiskey bottle was poised over the punch bowl. They called it a bowl though it was actually Mr. Russell's inelegant but useful white enameled dish pan filled with apple cider and fragrant spices.

Ed Garvey withdrew the bottle, but waggled a bushy brow at Tessa. "Now, Miss Jennings, don't you think a bit of Christmas cheer would do the punch good and liven the party?"

"I do not, Mr. Garvey," Tessa said, glad that the other ladies had gone off to put the last few candles on the tree before the lighting ceremony and were not witnessing Ed Garvey's outrageous behavior on Christmas Eve. "The children will be drinking from this punch bowl and I do not believe spirits would be appropriate. I'll ask you to mind your manners, sir."

Garvey laughed and shook his head as he walked away. "Don't know what you're missing."

Tessa huffed indignantly. She wished Sam was at her side. Ed Garvey would never have made such an attempt with him around. He hadn't at the tree-trimming party anyway. She wondered for about the umpteenth time where Sam was and if he was well and happy and playing cards with his friends or riding alone in the cold. She'd never know, but could she bring her heart to really accept that?

Many kind words had been said to Tessa about the selection of a fine, sizeable tree. She'd graciously accepted the appreciation always being sure to mention the part her brother and Sam Harper had played. While she was glad to know she'd accomplished what she'd wanted to do— no one seemed to suspect that she'd had any mean-spirited feelings about Nathan and Nellie—her pride in the accomplishment brought her little warmth.

Tessa could hardly recall what had annoyed her so about Nathan's defection to another or about the smiling adoration in Nellie's eyes when she took his arm. She should have been able to see that she and he would have never been happy together: he needing a wife who would mind her manners and make him look good to others; she seeking a man who could accept a father-in-law in a wheelchair as a perfectly ordinary circumstance. No, it would never have worked. It had been unfair of her to push her unrealistic expectations on Nathan.

Sam was another story. He'd taught her to be thankful for what each person brought into her life. That was all anyone had the right to expect from another—what he or she was willing to give. He'd taught her what it might be like to be a woman in a man's arms. Tessa sighed, wishing she'd learned the lesson sooner, not that it would have made how she felt about Sam any different, but it would have saved her some prideful pain. Still, there was no banishing the heartache of losing Sam.

A commotion at the front door of the school drew the children away from the tree. Tessa waited, holding her breath, hoping against hope that Sam would walk in. It was silly to even dream of such a thing, she knew. But wouldn't it be wonderful if he found some reason to come back to her and Prairie City.

"Here he comes," Danny whispered in her ear. He'd been appointed the man in charge of the water and sand buckets in case of fire.

Tessa's heart leapt with hope.

Santy Claus burst into the schoolroom with a bag full of candy and small gifts for each of the little ones. Tessa's hope evaporated.

But that didn't keep her from smiling at the sight of Nathan acting as Santy. Awe glistened in the eyes of the littlest boys and girls who toddled forward to accept their gifts when Santy called them by name. Suspicious delight sparkled in the eyes of the older children, who, like Danny, were beginning to understand who Santy really was. In time they, too, would become part of the adult conspiracy of Christmas.

After the gifts were given out, the singing began. Tessa considered not taking part. She missed her songbook and didn't feel like raising her voice in joy this Christmas Eve. Maybe by next year she'd feel more like it, but Papa smiled at her as if he understood. He drew her into the ranks of the singers, and she was soon lifting her voice in the lyrics of songs. Thankfully Papa never asked where the songbook was that her mother had given her. She didn't want to tell him yet that she had given it to Sam because she wanted him to have something that held good memories from her. Papa just held her hand.

"Sing, girl," he urged. "Singing is good for an aching heart."

So Tessa sang. Her voice was weak, but she lifted it first to the strains of "O Come All Ye Faithful" and then to

''Silent Night,'' Tessa discovered Papa was right, singing was good for an aching heart.

At the end of the first verse of ''We Three Kings,'' everyone heard the town dogs barking and the noise of a commotion among the horses in the shed reached them. Nathan who had changed back into his schoolmaster clothes stayed at the organ, pumping the bellows for Nellie, but he sent one of the older Asher boys out to check on the animals. Everyone continued singing. Just as they began the verse about Balthazar, Sam's verse, Tessa couldn't help thinking, the Asher boy was back. He came into the schoolroom, grinning from ear to ear. Behind him marched Sam.

Tessa's breath caught in her throat. She stared at Sam, unable to believe that she actually saw him throwing his dust-covered coat into the cloakroom, singing all the while, his rich voice adding depth and richness to the whole town's singing. He walked to Tessa's side and took her hand as if he'd only gone outside for a moment and was now back to spend Christmas Eve with them.

He pulled out her songbook and turned to ''We Three Kings,'' offering to share the page with her.

''I thought you might need this tonight,'' he whispered into her ear, his breath sending a tingle through Tessa's body. Only surprise kept her from throwing her arms around his neck in front of the whole town. She had no idea what words she sang. She only knew that Sam was there at her side, his voice full and rich in her ear. The chill she hadn't been able to shake off for the last two days disappeared.

Her heart which had been so heavy only a moment ago was light and fluttering in her breast. She stared at him all through the rest of the verse, taking in the familiar features of his face, burned by the winter wind. Exhaustion darkened his intense blue eyes, but otherwise he looked fine. He smiled at her. Tessa smiled back at him. He looked good—a little thin maybe, but unharmed by bullets or blows. Tessa stared, silently sending up a prayer of thanks.

"I can't believe you're here," she murmured the moment the singing ceased.

"I'm glad to see you too," Sam said, with a soft self-deprecating smile.

"Sam," Tina sang, skipping up to him. "I knew you wouldn't miss the lighting of the candles on the tree."

"You knew that, did you?" he said with a laugh. Tessa knew he hadn't planned to be here when he'd left them, but he had come back.

Tessa touched his arm. "What happened, Sam? Did you find Sanders?"

"I found him." Sam covered her hand with his and led her to the cloakroom where he told her a story about meeting the people along the outlaw gang's trail toward Denver; about finding the gang holed up at a deserted homestead. He didn't say much about the gunfight. The experience seemed to be something he didn't want to dwell on.

"But, you see, I had to write a letter to Cowan's girl," Sam said, without looking Tessa in the eye, as if he thought she wouldn't understand.

"What did you tell her?"

"That he wanted to see her," Sam said. "That her name was the last sound on his lips. That he was buried with her handkerchief."

Tessa nodded. There was more to the story than he was telling her, but she decided to let it go. Two men were dead, but Sam had little to say about the shooting. She longed to know the details. But Sam was here now, sharing what he could and she was grateful for that. "There would have been nothing to gain by vilifying Cowan to Bessie and leaving her with a tarnished memory," she declared.

Sam glanced at her at last. "I'm glad you think so."

Tina appeared in the doorway. "Hurry, the tree lighting is beginning. Come on. You can't miss this Sam." Then she disappeared as quickly as she had appeared.

Sam grinned at Tessa.

She laughed back at him, relieved to turn their attention to something more festive. "You can't miss your first Christmas tree lighting."

"The first of many to come, I hope," he said, as he allowed Tessa to lead him back the schoolroom.

The flames of the oil lamps had been turned down, and a soft darkness settled over the room.

One by one the candles on the Christmas tree glowed to life as the children took turns, each lighting a taper for his or her family. Tina lit a candle for the Jennings family. Danny, who was too old to qualify for lighting candles anymore, stood to the side, leaning on his crutch, the water and sand bucket near at hand in case of an emergency.

The sound of clapping hands carried through the room as the schoolmaster and his sweetheart lit their candle together, hand in hand. Tessa joined in the applause, truly pleased for Nathan and Nellie's happiness.

Then Tina did a jig by the tree and held out the long candle-lighting matchstick to Sam. "Here's a candle for you to light, Sam."

"For me?"

A murmur of approval hummed through the townspeople.

Sam took the matchstick and turned to Tessa. "Light it with me, Tessa."

"You don't have to feel . . ." Tessa protested, afraid of making Sam feel she wanted too much of him.

"Look, I don't know what the future holds," Sam said, too softly for anyone else to hear. He looked into her eyes as if he was searching for some truth. Tessa hoped he saw how much she loved him in her eyes. He glanced around the room.

Tessa followed his quick survey of the onlookers. Every eye in the place was on them, but that didn't seem to discourage Sam.

"Your papa says Prairie City needs a sheriff." He looked into her eyes again. "I thought I might give it a try."

"That would be great, Sam," Tessa said. "It would be nice to have you around town."

He shook his head. "But there's more to it than that. I'm willing to try my best to see that the future holds a place for the two of us together. You know, us out looking for a Christmas tree every year for the rest of our lives, if that's what you want. How about you?"

Tessa searched his eyes for the truth. Those blue eyes were no longer unreadable. They looked into hers with honesty and love. He meant what he said, she could tell, every word of it. Her heart did a little flip-flop. He would tell her in words when the time was right for him. She nodded, because she didn't trust herself to speak.

Sam took Tessa's hand and led her to the tree. With both holding the matchstick, they lit the last candle. With that added flame, the Christmas tree seemed to burst into a brilliant glow, warming the faces and smiles of all gathered around it. The beauty of it brought tears to many an eye in the room.

Applause echoed through the room again, but Tessa's heart was so full with love and wonder and Sam's words that she hardly noticed.

"Are you sure you want to do this, Sam?" Tessa was so breathless her voice was reduced to a whisper. "You don't have to. Are you sure?"

"I'm as sure as the sunrise." Sam vowed as he took her into his arms and kissed her—a long kiss full of warmth and promise and love.